Winter Jasmine

Nuala Reilly

Winter Jasmine

Dedicated to Keisha, Aislinn and Kathryn; my own beautiful little women.

In loving memory of Karen Stafford

Acknowledgments

I couldn't possibly thank all the people who have touched my life in one way or another during the writing of this book, so I'll mention just a few really important ones.

My sincerest thanks to Jordan Stratford. Without you I wouldn't have been able to keep my toes dipped into this amazing world. It is important to mention that this book, perhaps one of the most personal projects I have ever worked on, would not have been possible if not for a few of the strongest relationships I have had in my life. Most notably, the ones with my sisters and with my greatest friend Sarah. I have known you all through the hardest times in my life and through the most joyous. You have watched me fail, watched me triumph and watched me try to accomplish the impossible, sometimes successfully, sometimes not.

As this book is about women, I would like to mention a few women who have inspired me throughout my life in different ways. All of you made an impression on me that has stayed whether you are still with me or whether you have passed on.

Lucy Myers, Maeve Binchy, Stacey, Christine, Kelly, Kelley, Jolene, Kathy, Helen Comfort, Deborah

Skoggard, the ladies of Theatre Tillsonburg, Amber Reilly and Linda Myers.

Last but certainly not least, I again thank my family. Having a writer for a mother and wife is not always easy, but you have all showed me such unerring support and love as I continue on this journey that it would literally not be possible for me to maintain it without you there with me. For that I thank you.

Prologue

The summer I was ten years old, my parents took us to Nova Scotia to see our uncle. A confirmed bachelor, he was lamenting the passage of his adult life without children and wanted to spend a few weeks with my brother and me. We looked forward to it for weeks, bragging to our schoolmates that we were going to be flying on an airplane and swimming in the ocean.

Our very first day there, we jumped in his beat up old pickup truck and drove the twenty-five minutes from his house to the ocean; the real live ocean. It was beautiful. I was mesmerized, captivated by the beauty and majesty of it. The ebb and flow of the waves held my gaze like nothing I had ever experienced before.

Chuckling, my uncle and brother started to shed their clothes right there and, wearing only their jockey shorts, waded out into the surf. I eagerly followed suit, leaving on my underwear and t-shirt and charging in right after them.

As they splashed and laughed in the shallower water near the shore, I was overcome by a desire to immerse myself in the body of the ocean. I wanted to become a part of her. I had visions of gliding along with dolphins with tiny little minnows circling my toes and my fingers.

Nothing prepared me for the powerful pull of the undertow, a phenomenon that my ten year old self knew nothing about. At first it was exhilarating, feeling the underbelly of the waves tugging me in; like the ocean was trying to embrace me. I laughed, waved at my Uncle, and relaxed into the sensations.

Suddenly it wasn't funny anymore. In just a few short bursts I was much farther out than I was comfortable with. The water, which had been crystalline, was now black and ominous. My arms weren't strong enough to propel myself back towards the shore. Another strong pull yanked my head under the waves. I coughed and spluttered, grasping to right myself on the sky side of the world and away from the mysterious monster trying to swallow me whole.

A panicked sensation gripped at me. It was a scarier feeling than anything I'd ever experienced before, including the roller coasters at Wonderland, the feeling in my stomach when the plane had lifted off the ground and even the time my brother David threw a snake at me and it hit me in the face.

I couldn't breathe, I couldn't think and I was truly terrified.

Strong arms grabbed me under my arm and around my neck. My uncle had swum out to me and was pulling me back towards the shore. I turned my body and held onto him so hard, that in days to come red marks showed up around his neck where I had clawed him, trying to ensure that we wouldn't get separated.

He delivered me back to the safety of the shore where David stood with a shocked look on his face. Somewhere, from the depths of my fear soaked brain, I remembered hearing words *of warning about the ocean, where it was safe for me to play, and where it wasn't. David didn't want to tell our mother, as he was sure part of the blame would fall on him as the older child for not watching his sister properly.*

As for me, once I was safely back on that shore and the pounding of my heart had settled into something more normal, I remember feeling more alive than I had ever felt before. Once again, the ocean seemed to call out to me, teasing me to come and try again to best her.

That summer, we stayed for two whole weeks with my uncle. That summer, I learned to swim better than I ever had before. That summer, I went back to my ocean several times, always with the guise of staying within my boundaries. But my feet sought out that feeling of the undertow, and although once or twice I thought I had caught it again, I never again allowed the ocean to win.

Perhaps that's why I've grown to be a pretty tough girl. I don't feel that shaking fear at all anymore, over anything. I've been my own person since that summer that I was ten, and I don't make apologies for it to anyone. I take care of myself, and I respect people who can do the same. It's one of my best strengths, but it's probably also the reason why I left that restaurant in such a bad mood after my fight with Rick, and why I wound up nearly losing my life. That damn ocean undertow has followed me, angry that it didn't claim me the first time around, furious that I had the audacity to flirt with it once out of its vile clutches, and dying for a chance to get me back. If you go looking for danger, it will always find you when you least expect it.

Chapter One

January: that time of resolutions and good intentions for the year ahead when we all plan how we will make our lives better, or healthier, or whatever we feel might be lacking already. For Jaye, it was the time of year when her business usually slowed down just a little. Well, her business and her best friend's. Several years ago, Jaye had loaned her best friend Moira some money when she decided to open up her bakery, and had joined her working in the kitchen of the warmly inviting shop. Together, they had taken it from a business hardly anyone knew about, to the one of the most prosperous stores in the area.

All throughout the year Moira and Jaye made breads, cookies, squares, pies, and almost anything else you would expect to find in a bakery, but especially cakes. Indeed, the very name of the shop was The Cakery, and everyone who was anyone in the town of Fayette went to the girls for their weddings, their birthdays, anniversaries and anything else worth celebrating.

While Moira herself lived in a quaint little apartment above the shop, Jaye lived across town with her boyfriend of four years, Rick Abbott. They shared a tiny, cozy little place just a few blocks over from Fayette's uptown.

Jaye was standing at the back door of her building, taking her time putting her key in the lock. There was a light covering of snow on the ground and the air was alive and crackling in the kind of wintery anticipation of an impending snowfall.

It was a glorious winter's evening. Jaye had finished her orders at the Cakery early and her business partner, Moira, had offered to close up the shop so that she could go home and start getting ready for a well deserved night out. As much as she loved the smell of fresh baked bread and goodies, it would be nice to take the time to stand under a hot shower and smell like a woman again instead of a bakery. Jaye's mouth twitched in a sly smile. She had already planned out her outfit for tonight, and since Rick wouldn't be home until very close to seven, she would have plenty of time to glamorize herself. She wanted to surprise him when he walked in. For a man so used to seeing her in clothing dusted with flour or sugar, a polished and prettified version of her would be a treat.

Rick mainly worked in a neighboring town, but did some travelling in his job. It was complicated. He was a biomechanical engineer who worked in prosthetics. He frequently left his office/lab to personally fit high profile clients or children for their artificial limbs. He loved his job, and Jaye loved that he did something that he was passionate about, as she did. It wasn't hard to be zealous about a job that you had seen grow into something real right from the get-go. The store itself was almost like a child to her and to Moira. Finally, it was coming out of the awkward teenage stage and growing into a real adult business. The girls had recently expanded to include more internet orders and sales, and had taken on Moira's sister Sloane as counter help, since the two girls now needed to spend the bulk of their time in the spacious kitchen. For a short time they had taken on a couple of students, but found that they really wanted someone a little older, and Sloane was working out just fine, for the moment.

Jaye didn't mind Sloane, per se. At least, not as much now as she used to. Sloane had settled down a lot since getting married three months ago, and was five months pregnant with her first child. Jaye was sure that the impending little one was doing more for their sales than the new website. Sloane just loved to gently touch her belly with that wistful look of an expectant mother while talking to the customers. Something about her beatific face made them think that they needed twice what they might have come in for, so as to keep this delicate blonde beauty from starving to death whilst incubating a baby.

Whatever it was, Jaye was not complaining. The business had nearly doubled now from what it was a year ago, and at this tempo, she had no doubts Moira would talk to her soon about taking on more permanent kitchen help.

Jaye let herself into the apartment and looked around. Sure, it was cozy and nice. But it was also small. It was a perfect place for them four years ago, when they were both starting out and making little money. Jaye knew that she personally had saved enough now for a down payment on a small house. She knew that Rick was saving too, but money had always been one of those things that they kept separate. She had no idea what he had put aside. The only thing she did know was that in his particular line of work he made a very decent income, which over the last several years had increased significantly.

She had felt for about a year now that the time was coming that they should begin to think seriously about moving. Rick usually shied away from this conversation. Jaye had a pretty instinctive feeling that had he known she was quickly becoming one of those women interested in marriage, he would have shied away from that conversation too. Thankfully, it was a topic that was not brought up often. Jaye didn't think marriage was necessary, yet, but she did think about it, and she was sure that they needed a place with more than eight hundred-and-fifty square feet.

This 'problem' was a problem unto itself though; Jaye mused as she stood under the therapeutic blast of the hot shower. Recently, with the tough economic times, more and more homes had appeared on the market around Fayette. Jaye drove by them with the same gleam in her eye that Sloane had when she saw other women with babies; the same look that older women had when they came into the shop and drooled over the strawberry mousse cakes or the chocolate truffles. It was the same look Jaye had given Rick the first time she saw him. Pure, unadulterated desire is what it was.

Fayette was a town that was over a century old. Many of the residents had lived in their homes for twenty to thirty years or more. Now, as a lot of them retired, they wanted smaller places that were easier to manage. Indeed the new homes being built on the other side of the river near the industrial section of town were just that, tidy little bungalows not terribly far from the hospice and the hospital.

Jaye got out of the shower and wrapped a towel around her hair. In the fall, she had been sporting a bright streak of cobalt blue. Now it was a cheerful pink which shone spectacularly against the darkness of the rest of her hair. She grabbed another towel and dabbed the beaded water from her body. Then she wiped the steam from the mirror and glanced at the small clock on the back of the toilet. It was already 5:45.

Back in the bedroom, Jaye dabbed perfume behind her knees, on her wrists, neck and between her breasts. She dug in the back of her underwear drawer for her fancy stuff, vivid purple lace panties and a matching bra. She pulled the stay-up stockings, the kind that drove Rick mad with desire, onto her legs and then slipped her feet into the shoes she usually saved for weddings.

In the back of her side of the closet was the piece de resistance, a soft skirt the colour of molten gold. The fabric was rich and thick and something about it made the colours reflect on her skin and change slightly depending on the light. Moira had lent her a black low cut blouse to pair it with. Even Jaye had to admit to herself that the result was stunning. She went back into the bathroom to begin putting on some makeup.

Jaye almost laughed to herself when she dug out the old cosmetics bag from under the sink. She rarely wore makeup anymore. She hardly ever wore skirts and heels anymore. She was more of a jeans and an old pair of combat boots kind of girl, and wore clogs for work, since she was on her feet for so long. Her hair had long been her only accessory. She still liked old band t-shirts that she had gotten while in high school or the years since then.

The tip of the eyeliner was dulled, and since she never needed it for upkeep, Jaye didn't have a pencil sharpener anywhere that she knew of. She wound up going into the kitchen and chipping at the sides of the thing with a knife.

Rick walked through the door just as she was finishing up with the makeup. Jaye stepped out of the bathroom just in time to see him come in and hang his keys on the hook near the door. He turned, and they looked at each other for a moment.

"Wow. I mean, just, wow. You look amazing" he told her, crossing the room and planting a kiss on her cheek.

"Thanks. You better hop in the shower. Our reservation is in half an hour."

Rick disappeared into the bathroom and Jaye could hear the water coming on. She leaned on the edge of the counter in their tiny kitchen. Tonight was going to be a great night. She planned on bringing up the subject of moving again over dinner. If his reaction to the way she looked was anything to judge by, this would probably be a good night to bring it up.

The last time she had mentioned it, Rick had not been eager to talk. He didn't care much for changes at the best of times.

After fifteen minutes, Rick emerged from the bedroom showered, shaved and dressed in crisp clean clothes. Jaye took a minute to admire her man, still with the edgy good looks he had that first time they met. It was nice to see him dressed up and relaxed looking. Okay, maybe not totally relaxed. He had a busy job that was often a little stressful and more than a little depressing, especially when he was designing for a child. But the brooding dark look on his brows was one of the things that had attracted her to him in the first place. She just hoped that today had not been one of those hard days.

"All set, babe?" he asked her.

She nodded and headed for the door, enjoying a private grin to herself when he swatted her ass as she passed in front of him.

Oh yes, it was going to be a good night.

Chapter Two

Jaye and Rick pulled up to the new French restaurant that had recently opened at the far end of the downtown sector. It was already bustling with customers and the only parking spot they could find was the one next to the alleyway for the large post office. Jaye didn't wait for the car to come to a complete stop before she unsnapped her seatbelt and grabbed for the door handle.

"Jeez, can you wait a damn minute?" Rick asked her impatiently.

Jaye shot a look at him that she hoped said 'Don't mess with me' and climbed out of the car as Rick turned off the ignition.

The great start to the evening back at their apartment had suffered a serious blow on the way over, which didn't bode well for their romantic dinner plans. This was supposed to be a night out to celebrate four whole years together, and yet they had barely spoken to each other since they had driven by 'the house'.

The house in question was the beautiful two-storey white sided colonial house that was just a block and a half from Moira's mother's place. Jaye had loved that house for years and now it was finally on the market. It was probably the most clichéd house in the whole town. It actually had a small white picket fence that encircling the lovely garden in the back, which you could see from the road. There were dark blue shutters and a boldly painted door. There was even an old weather vane on the roof with a rooster to show the wind direction. As unconventional as Jaye could sometimes be in her appearance and attitude, this house was the most normal looking thing she had ever fallen in love with.

She of course had mentioned this house to Rick numerous times over the course of their relationship. He in turn had seemed to agree that it was a lovely place, the kind of place that he would like to live in. But tonight when they drove by it on their way to the restaurant, Jaye had sat up in glee when she saw the sign and, looking at Rick to gauge his reaction, was completely deflated to see him roll his eyes.

The rest of the drive was spent in slightly frosty silence.

Now the two walked into the restaurant, not as a couple in love holding hands or nuzzling, but almost as cold strangers on a reluctant first date.

Jaye watched as Rick followed the maître d' to their table and then sat down and folded his arms over his chest. She didn't pay any attention to the wine list, and instead asked for vodka on the rocks. Rick took his cue from her and ordered beer. They both stared at the waiter trying to tell them about the specials, probably making the poor man completely uncomfortable. Jaye didn't even bat an eye when Rick uncharacteristically ordered first, a steak, so she looked him straight in the eye and ordered the lobster. If he was going to be an ass, two could play at that game. At least she would get a great meal out of this evening. Jaye nibbled on a breadstick as she waited for their food to come and watched Rick carefully. He was thinking about something, and not something that was making him happy. She could read his face so well now, she knew that the wheels of his brain were turning and that sooner than later whatever it was would come rising up to the surface. Not wanting to wait for him, she decided enough was enough.

"What?" she demanded finally. "Why are you all of a sudden so grumpy?"

She watched him take a decent sized pull on his glass of beer and take a deep breath.

"I'm not grumpy," he told her, "I'm just starting to wonder when all of this is going to wear off."

"This? What are you talking about?" Jaye was confused by his statement.

"All this residual stuff from Moira's sister's wedding. You've been dropping all these hints lately about buying houses and weddings and babies ever since that night and quite frankly, I'm getting sick of hearing about it!"

Jaye was in a bit of a daze. She quickly ran through her mind the conversations that had been going on between them lately. Okay, so she might have mentioned what a great wedding it had been a couple of times. Perhaps she had dropped one or two hints more than usual lately about moving somewhere in town that had an actual yard to it. Maybe there had been an insinuation or two spoken about babies and how nice it might be to have one someday. In all honesty, she didn't think that she had been all that annoying about it. She thought she had been rather cute. Apparently not, judging by the sour look on Rick's face.

"Sorry, I didn't realize that I was bugging you," she said, "I was under the impression that after so many years, you might naturally start thinking about these kinds of things too."

She watched her man fiddle with the breadsticks and take another swallow of his beer.

"I might have thought about some of it, once or twice,' he gruffly admitted, "but that doesn't mean that I'm ready for anything to change."

"What does that mean?" Jaye asked, albeit much more politely, as their waiter had just arrived with their entrees.

"I mean, I don't see what's so wrong with our life now" he told her, and then dug into his plate of food without even blinking.

Jaye looked at her plate. Suddenly she didn't much feel like eating, which was a shame since her lobster looked and smelled amazing. She grabbed the tongs and half heartedly began cracking the shell of the claws. It was satisfying to feel that hard red shell shatter between her fingers and by her doing. Jaye kept cracking harder and harder, piling the meat on the side of her plate and leaving the shattered remains of the crustaceans' exoskeleton on the side plate before her.

Rick eventually looked up from his steak to see what she was doing. By the time she had finished extracting anything edible from the poor creature, she looked up to find Rick staring at her.

"Now what?" he asked her.

"What? Don't you like your food?" she asked him sarcastically.

"It's just fine. Are you going to eat yours or just perform an autopsy on it?"

Jaye muttered under her breath. She was not in the mood for him to get all funny on her.

"Goddammit Jaye, just tell me what's going on in that head of yours right now" Rick demanded.

"Fine. I'm pissed at you, okay? There's nothing wrong with our life right now…" she began.

"Good, then that's settled" Rick said, raising his fork for another bite.

"I'm not finished. There's nothing wrong with our life right now, really. But nothing has changed, nothing is new, and it seems that there is nothing to look forward to." She grabbed a big piece of lobster from her plate and bit into it. Damn. Now she would actually have to work at staying mad. It tasted like heaven.

"Great, so I'm boring" Rick said, grabbing his napkin and wiping off his mouth.

"That's not what I said" Jaye told him.

"Oh no, of course you wouldn't actually come out and say that, you just said that there was nothing new going on with us and nothing to look forward to. Sounds like the definition of boring to me."

"Well, you tell me different. We do the same things all the time, we've been together four years, lived together for three in that same small apartment....don't you think we're in a rut?"

"No, I don't think we're in a rut. I think that we have a nice place, that we're pretty happy-happier than a lot of people. I think we both have decent jobs and make decent money and that we're able to take off and enjoy a steak and lobster dinner whenever we want to. I thought shit was pretty good, actually" Rick told her, and promptly took another large bite of meat.

Jaye was getting more than a little angry now. "Shit is pretty good, Rick? Shit? Well, you really know how to pour on the charm, especially on our anniversary." She looked down at her plate full of succulent lobster and aromatic rice. Using her fork, she pushed the food around a little. She was having a hard time figuring out why the evening had gone so wrong, so quickly. She stole a glance at Rick. He was still chewing his last large bite, but he had a bit of a sad look in his eyes. Perhaps he realized how harsh his comment had sounded, or how inappropriate it was to say something like that to her in this beautiful place and on their anniversary to boot.

Jaye shoved a forkful of lobster into her mouth and looked around at the other tables. All around her were happy couples. Young couples, like herself and Rick, holding hands across the table, gazing into each other's eyes. There were older couples trading bites of each others' food back and forth across the table. At one table, a group of girls sat cooing over a tiny little baby, the proud mother of the child beaming around her and barely concealing her joy. Jaye felt inexpressibly sad that there were so many people here enjoying this place for what it was meant to be, and here she was having a conversation about why her relationship didn't need pressure put on it, because 'shit was pretty good'. A tear started to form in her eye, and then another. She got up and mumbled out an excuse about the bathroom.

Once inside, she stared at the reflection in the mirror. What is wrong with me? she wondered. I used to be one tough bitch! I didn't go in for all the mushy crap that I've been feeling lately. Rick is right, we do have a good thing going on. So why am I so fixated on houses and babies?

But she hardly needed to ask the question. It was simple. Jaye would be twenty nine this year and she had been feeling those pulls, those yearnings for at least a year now. It was what her mother used to refer to as the biological clock. Well, she didn't much care for that term, but the sentiment was the same. She wanted stability and probably someday soon a family.

All around her were the reminders of people moving on with their lives and….growing up. Okay, so she was a fairly significant shareholder in her best friend's business. That was pretty grown-up. But the bad-ass Jaye of the past was rapidly fading away in favour of one who was starting to feel the need to put down some roots. She and Rick had met at a rock concert. They had ridden motorcycles together and gone rock climbing. They partied all weekend long sometimes in Toronto, taking off whenever the need for noise or the opportunity of a good band came up. Sure he would be a little surprised that she suddenly felt a yearning for white picket fences, but after so long together, the key question should be why isn't he feeling it too?

Jaye went back to the table and sat down. Rick had evidently asked for the waiter to clear their plates, since there were now two Styrofoam packages sitting where their food had been just a few moments before.

"Gee, thanks. Couldn't you have waited until I came back to decide that we were ready to leave? What if I wanted to finish?" she demanded.

"You didn't seem to be eating, so I figured we'd just take it home" he shrugged.

"Yeah, 'cause reheated lobster is just oh so delicious."

"For fuck's sake, Jaye, I can't win with you tonight. You're mad at me, you're mooning over shit, and you think we're in some kind of rut. What the hell do you even want me around for anymore then?"

"Maybe I should start asking myself that" She spat out at him.

"Maybe you're just getting your period" He threw back.

"You're an asshole" She told him, and turned on her heel to leave.

Jaye stormed out of the restaurant feeling white hot with anger and frustration. How was it that a simple conversation these days seemed to erupt into arguments and accusations, she wondered.
She shivered a little as the crispness of the air bit into her arms and walked purposefully towards the car.

Grabbing the handle, she realized that Rick had the keys. She crossed her arms to try and warm them and waited, facing the restaurant door for him to appear.

Jaye gave a tight smile as Rick started crossing towards her. He dug the keys out of the pocket of his coat, and then patted his other pocket, looking perplexed.

"What now?" she asked him.

"Forgot my wallet. I'll be back in a minute."

"Wait…" she barked at him.

"What?"

"Give me the keys so I can get in. I'm cold."

Rick gave a shrug and tossed the keys at her, which hit the ground just behind her. Jaye grunted and turned, bending down to pick them up. She scraped her nail along the pavement and swore slightly at the annoyance of having to re-do her polish.

From somewhere in the alley beside the car, there was a scuffling sound. Jaye shrugged it off as some nocturnal animal foraging in the garbage.

She stood up and straightened out the bottom of her skirt, clutching the keys and squinting at her nail in the scant glow from the streetlight. The noise got a little louder, and this time Jaye turned to look in its direction. She didn't see anything, but she heard what sounded like whispers. Feeling ever-so-slightly frightened, she flipped through the keys to find the right one and hastily pushed it into the lock.

The smell of sour whiskey hit her first.

The piece of wood hit her second.

And then all was black.

Chapter Three

In thirty years of life, Rick had never visited anyone besides clients in a hospital before. He was the youngest of three children in his family and younger by quite a bit; a second honeymoon baby. Rick had an older brother and an older sister who were already into their forties. They lived on opposite coasts of the country with their own families. Between them, Rick had three nieces and a nephew. Rick had all their pictures on his computer, but had never met them. Even they were growing up; now all of them were teenagers.

His parents had retired years ago and now lived in a cheerful little retirement village in Florida, as they had always dreamed. He visited them twice a year for a week, always staying in a hotel. Even in their mid-seventies, they were both as healthy as could be. They filled their time playing golf, senior's tennis and a myriad of other retirement type activities. His mother, a retired nurse, often looked in on residents that were under the weather or going through treatments for cancer or severe diabetes. His father ran the book exchange. Rick often wondered about the point of retiring if you were going to stay just as busy, if not busier, than before.

Regardless, serious illness or extended hospital stays were not something within his comfort zone, nor were they anything he did with any comfort, even where work was concerned. Rick preferred to see his patients in his office, or in their homes. Only an emergency could get him in a hospital these days.

That was probably why it was so hard for him to come into this hospital room and see Jaye lying on the bed with various bandages covering her body. She had a needle in her arm attached to a tube, attached to a bag of something. There was a clip on her finger that glowed, attached to a machine that blipped beside the bed. She looked shrunken. She looked broken.

The doctor had warned him that it might be difficult to see her like this, but that hadn't prepared him nearly enough. Rick clutched the bag of clothes he had brought for her, mentally questioning his choices. Would she want the jeans he had selected, or would sweats have been better? He looked around the room and noticed that all of the lovely clothes she had taken such pains to get dressed up in were nowhere to be seen. Something had been mentioned about evidence. Honestly, so much had happened in such a short time that his head was swimming.

He had been told that Jaye had been given a sedative to help her sleep while they monitored her injuries. He had been down in one of the private offices of the hospital with two police officers for the last hour and a half answering questions. He was tired, he was angry and he just wanted more than anything, for Jaye to sit up in the bed, pull off her equipment and tell him to take her home.

Sinking down into a chair, Rick looked out the window. He had already called Moira and told her what had happened, but not to come tonight. He had left a message for Jaye's father, but doubted they would hear back from him before next week. He felt so impotent. There was literally nothing he could do right now. The thought crossed his mind that this whole debacle was his fault. He'd had a bad day. The little girl for whom he was creating new arms had died. She had been born with many complications and no arms below her elbows. She was a cherubic little thing with a spitfire attitude and he had adored her. The call from her doctor to cancel the order had stunned him more than he had thought possible.

Maybe if he hadn't been so worried about change, so terrified of owning something concrete and constant as a house and all it represented. He was worried that a house would lead to a family, and that maybe he and Jaye might have a child just like dozens that he saw week in and week out at work. Just like the one who had died so many hours earlier that day. Maybe if he hadn't been so obstinate with her, she never would have left in a huff, he never would have forgotten his wallet and the attack never would have happened. No bums high on anything would dare have attacked her if he had been standing right there.

It was heart wrenching to see Jaye lying there helpless. The first bit of her that had made him fall in love was her fierceness. She did nothing half-assed including love people. She was a fighter, not some poor broken girl lying in a hospital bed. Shit, he didn't even know how to be in a situation like this. Rick had never seen anyone really hurt before tonight, unless you counted a guy he had once punched in the nose for spilling a drink all over his current girlfriend. But that guy had had it coming, and man, did his nose bleed.

Outside the darkness was all-encompassing. As he stared out the window, Rick wondered if the velvet blackness would simply reach in through the window and swallow him whole as well.

Every so often, Jaye twitched or moaned. It made him jump a mile. Every time he thought that perhaps whatever drug they had given her had worn off, or that she was simply waking up to tell him that it had all been a big misunderstanding. It had made him sick, what those two guys had managed to accomplish in just a matter of minutes. One of them had hit her on the head with a piece of wood and then hit her or kicked her in the chest. And when she had hit the ground and her skirt had fallen around her waist, well, let's just say that when he came upon the two men, one of them had wound up with his face smashed against the side of the car. Someone else from the restaurant had called the police, thinking that he was in some kind of fight with another man. It had taken some time to explain that Rick was not the instigator. Even now, he knew that there would be at least one more time that he would have to retell the series of events, as soon as the arresting officer, or investigating officer or whoever he was, made it out to the hospital to talk to Jaye.

Rick still had flashes of the other man, running on shaky legs as far from the car as possible. It had been too dark to get a good look at him, but judging by the smell of him, the police would find him either in a crack house or a homeless shelter. If Fayette even had a crack house, that is.

*****

Jaye's head was throbbing. Lights seemed to be flashing over her face, but try as she might she could not open her eyes to see where they were coming from. She could hear voices all around her.

"….female, late twenties, early thirties…."

"…two assailants…..custody…..warrants…."

"….fracture….abrasions…assault…"

From what she could tell through the foggy haze that was her brain, someone had been assaulted, and hurt. There were at least three voices that she could hear. Why couldn't she open her eyes?

Jaye tried to move. She willed her body to sit up, but nothing happened. She tried bending her knees, but they wouldn't cooperate.
Feeling frantic, she tried to wiggle one of her fingers, one of her toes. Nothing was cooperating.

Jaye's head began to swim. What if they were talking about her? Where was Rick, what had happened to her? Her head throbbed with the effort of trying to recall, well, anything. She tried to cry out, but couldn't find her voice. Finally, she let the dark blanket of unconsciousness cover her once again.

Time had absolutely no meaning. For the next several days, or hours, she couldn't be sure, Jaye drifted in and out of awareness. Sometimes she felt severe pain shooting across various parts of her body. Sometimes her head hurt so much she simply passed back out again. Sometime she was vaguely aware of someone else being in the room with her.

She had figured out that she must be in a hospital and that the voices over her were those of doctors and nurses. She had also realized that she had been in some kind of accident. But she couldn't remember anything about the drive home from the restaurant. She didn't know whether or not Rick was hurt, or even still alive.

What really bothered her was hearing the word assailant over and over. Or was it plural? Were the people talking over her body trying to refer to whoever had hit their car?

It was all too much to take in. Most of the time she simply let the white hot streaks of pain take her back into a world of fuzz, where nothing hurt and no tears ever slipped unbidden from her eyes.

It must be morning, Jaye thought to herself, since there was a bright light pinpointed on her face. She could feel its heat licking over her cheek and ear. She made what she hoped was a sighing sound and turned over before remembering that any previous attempts to move had been thwarted. Pain shot through her like a lightning bolt.

But I did it, I moved! She thought to herself triumphantly. There was a noise from the end of her bed.

"Easy now, don't try and do too much, sweetie," said a soft female voice that she didn't recognize.

Jaye loathed women who called her sweetie or dear or any other kind of saccharine term of endearment. And she especially detested it when she had no idea who the other person was. Strangers just don't call strangers sweetie.

She struggled to open her eyes to see who it was talking to her. Her left eye fluttered, and then opened slowly.

Bright light was indeed pouring in through a window near her bed. There was a nurse leaning over her holding her wrist and checking what appeared to be an IV needle in her arm.

"Nice to see you awake. Just let me go through a few of your vitals and we'll see about getting you something to eat and tracking down your doctor."

The nurse bustled around for a few seconds and then Jaye became tired again.

"Excuse me," she started to say, but became momentarily lost in the raspy sound of her voice. The nurse looked up at her.

"What happened? Was I in a car accident?"

The nurse gave her one of those sad smiles. The kind Jaye had seen on dozens of faces when people talked to her best friends' boyfriend, who had recently lost his father.

"I think it's best to wait for the doctor to explain," the nurse told her. "Right now why don't we try and get a little breakfast in you, hmmm?" She disappeared into the hall then reappeared with a tray that bore a cup of hot water, a tea bag and a bowlful of jello.

Jaye was pissed. She was in pain, her eye wouldn't open and this perky little nurse was making her feel about six years old.

Jaye lifted her right arm to put the tea bag into the cup of water and winced. Her wrist and forearm were covered in a bandage and wrapped very tightly.

Turning her head slightly, Jaye looked at the controls for her bed. She carefully pushed buttons until she was sitting almost upright and tried to take proper stock of her surroundings. Her right eye not only wouldn't open, but appeared to be bandaged as well as her wrist. She had some bruises on her left arm, scrapes and bruises on her knees and her chest hurt when she tried to breathe deeply. How in the hell did all this happen and why couldn't she remember anything? Praying for the doctor to show up sooner rather than later, Jaye mustered up the will to eat the quivering mass of red jello on her tray. Thanking her lucky stars that she was left-handed, Jaye only managed one bite before she was again overcome with the desire to escape into the deep pit of unconsciousness. She forced herself to stay awake, however, as the need to find out what exactly had happened, and when, was trumping the urge to close her eye and sleep.

It was going to be a difficult battle, she thought, as there was nothing of interest to look at in the room. It was a standard hospital room with mint green walls and horrible linoleum on the floor, ugly bed with pale blue blanket, or what passed for a blanket draped over her, a crinkly pillow and a boat load of equipment beeping.

Jaye never had really been one to pay attention before and she hadn't ever had to stay in a hospital but she challenged herself to see if she could figure out what all the gadgets were for.

The IV was easy. There was a big bag and a smaller one with a big sticker on it attached to her IV pole. Probably some kind of antibiotic in case any of her wounds got infected, she figured.

There was a white circlet of a sticker stuck to her chest with a wire coming out of it. It was attached to a machine on her left side, which made little blipping noises. Most of the other stuff in the room looked like it wasn't being used. There sure was a lot of it though. Her bandaged arm had track marks in the crook of her elbow, probably from having blood drawn.

Jaye started to feel around her face which had hurt even as she had tried to chew the horrible red gelatin moments before. She wasn't sure, but thought that she could feel swelling around her cheeks. There were definitely stitches on her forehead.

Jaye dropped her arm. She didn't want to know anymore. She used the buttons on the bedside to drop it back down into a sleeping position and prayed for the shadows to take her over once again. She didn't want to talk to the doctor. If she was this bad, what on earth had happened to Rick? It was far safer to cocoon herself in a blissful state of denial and unawareness than find out what had caused her body to become this broken frankenstein-esque creation. Jaye let one hot tear escape her good eye and then tried as hard as she could to disappear into the bed.

By the time the doctor finally made it into her room, Jaye had brushed aside her earlier feelings and was back to trying to be her usual self. In short, she was pissed and she wanted some answers.

Chapter Four

When the doctor finally got around to talking to her, Jaye was astounded by the laundry list of injuries she had sustained the night she was knocked unconscious. There were the two fractured ribs, the broken wrist, and the multitude of bruises and cuts not to mention the gash on her head from being hit with a broken piece of wood. She had stitches from that one. Most shocking was the evidence that some sort of sexual crime had been attempted, but it seems that the appearance of Rick had thwarted the efforts. Jaye was confused but grateful that her doctor was a woman. She couldn't imagine how this particular piece of news would feel coming from a man. Of course the doctor had also informed her that she very likely had a mild concussion from the initial hit. Rick couldn't possibly have been away from her so long in the restaurant that they would have had time to hurt her so badly? But the doctor had assured her that such an attack only took two or three, maybe five minutes at the most.

Jaye bit back the tears that were starting to burn behind her eyes. She was tough, everyone knew that. There was no way she would let this event dissolve her into one of those simpering little girls. She was a fighter.

The meeting lagged as the doctor droned on a little bit. Once she had gone through with her the 'highlights' of her afflictions, she wanted to call the police back into the room to speak with her in her presence, sort of a way to put the attack together like a really messed up jigsaw puzzle.

"I understand your reasons for wanting to do this, but there's no way I'm doing it without Rick here," she told her.

There was a moment of silence and the doctor shuffled her feet uncomfortably.

"What's the matter?" Good lord, she hoped that he had not been hurt.

"Um, I think I'll send the officer in to speak with you on that," the doctor told her, and she left the room.

This all just got weirder and weirder. A young police officer sauntered into the room. He was very good looking. Probably knows how gorgeous he is. She thought to herself. She hated guys like that. One of the most attractive things about Rick was that he had no idea how hot he was. This guy pissed her off on principle. He took a long time staring at her, probably trying to make her blush in some girly type way, but

Jaye was having none of that. She stared right back at him, sure that it was going to make him uncomfortable with all her scrapes and bruises and bandages.

"Good day ma'am."

Fucking Ma'am??

"I'm Officer Daryn Stewart and I've been assigned to your case along with a couple of my colleagues. I believe we are going to have a bit of a chat about your episode with your doctor."

"No, I believe that you are going to tell me what happened to my boyfriend, Rick."

"He should be along shortly. He had some things to settle downstairs first."

"What things?"

The young buck actually smirked at her. God she hated him.

"That's not really important ma'am. I'm sure he will fill you in if he feels it necessary when he gets here."

"I think you better tell me what's going on with him," Jaye told him.

"I'm not authorized to divulge that information."

"Bullshit! I'm sitting here in the hospital, I've been attacked and you are supposed to be on my side. Now my boyfriend is not here and you think I'm going to talk with you and the doctor without him? No way. You tell me right now what happened to Rick or I'm not going to cooperate with you at all." Jaye kept staring him down. Officer Daryn chuckled softly to himself. "You don't like backing down from anything, do you?" he asked her.

Jaye continued to hold her ground.

"Okay, the truth is Rick is just down ironing out a little scuffle he got into last night when you were attacked. It seems that someone heard him shouting and called the cops, and he was so busy beating the hell out of the one of the guys who attacked you that he got carried away and hit one of our guys. There's not going to be any charges, under the circumstances, but he does have to fill out a report and sign it."

Jaye struggled to comprehend all this information. Did he really say 'one of the guys' who attacked her?

"Is he okay?"

"Oh sure, bit of a black eye, but we're used to stuff like that on the force."

"You jackass, I don't give a shit about the policeman he hit, I was asking if Rick was okay."

"Yeah, your boyfriend is fine." He sounded amused.

"I don't like you much," Jaye told him.

"Really? Most women do. That's why they usually send me in to meet with them."

"Them…you mean people like me…victims."

"Well, yeah. The lady ones."

"Listen buster. All I want is to catch the guys that did this and get their asses in jail. I don't need to know the gory details of what happened to me. Maybe you and the doc can have your little chat without me."

He sat down on one of the chairs. "You don't want to know what happened?"

"Nope." Jaye crossed her arms, wincing at the pain that shot through her chest, but determined not to show it.

"But," he sputtered a little. "It's my duty to inform you of the circumstances of your attack."

Jaye stared him down a little more. Good, she felt better that she was in control of this little interaction. Something was bubbling in the hot anger behind her eyes. She tried to ignore it. The officer was obviously getting uncomfortable. He mumbled something under his breath and left the room.

Through the space of the doorway she could hear muffled voices talking, definitely the office who had just been in there, and a woman's voice, either the doctor or one of the nurses. They must have been trying hard to keep her from hearing what was being said, because try as she might, she could not make out any actual words. She eased herself back onto her pillows and tried to assess what was going on for herself.

Okay, so it was not a car accident, as she had originally thought. Her head still hurt when she tried too hard to remember that night. Bits of it had been coming back to her in flashes. She remembered a stupid fight with Rick. She also remembered walking out by herself. Someone, her doctor maybe, had said something about him going back in for something. Or did she? Maybe she was remembering it, or maybe her mind was making it up. Regardless, she had been out at the car alone and someone had hit her on the head. Someone else had apparently been there too, and the two of them had assaulted her with a broken piece of wood and probably their fists and feet as well. She didn't like to dwell on the allegation that some kind of sexual assault had been tried. She certainly didn't want any details on that from the cops. She shifted slightly, trying to feel if she was uncomfortable down there at all. It was too hard to tell. Everything on her body was one big ache, it made specific spots besides her head and her lungs too hard to pinpoint.

She hoped Rick would be back soon. She didn't like being here, her wounds were dressed and she wanted to go home. It occurred to her that Moira would likely be freaking out. She was sure Rick would have called her. They had so much work to do over the next couple of days; Moira would never get it done on her own. Chewing on her lip, Jaye watched the door and waited for the next person to come in and speak with her.

It must have been a bit of time, because the next thing she knew, there was a gentle hand on her shoulder and a soft woman's voice calling her name.

She opened her eye, cringed slightly when she remembered that she couldn't open her right eye, and looked up. There was an older woman standing over her, and behind her was Rick. Jaye ignored the woman and smiled at her man.

"You're here," she said.

"Yeah, I'm here, sorry I had to leave. Must have pissed you off to wake up and find yourself in here alone." He was sheepish.

"I wasn't alone, Officer Testosterone was here too, but I sent his ass packing."

Rick chuckled softly. "Yeah, I'm not really his biggest fan. He thinks you're nuts."

Jaye harrumphed, but finally turned her attention to the woman.

"I guess that would be where I come in. Hello Jaye, my name is Dr. Kate Spiers, I'm the hospital psychologist. I often come down her and consult for victims of violent crimes. Is it okay if I sit and talk to you for a bit?"

"Suit yourself," Jaye told her.

Rick pulled out a chair for the woman, and then sat himself on the end of Jaye's bed. He was wearing a look of concern that Jaye didn't care for one bit.

"So, are you supposed to sell me on some kind of support group or something? Because I don't need that." Jaye smiled at her, but there was no warmth in it whatsoever.

"No, I just wanted to check in and see how you're doing."

Jaye patted the bandage on her head. "Fine, thanks, how are you doing?"

"I understand you haven't been cooperating much with the services that are here to help you."

"You mean with Officer Good Body and his smarmy attitude? Forgive me if I don't want to hear details of 'how' I was attacked by a guy who looks like he'd rather be making love to a mirror."

She looked like she was trying not to laugh at that. Probably she knew the guy, which meant that kind of description was pretty much bang on.

"Well, it is a little unusual. Most people in your position generally want to know exactly what happened to them, the depth of their injuries, both physical and mental."

"Well, I'm not most people." She glanced down at the end of the bed. "Am I, Rick?"

He appeared to be studying his hands for a moment. "No, you're not, but don't you think maybe you should listen to this? You know, she is a professional."

Jaye shot Rick a look that she hoped told him to shut up.

"No, I don't think I need to. I don't want to know. I already know the gist of it, why would I need specifics? It'll only upset me. Besides, didn't they get the guys?"

"They got one. The one I caught. The other one got away." Rick had a very pained look on his face when he said this.

Jaye lifted her hand towards him, which he reached out and held. She turned to face the psychologist.

"You can go now. We'd like to be alone."

The woman got up, turned on her heel and walked out of the room.

Then, for the first time in their four year relationship, Jaye carefully leaned into Rick's arms and cried as if her heart was breaking.

Chapter Five

On her first night home from the hospital, Rick put Jaye to bed with care. She was still taking some fairly substantial painkillers and was like a floppy bunny, her head lolling off to the side. She spoke almost as if drunk, making little to no sense at all. Scattered throughout her marred speech were references to her brother David, Moira and himself.

Rick tucked the blanket around her battered body and wondered what thoughts were going through her head. He had promised to call Moira when they arrived at home, so, reluctantly leaving the bedroom, he headed into the living room to find the phone.

He picked it up, and then put it down again. What do you say, he wondered? What could he say? There was no doubt that he was feeling the bulk of the guilt for what had happened. But how was he supposed to tell Moira that her dear friend was almost unrecognizable from her regular self. He didn't really want to talk to her again. When he had called her after the attack from the hospital, it was all he could do to get the words out of his mouth without breaking down in tears.

What he really needed right now was a stiff drink, even though he rarely touched the stuff. In the kitchen there was a bottle of whiskey in the back of one of the shelves. He took it out, opened the lid and poured himself a glass. Rick swished it around, staring into the amber liquid as if transfixed. Finally, he downed it in one burning gulp, swiped at his mouth with the back of his hand, and crossed the room to pick up the phone again.

Moira answered on the second ring.

"Hello?"

"Hey Moira, its Rick. We're home, just thought I would let you know." The words tumbled quickly from his lips.

"Oh thank god! Is she okay, do you need anything? Do you want me to come over?" she asked.

"No, no, no, we're fine. They gave her a really strong painkiller to get her home and she's passed out in the bedroom. Probably she'll sleep until tomorrow. I just didn't want you to worry," he told her.

"Okay, thanks." Moira was quiet for a minute on her end of the line. "Rick?" she asked, nearly whispering.

"Yeah?"

"She's going to be okay, right?"

Rick took a deep breath. Thank goodness for the drink before the call. "I hope so Moira, I hope so. Will you be okay at the store tomorrow?"

"I should be fine. I can get more help if I need to. Just tell her…just tell her that I love her and I want her to get well."

"I will," Rick promised. "Bye Moira." He hung up the phone without waiting to hear her say goodbye in return. There was no way he was going to let her hear him being weak. Heading back for the kitchen, he poured another measure of whiskey and drank it down. Refilling his glass one more time, he carried it into the bedroom.

Jaye was out cold on the bed. Rick looked at her lying there, so eerily motionless it was as if she were dead. Trying to banish such thoughts from his brain he quickly finished the last bit of his drink and set the glass down on his bedside. His brain was fogging up quite nicely.

Rick disrobed quickly and sat gingerly down on the bed on his side. Jaye was still wearing her clothes. He hadn't wanted to disturb her or do anything to exacerbate the wounds she already had. Now, he pulled back the blankets, pausing as she let out a quick little moan, and then tried to remove some of her clothes without upsetting her sleep.

Her socks were easy. Then he undid the dome of her jeans and tried to ease them down over her hips. Slowly he shimmied them under her bum until they were sitting just over her thighs. Rick couldn't help but think about any other time he had removed her clothes for her. Always it had been in the guise of foreplay. He bit the inside of his cheek hard to focus his brain away from the automatic response of the erection that was already building between his legs and finished removing her jeans altogether.

There were scrapes and cuts all over her legs. Standing out from these though was the one bruise that made his blood boil in anger; the thumb shaped deep and angry looking one on the inside of her upper thigh and the four finger-shaped ones on the outside. Exactly where that monster of a man had grabbed her, trying to force her legs apart. It didn't bear thinking of what might have happened had he not gotten back outside when he did. Rick very carefully wiped his hands across Jaye's leg to dry the few tears that had dropped there. He hadn't even realized he had begun to cry. Curling up in a tight ball, so as not to bang into her, Rick pulled the covers up over them both, and fell asleep.

Dreams of the night it all went so horribly awry haunted him. It was like re-living it all over again.

He was taking his time in the restaurant. His wallet was still sitting on the table beside his plate. The waiter had appeared briefly by his side, and Rick had pressed an additional five dollar bill into his hand, apologizing for the behaviours of Jaye and himself and assuring him that it was neither the food nor the service that had caused them to leave early and in a bit of a huff. The waiter was young, probably late teens or early twenties. It wasn't his fault. Rick felt bad for the kid. He himself had spent a good deal of time working the floor of a restaurant while putting himself through university. It wasn't always an easy job.

Finally, after tucking the wallet back into the inside pocket of his jacket and lingering another moment or two to give Jaye time to cool down in the car, he sauntered back out the front door.

There were noises coming from the spot where he parked. It was hard to understand as a group of four loud people were just on their way to the entrance to the restaurant themselves. Rick stood for a second listening. And then something in his brain clicked over and he ran for the car, startling the other would be diners and very possibly shoving one of them out of his way.

Thunder filled his ears. Snatched words made their way into his brain. It seemed to take a hundred years to reach the car which was only about twenty feet away.

"…hey…." Rick ignored this voice. It came from behind him. Not from the car.

As he rounded the side of the vehicle, he noticed two dark figures, neither of whom were Jaye.

"…money…bitch…"

"…move her legs….dammit…."

The contents of her purse were flung around on the ground. There was the broken leg of a table or chair lying nearby. The two men reeked of stale old whiskey, unwashed feet and some other sickly-sweet odor that his brain couldn't process. They were in crappy clothes, big baggy pants, huge sweaters with the hoods pulled up. One of the guys had his pants down and was kneeling over Jaye, who was lying on the ground at an awkward angle. Her head was tilted in an unnatural way and there was blood trickling down her face. Her wrist was red and looked wrong. Rick was trained to know how limbs should look and nothing about Jaye's limbs looked right. She had fallen so that her skirt was up so far as to reveal a glimpse of what should have been her panties, but these had been ripped and were hanging off her thigh in tattered pieces. A huge red welt was burnt into her side, probably from where the elastic and fabric had been torn against her skin.

Rick took this entire scene in within seconds, maybe even less time than that. His voice seemed to boil up from somewhere deep inside him, an alien shouting from his borrowed lips.

"GET OFF, GET OFF HER," he screamed. He could hear the people who he had pushed into to get here muttering and the electronic beep of their cell phones going off. It barely registered.

"You motherfuckers!" he yelled. One of the guys, who had been rummaging through the purse and throwing things about, took off right away. Rick could only pray that one of the onlookers would stop him, because this other guy was his, frozen in place with his fingers somewhere they NEVER should have been. Saliva dripping off his mouth in fetid stank. The kid, for he must have been just a kid, stared up at Rick with red rimmed eyes.

"Relax man, you can go next," He managed to garble at him. With unbelieving eyes, Rick watched this kid lean down as if to…

Grabbing the back of the kid's sweater, Rick hauled him up to his feet, shoved him against the car and punched as hard as he could into the kid's face.

There was a sickening crunch of cartilage and the kid's nose immediately started to bleed.

"What the fuck, dude?" He swiped at his face. Something must have clicked in this vagrant's cloudy brain. He must have noticed that the face of fury staring back at him was no longer his companion. Or maybe it was the wail of sirens already on the way towards them, the sound reverberating in the quiet of the night. Whatever it was, he tried to clutch at his pants and looked frantically from the crumpled form of Jaye to the purple and furious face of Rick holding him up from the back of the neck.

"Dude, it wasn't…" but no more pleas would leave his mouth that night. Rick's second blow landed squarely against his jaw.

If not for Rick's grip on the back of this guy's neck, he felt sure the kid would have fallen to the ground right then and there. But he would not allow it, would not allow this guy's body to fall anywhere near Jaye. Rick wrenched him towards the front of the car and threw him over the hood. He could hear other voices now around him, but they mattered not. All that mattered was beating him to a bloody pulp.

As he raised him arm to land another blow, strong hands tried to grab him mid-swing. Without thinking, Rick swivelled, allowing the kid to slide to the ground and hit out at whoever was trying to impede his justice.

The second his fist found purchase, another pair of hands grabbed him from behind.

"NO, NO....YOU DON'T UNDERSTAND....SHE'S MY..." Rick struggled to get words out even as he was pressed down onto his knees. There was a whole crowd around now, but he didn't notice anything other than the face of a police officer that suddenly appeared before him.

"Get her, help her," he said.

"We got her," a voice said from behind.

Arms were still holding him. Rick tried not to struggle, but it was hard when he saw them pick up the bum who had been left in a slumped heap on the ground. This guy did not deserve help. Rick hoped that he had broken his nose. The bastard. He was starting to shake now. It wasn't that cold. Must be the adrenaline wearing off.

Rick was desperate for the officers there to know he was a good guy. He stayed put, every muscle of his body screaming out to go to Jaye, to pick her up, to hold her.

More voices milling around. More sirens. Someone, perhaps one of those unfortunate would-be diners, was talking to one of the officers in front of

Rick. Whoever was holding him let him go. He stood, turned wildly and looked for Jaye. She was being lifted onto a stretcher. There were now paramedics, police and who knew who else milling around the scene. People were staring at him, but he didn't care.

Someone came towards him. A police officer. There were questions, and more questions. Rick didn't even know what they were asking him. Someone told him that he had hit one of the officers. He didn't even care.

A movement caught his eye and he turned in time to watch another of the officers' guide the kid with the now bloodied face, arms bound behind his back and shove him down into the back seat of the cruiser. Rick tried desperately to explain that there was another guy, somewhere out there, running away from this heinous crime, but the words wouldn't form in his mouth. He lips felt dry, his tongue tasted salty and warm. He must have bitten it at one point or another. He could hear voices talking to him and felt the steely grips on his own arms loosen.

Rick stood helplessly next to the police officer as the entire scene was roped off with police tape and an Ident team went through and picked out anything that could be used as evidence. His eyes watched with a blank expression as he watched them reclaim items from Jaye's purse; her lip chap, a portable calendar that she kept cake deadlines from work in, a small picture of them both, bits of a broken mirror and tons of little papers flying in and about the car. There was a small bit of blood on the ground; Rick could barely stand to see it. But what really broke him was watching someone bend down and with tongs and a be-gloved hand, pick up one of the fragments of her panties and place them in a plastic bag.

His knees went weak and he felt himself starting to fall.

Rick abruptly awoke, breathing heavy and sweating like crazy. The room was completely dark. He swiped at his face and tried to slow down his breathing. He had been having the same nightmare, reliving the events for the last three nights in a row, ever since it had happened. He had hoped that with Jaye back home and by his side in the bed, they would subside. Terrified of waking her up, he stumbled out to the bathroom where he splashed his face with water.

"Pull yourself together!" he hissed at his reflection in the mirror.

Rick crawled back into bed. He reached out his hand under the covers and tentatively touched Jaye on her arm. She flinched, moaning briefly, and then went back into whatever thoughts were swirling around her own sleep and drug-fogged mind. Hating himself, Rick stared at the ceiling until his heavy lidded eyes once again claimed him and dragged him into the torturous caverns of his worst nightmare come true.

Chapter Six

Daryn Stewart

The first memories Daryn had were of women. He came from a large family of women; a mother, three sisters-all older, two aunts who seemed to be semi permanent fixtures of his house and a grandmother. His father wasn't around much. He was a high ranking detective on the police force in Toronto. He worked a lot of nights and was rarely home on the weekends, choosing instead to fill his time with fundraisers for the Police Widows Association, or another quality charity associated with the force. Daryn knew that his father had hopes of becoming chief one day as his mother spoke of it often. Nothing made him prouder than watching his mother sit in the kitchen in an afternoon, shining his father's shoes or his belt buckles. When he was old enough, he was allowed to help.

By the time Daryn was six years old, he was aware that there was something different about him, something unique. He never seemed to get in trouble in school the way other boys did. Teachers doted on him, as well as a good portion of his classmates. He was aware of being a handsome boy, weren't his mother, aunts and grandmother always telling him so? But it was around this time that he began to understand that it might mean something beyond being a simple fact. Being handsome meant that people naturally like you, and trusted you. It was intoxicating, even for a six year old.

When Daryn was eight, he started stealing, nothing big, just little things, to see what he could get away with. Usually he put the items back after the puzzlement of the theft had run its course with whomever he had picked as his victim. Once or twice, his sisters voiced their opinions about who was behind the vanishing hairbrushes, or missing pair of shoes, but they were silenced by their mother, and even their father.

"The boy spends too much time with women," he had boomed good naturedly one evening. "He needs more male influences in his life."

"Maybe you should spend more time at home then," his mother had quietly put in.

It was a very late night in Daryn's eleventh year, and he was supposed to be in his bed. Instead he was crouched down at the top of the stairs listening in on a rare conversation between his parents. Earlier that afternoon, his mother had caught him spying on a neighbour girl through their fence and taking pictures of her with his instant camera. She had taken him by the ear and dragged him into the house where she had sat him on a chair without allowing him to move at all until his father got home.

Daryn spent a very uncomfortable two hours sitting stock still waiting for his father to drive home after his mother had put in an emergency call to him. He wasn't even allowed to get up to go to the bathroom. It was his first real experience with discipline.

The second his father came in the door, he bolted from the chair and into the bathroom. From beyond the sound of the running water, he could hear his parents arguing about his transgression. It was there that he heard them agree to discuss his behaviours after he had gone to bed that night, and there that he had vowed to find a way to listen in.

"You know I'm home as much as I can be. I can't be everywhere at the same time." He was starting to sound angry. "I don't know how much you expect of me, you knew this job wouldn't allow me to be home much when we got married, didn't seem to bother you then."

"This isn't about your job so much as it is about Daryn. He has no man around here to show him a role model. He needs a father for that."

"Fine, I'll take him into work with me this weekend. It'll mostly be a paperwork day anyway. He can meet some of the guys and go for a ride in the cruiser with me. Do him the world of good."

"Fine. Now what do we do about his behaviour today?"

"Did the girl catch him?" he asked her.

"Not that I know of."

"How about her parents?"

"I don't think so."

"Did you at least have the common sense to take his camera away?"

"Of course I did."

"Well then, no harm done this time. The boy's just curious. Not that I'm surprised, surrounded by all you hens all day. At least he had the decency not to try it with any of his sisters," he chuckled.

Daryn took this opportunity to high tail it back to his room. Caught by his mother and the punishment was a whole day with his father at work! It was too perfect.

Daryn did indeed spend an entire Saturday with his father in the bustling Toronto police station. He was doted on by the other officers, got to ride in a police car and make a few calls on the police radio to cars already out in the field. He watched his father flirt with the women who flitted around the office carrying stacks of papers or typing away on the computers. One of them even sat on his father's lap as he teased her about some boyfriend or other. Daryn was captivated. If anything, the day had firmed up his belief that good looks and a charming nature could get you pretty much anything you wanted in life. His father was walking proof.

After that day, over the years, his father made it a habit to bring him in to the office. Daryn finished up his formative years surrounded by doting women at home and in his father's workplace. He made sure never again to do anything as obvious as snap shots of a neighbour in the near presence of his mother. He did however, by watching his father and the other men of the force, learn how to slick talk women and flatter them into doing his bidding. In high school he always had a smart and pretty girl typing up his essays. One year he even got out of writing mid terms from two of his female teachers. He sailed through the police sciences courses in university and broke several hearts along the way. On the day he graduated from the police academy in Orillia, he was a bona fide heart breaker with the face and body of a matinee idol.

His first post was in Toronto, working the beat out of the same office where he had cut his teeth on the profession with his father, now retired. He was doing just fine, and probably would have risen through the ranks there with grace and speed had it not been for the incident.

There was a woman working as an office liaison while she paid her way through college. She had long blonde hair, devilish blue eyes and a wicked grin. Daryn wanted her from the moment he laid eyes on her, but the darndest thing had happened; she wasn't interested. He tried all of his old tricks to get her to loosen up. She wasn't biting at all. Oh sure, sometimes she would playfully swat him away or tell him off, but there was a hint of steel behind her laugh and Daryn was thoroughly frustrated by it.

One night, almost four months into her job post, Daryn was working late at the office to finish up some overdue paperwork for himself and one of his superiors. It never hurt to grease the right wheels. He had thought that he was one of the only people in, apart from the dispatch staff who were located in an entirely different part of the building.

Leaving his desk to stretch his legs, he wandered around for a few minutes when he spied her. She was in one of the detective's offices sitting on the chair with her lovely long legs up on the desk. He didn't even think twice about it, just eased his way in the door and sat down on the corner of the desk, one hand resting just beside her legs.

"Late night?" he asked her.

"You could say that." She went to move, but he put his hand on one of her shins.

"I won't tell if you don't," he grinned.

"Hmm, actually, I really should be getting back to work and then getting out of here," she told him, and she swung her legs back down onto the ground and went to stand up. Daryn stood up at the same time and blocked her way.

Later, if you listened to her side of the story, he had all but tried to rape her right there in the office. If you listened to his, he had simply made a few slightly stronger suggestions than usual and tried to go in for a kiss. She said that he grabbed her arms; he said that she kicked him in the balls. She threatened to sue for sexual harassment, and he was sunk. You couldn't fight that. Oh sure, Daryn had seen some new age type movies where a guy could counter sue for physical harm or whatever, but that was just in the movies. Here, he was a tough, white male cop and she was a woman. Case closed. Since he was the son of a prominent and well known and respected veteran, Daryn was simply transferred to a small town about two hours north of the bustling metropolis. Somewhere that it would take much longer for him to rise up in the ranks and where he would have to cool his jets on twice the paper work with only a fraction of the action. He was moving to Wells County, specifically the small town of Fayette, population ten thousand.

Daryn detested it there. The sticks, he called it whenever he talked to his father on the phone. Neither his mother nor his sisters knew the real reason for his transfer. His father had laughed at him and told him that he had to pay for playing like that and said that he thought he had brought up his son to recognize the ones that were more trouble than they were worth. The humiliation was mountainous.

Daryn employed all the charms in his power to ingratiate himself with his new ranking officers. He fit in just fine. One of the youngest on the force and the only one not married, he was back to working a lot of nights, but he didn't really mind. One of the more frequent calls he got was to the only strip club in the tri-county area, and he quickly became friendly with a lot of the girls who worked there.

It was a nearly a full year before he met Rebecca, and right away he had her pegged as the perfect girl to keep him company in his banishment.

She was obviously straight laced, one of those button collared girls like the ones he had known in high school who did his homework. But there was something else about her that screamed looking for a bad boy. He pounced, and was dead on the mark. She was everything he expected her to be and more.

In fact, as time went on, she became more than just a fling to him. He found himself spending less and less time with the girls he had met at the strip club and more time with Rebecca. He even took her out on dates occasionally. It was completely out of character. Many times he told himself that he should set some distance between them, if for no other reason than to discourage any thoughts she might have had about the future for them. But she was just so damned addictive. She was smarter than any other girl he had ever spent time with, and he found their conversations every bit as engaging as their steamy sex life.

Daryn lived for the days when they spent time sending racy emails or texts back and forth to each other only, to end the day wrapped around each other in his apartment or hers. Once even in the back of his squad car after his shift had ended.

Finally, with all of his hard work being recognized, and endless boring conversations with the chief where he pretended to care about the most mundane hobbies of the chief's wife, Daryn was made a full investigating officer. Junior detective, in effect. He was on top of the world. His schedule filled up again, almost to the same pace he had enjoyed in Toronto, and he reveled in the new challenges of his work. It meant less time with Rebecca though, as his erratic calendar left little time for anything social, let alone a sex life.

Months went by and gradually he began spending time with one or two of his stripper friends again, if for no other reason than to get a release without the conversation or sleepovers that might drag his mind away from his all important job. So it shouldn't have come as a shock when he showed up one night at Rebecca's apartment only to be told that their little affair was over, but it was a shock all the same.

Daryn dealt with the blow by charming the pants off every woman he could, literally. The way he burned through the eligible women of Fayette, it was a wonder there were any left who didn't know of his reputation. He was hardly challenged with the petty crime in the area. Scarcely anything happened around here where at least one person didn't recognize the perpetrator within days, sometimes even hours, the hazards, or benefits, of small town living, depending on how you looked at it.

Even still, he missed Rebecca's smile and the way she made him crazy just by letting her tightly wound hair down at the end of her day. He lamented the fact that they had never had the chance to work together. When he was a beat cop, he had given plenty of affidavits, but was never in court at the same time as she, or involved in the same case, until the day a young woman was attacked right outside a popular restaurant, practically in front of witnesses. Daryn was closest and was the first on the scene. Finally, he was going to deal with an actual case. All the meaty components were there; female victim, two assailants, physical assault, attempted sexual assault, possibly a connection to the drug trade. And the woman in question was very easy on the eyes. It was a real career maker, and he intended to use it to his full advantage.

Chapter Seven

Jaye awoke in her own bed in the apartment and for a brief moment, she forgot that anything was different. That is, until she tried to move.

"Oohhh." She groaned.

The second she tilted her body to the side to get out of the bed, a sharp pain shot through her chest, her head and her wrist. It was like being electrocuted. Too late she remembered that there were bandages on her body, broken bones to be aware of and no painkillers keeping the sharp stabs from twisting through her limbs.

Beside her in the bed, Rick sat up at the sounds of her trying to move.

"What? What is it? Are you okay, do you need me?" he babbled.

Jaye took in his rumpled hair and the dark circles under his eyes. She doubted that he had managed more than an hour or so of uninterrupted sleep.

"I'm fine. I just forgot about all this stuff." She said, indicating her bandaged wrist. "I just have to get to the bathroom." And she twisted herself carefully so that she was on her side and could use her good hand to help push herself up into a sitting position. Jaye could feel Rick's hand on her, trying to help her sit up. He was pushing on her ribs.

"Ouch! Rick, let me do this." She told him.

"Sorry." He murmured.

She continued to push her own way out of the bed and managed to stand up for a few seconds. Almost immediately, she could feel the blood rushing into her face and knew that if she didn't sit back down, she would pass out. Her bottom barely touched the bed when Rick had whipped around and was crouched on the floor in front of her.

"Are you okay?" his eyes were super wide and his arms were out to the sides, as if he were a basketball player going for a block.

"I'm fine, I just need a second." Jaye was starting to get impatient. "Just let me do this, okay?"

She tried not to feel guilty at the look of hurt on Rick's face. Staying put on the bed for the moment and breathing deeply as she was able, Jaye tried to compose herself. She watched Rick get up in one fluid motion and head to the bathroom. It made her ever so slightly angry that he could just move like that, and right now she couldn't. Hearing the flush, she once again made to get up from the bed, albeit this time much more slowly.

Gritting her teeth against the pain, Jaye rose with care and took a few steps towards the bathroom. She saw Rick appear and make a motion as if to come over and help her walk, but she didn't want that.

"Babe, I'm starving. That hospital food was heinous. Why don't you go make us some breakfast?" she asked him, mostly to stave off another attempt at help. She wanted to do this on her own.

She waited until she was sure Rick was in the small kitchen before she tried to walk on her own again. Now that he wasn't standing over her, she allowed herself to make small noises to handle the pain of walking. Her wrist was aching, her head throbbed and it hurt to breathe too hard. She had slept in her underwear and the loose t-shirt that Rick had brought to the hospital for her. There was no way she was going to be getting into a bra anytime soon, but that made no real difference. Figuring out how to pull down her panties to pee with only one hand was going to be a chore though. Especially since her bladder was all but screaming at her to go.

Stumbling ever so slightly, Jaye made it to the toilet and wrestled to get her underwear down so that she could sit. What she wouldn't give right now for one of those safety bars on the wall like they had in the hospitals, or like there was in Moira's mother's house for her grandmother. Here in the apartment, the toilet was tucked in between the wall and the shower, so there was nothing to hold but slick walls.

Unfortunately, the urge to pee was not to be put off any longer. Maybe it had something to do with her body being in such a beaten state, or the fact that Jaye could only remember having gone last at the hospital late in the afternoon the day before. But whatever the reason, it made Jaye scream out in frustration as she felt the warm trickle of her own urine pass over her thighs and fingers while she was still trying to get out of the damn underwear. She pinched her muscles together and tried to hold it back and dropped down with her panties still stuck at the tops of her thighs. It didn't matter, they were already soiled.

Rick came tearing in from the kitchen at the sound of her distress.

"What happened? Are you hurt?"

"Oh for fuck's sake, Rick, I pissed on myself." God, she was so embarrassed. What next? She looked down and noticed that some of the mess had ended up on the floor. "Just get out. I'll deal with it." She said, not meeting his eyes.

Rick left the room and Jaye bit her inner cheek hard. She would not cry again. This was stupid. Sitting, she wrestled the soiled panties the rest of the way off her legs and threw them in the sink. She noticed a series of bruises on her leg and had to bite down again as she realized that they were exactly the kind of marks that would have been made by someone grabbing her thigh, hard. Rick would never do that. Someone else's hand had been on her, touching her, grabbing at her. It made her want to punch something.

Jaye was careful to clean up as much as she could with toilet paper before she tried to get up again. She mopped up her legs, the floor and for good measure wiped down the front of the toilet. She knew the smell of urine would stay embedded in her nostrils for ages now. What she needed was a shower. She felt so dirty. She stood up, flushed the toilet and tried to take off her t-shirt.

"Holy mother fucker!" she swore under her breath. There was no way she could raise her arms up enough to take it off. The pain was too much. Jaye had never broken any bones before. Broken ribs had to be the worst. And there was no way she was going to call Rick in here to help her. Mentally shrugging, she made up her mind to get in the shower with her shirt on.

As she bent over carefully to turn on the water, she felt her ribs scream at her. Jaye ignored it as best as she could. Right now, getting rid of the feeling of being completely dirty was a higher priority than paying attention to the pain.

She got in under the steamy hot water and imagined Rick was probably in the kitchen right now fighting a battle with himself. The sound of water running would make him want to come running to her aid, but since she had been biting his head off all morning so far, he was probably trying to give her some space.

The water felt so good. It was hot enough to burn her skin pink, something she normally would have hated. But today all it felt like was a purge, getting rid of the traces of whatever tramp had touched her, washing away her own inability to do something as simple as pee. Jaye decided that she would not let these stupid injuries hold her back. She would carry on as normally as was possible to do. Determined not to turn into some sad sack of woman, lying in bed moaning and making her man do everything for her, she was self sufficient, a fighter. Hell, she would make herself heal. Very little in her life had failed to succeed when approached with this attitude. It was hard to see why this should be any different.

Jaye grabbed the soap and scrubbed as hard as her injuries would allow. The entire shower was filled with so much steam; she could barely see her own skin.

Sucking up her pride, Jaye pushed down the tap with her foot to turn off the water and called Rick. He was there in mere seconds.

"What, were you just waiting outside the door?" she mumbled at him. She was soaking wet and the shirt was clinging to her.

"Not really. Breakfast is ready and I thought you might need a hand in there. I didn't want to impose though, seeing as you're bound and determined to do everything for yourself."

"Yeah, well, I can't get my shirt off and I'll need help drying. If you don't mind, that is."

Rick came in and grabbed hold of her shirt. He tried to wring it out a bit first, and then carefully pulled it up at the back so that it came over her head first and then slid down over her arms and off her body. Jaye couldn't help but notice that Rick had suffered the exact reaction he normally did when handling her naked body. Seeing it first encased in a wet t-shirt probably didn't help matters either. She decided not to make comment on it. Instead, she watched him grab a towel from the rack and pat her skin dry. He was especially tender with her rib cage and with her hair, probably trying not to aggravate her injuries. Truth be told, Jaye was enjoying it just as much as Rick was and she fought to keep the flush off of her face as he lightly touched her all over with the towel. It was both sweet and sensual.

As he rose up to finish, Rick was standing so close she could feel his breath on her ear. Jaye reached out and put her hand on his shoulder to steady herself. She was starting to get just a little cold. It made her nipples stand up.

"I'll need help getting dressed, too." She whispered, nudging her nose into the cleft of his collar bone.

"Come with me."

Rick helped her into the bedroom again where he fished out clean clothes from the drawer. Just the feel of him running his hands up from her calves to her thighs and over her hips in order to put panties on her, instead of taking them off, nearly made her climax on the spot. It was the most sensual action she had felt in a long time. Rick must have felt it too, because he began to trace the geography of her body with the palms of his hands.

And then his hands met with the red mark on her hip. He paused and then dropping them down slightly to the bruises on her thigh. Jaye looked down at him.

"What? What is it?" she asked softly. Broken ribs or not, she was seriously in the mood now for some good loving.

"I just...I can't Jaye. I keep seeing him." Rick turned away from her. "The doctor said you shouldn't wear a bra for a few days."

He grabbed another shirt and helped her put it on while she sat on the side of the bed with her teeth clenched. Silently she let him finish putting clothes on her and then stood up.

"I'm going to go eat." She said bitterly.

Turning from the room, Jaye silently seethed into the kitchen. Rick had made a full breakfast for her. She couldn't remember the last time he had done that. She grabbed a plate and tried to put some scrambled eggs on it, but her wrist couldn't take the weight and she dropped it, splattering egg on the counter and floor.

"Shit."

"It's okay, I'll get it."

Rick had come into the room behind her and quietly filled her plate with food, set it down on the table and then began to mop up the mess. Jaye just watched him. When he stood up, she was still rooted to her spot. Moving around her to the garbage, he threw out the paper towels he had used and then put his hands on her shoulders and guided her to the table where he pulled out her chair.

"Stop it!"

"What?" he asked.

"Stop treating me like a baby. I can walk. I can sit. You don't have to do everything for me, you know."

She sat and forked up a piece of bacon, stuffing it in her mouth. She couldn't even taste it. There was no marvelous salty flavour, only crunchiness. The eggs were the same, only texture and no flavour. Maybe it was the meds she had been given in the hospital. Maybe it was that she was angry, but whatever the reason the food didn't taste like food and it made her lose her appetite.

Pushing back her plate, Jaye got up and walked around the apartment for a minute or two. She could feel Rick's eyes tracking her.

"You should go and lie down. The doctor said you should be getting rest right now."

"I'm not tired."

"Or hungry," Rick muttered.

She ignored him. It was terrible to feel so restless. She hated not being trusted to do anything, or not able to do the things she wanted to. Eventually,

Rick got up from the table, took their plates into their tiny kitchen and then retreated to the bathroom.

As soon as Jaye heard the shower come on she took the pills Rick had left for her on the counter and swallowed them dry. Then she crept into the hall, shoved her feet into her shoes, took the keys and left.

Chapter Eight

Moira

Inside the warm kitchen of the Cakery, Moira was busily instructing her sister Sloane on how to prepare basic dough for the many types of bread that would be done in the course of the coming week. They were bickering good naturedly at one another and Sloane kept jotting down little notes to herself in a pink sparkly notebook.

"It's like you're still in junior high," Moira told her sister. "Are those feathers on the end of your pen?"

"Yeah, I think they're kind of cute," Sloane defended her choice by gently rubbing the fluff on her cheek. "There's nothing wrong with enjoying being a girl."

Moira harrumphed at her. "You're never going to learn by writing stuff down. The best way to do it is just to do it. I've been telling you this for ages now."

Indeed, ever since Sloane had come on board to help out with the increased business at the store, Moira had been trying to make her take a more active role in the actual baking of goods. Sloane had of course been for the most part brushing this off as unnecessary. She much preferred working out front and talking to the customers. And she was well suited to it. Her bubbly good nature endeared her to the older patrons and her shining good looks appealed to the younger ones. Frequently her friends had popped in to marvel at the great and golden friend of theirs, newly married and working of all things, but Sloane had never let them leave without making a purchase. It warmed Moira's heart to see her sister begin taking on a serious, or semi serious role in her life.

"Whether you like it or not, you're going to have to learn some of this now. Put down the pen for a second and come over here." Moira was serious, but spoke with a smile.

"Okay, okay. Sheesh. Never go to work for your big sister." Sloane giggled, but she put away the pen and pad and walked over to the large floor sized Hobart where the dough would be mixed.

Moira talked her sister through the process of adding the flour, water and yeast. She explained how this would be a beginner dough, used as a base for both regular white breads and later for specialty combinations when they added other ingredients.

It wasn't hard to see that, patient as she was; Moira was clearly missing her partner in the kitchen. Orders were falling slightly behind and she had instructed Sloane not to accept any more than five cake orders a week for the next little while.

With the dough started and the machine whirring away, Sloane stood back from her efforts and beamed. Her face fell only slightly when she realized that Moira was not smiling.

"Have you heard anything new?" Sloane asked.

"Not really. I do know that she went home two days ago, but Rick called and said that she wasn't up to seeing or talking to anyone yet. I really miss her."

"I know. So what's the verdict about her…wounds?"

"Um, she has a mild concussion. This is pretty amazing considering how hard she got hit on the head. I always said she was thick headed…." Moira tried to laugh, but the sound was too flat and hollow. "Couple of broken bones, cuts and such, you know."

"Yeah, I heard some of it on the news. Martin was saying the other night that if you read between the lines of what the police are saying, and not saying, and the way it's being reported…you know the way lawyers speculate about stuff, always looking for the next big lawsuit…"

"What are you getting at, Sloane?" Moira didn't quite like where this line of conversation was headed.

"Maybe it's nothing."

"I think you better spit it out."

"Okay, well, the word being tossed around a bit in Martin's office is 'sexual assault'. You don't think one of those creeps tried to…." Sloane lowered her voice. "rape her, do you?"

Moira turned a slightly pale shade. She had heard this term tossed around too, though not confirmed by either Jaye or Rick, not that she was going to ask them outright.

"I don't think so," she said, trying to steer both the conversation, and her thoughts, away from such a dark place. "Rick was only gone from her for no more than five minutes, he says. I know it's enough time to get beaten up, but it can't be enough time for that."

"I hope not." Sloane murmured.

"I don't want to talk about this anymore. Let's just figure out what else we have to get done this morning.

Without her work partner, Moira had been finding it a challenge to keep up with the new demands of her expanding business. A couple of months ago, her boyfriend Jack had helped her create a whole new website, complete with web ordering capabilities and the work was literally rolling in. She and Jaye had even had to bring in extra help from time to time just to keep up. Sloane had started working in the front to enable the girls to spend the vast majority of their time in the kitchen. While the business was mainly Moira's, Jaye was a substantial contributor to the start up, and Moira always gave her a fair share of the profits, instead of a mere salary. It was an agreement they had drawn up when Jaye had loaned her some money to get started. Moira held the deed to the building; the loans had been taken out in her name and the business run under her name, as well as being the creative director. Jaye, who had already made back her initial investment, and then some, enjoyed a 40% cut of the profits as her pay. What had seen her making almost no money in the first few months, a huge sacrifice on her part, now netted her quite a tidy sum every year. As of now, they could afford to take on full time help if they wanted to, but the friends still enjoyed too much their camaraderie in the kitchen and were loathe trying to introduce anyone else into the dynamic.

Besides, it wasn't unusual these days to find Jack in the back of an evening, watching the girls design a fancy cake while himself putting icing on cupcakes or sprinkling cinnamon and sugar on some pastries. It was a real family-feeling operation.

Jaye and Moira had been friends for ages. It was breaking Moira's heart that someone she loved so dearly was so hurt. She couldn't stand that Jaye had to go through this, couldn't believe that it had happened to her. Life just wasn't fair sometimes at all.

The biggest slap in the face, now that she knew from the doctor that Jaye would be all right, physically anyway, was this idea that Jaye didn't want to see her. Didn't even want to talk to her. It was eating Moira alive that she couldn't go and visit her friend. All those times when Moira had needed someone and Jaye had been right there, and now she wasn't even being allowed to return the favour.

That's friendship for you though. If Jaye needed her space, her peace and time to heal, Moira would give it to her. No matter how badly she wanted to be there and lend her hand to help in the recovery process. Being a good friend like that meant doing what the other one wanted, even if it wasn't what Moira though she needed.

She decided to call Rick again later on in the morning, just to check in. Rick had said that he was taking the rest of the week off from his job, so she knew he would be there. She also knew he would tell her the truth about how Jaye was doing, and not try to sugar coat it or brush it off.

Rushing around to finish off the jobs that still needed done, Moira barely even noticed when another person entered her kitchen from the back door.

"Hey there, falling behind in my absence?" the familiar voice enquired.

Moira whipped around and stood with her mouth agape to see Jaye.

"What are you doing here? You just got out of the hospital two days ago!" Moira said, but she crossed the room and enveloped her friend in a cautious hug.

"Well, I didn't want to see us go under just because you're down to one back here." Jaye teased her.

"It's not as bad as that yet. Sloane's been helping me out, and Jack and even my mom. We're getting by."

"Getting by isn't good enough. What needs to get done?" Jaye removed her coat, and although it seemed she was trying to hide it, Moira saw her wince at the effort.

"Are you sure that's a good idea? I don't want you to make your wrist any worse than it is."

"Whatever, I can handle it." Jaye started looking over the printed sheets of orders and needs that were always posted on a large corkboard near the door from the kitchen to the store front.

"Good lord, you'll be at this all day and night if it weren't for me." Jaye muttered. She grabbed an apron from the hook on the wall and went to the walk in fridge. Gingerly, she opened the door and disappeared inside for a minute.

Moira was too stunned to move. She couldn't believe Jaye was acting like there was nothing wrong. Finally, her feet became unglued and she rushed to get Sloane.

"Call Rick right now and see if he knows she's here." Moira hissed at her sister.

A large yelp emanated from inside the fridge.

Moira dashed over and threw the door open. Jaye was slumped back against one of the fridge's inner shelving walls. She had a basket of strawberries in her good hand and a large spill of cream down her clothes and puddling at her feet while the empty container had rolled near the door.

"What happened?" Moira asked her.

"I don't know, I was just grabbing the strawberries and cream and it…it…just fell out of my arms. Sorry Moira."

"It's fine. I'll grab you something to wear from my place." Moira lived over the shop. "In the meantime get out of there when you're all wet and we'll get this cleaned up."

"I'll clean it up, it was my fault." Jaye said, stepping around the white puddle on the floor.

"No, no, don't worry about it, I got it."

"FUCK!" Jaye yelled.

Moira was stunned. "What?"

"Stop treating me like a baby! God, that's the whole reason I left the house and came here in the first place, I thought at least you would treat me normal!" she pushed past Moira and stormed into the middle of the kitchen where she promptly began taking off her shirt.

Moira watched her struggle to lift it, soaking wet, over her head with the bad wrist and ribs that were making it difficult at best.

"Want me to help you?" she meekly asked.

"NO, jeez!" Jaye barked at her. "I can do it myself."

Scanning the room, Moira watched in horror as Jaye spotted the large industrial scissors, grabbed them from the holder and proceeded to chop away at her shirt, cutting it off. Jaye was left handed, but the scissors were not. She couldn't hold them properly. With her heart breaking, Moira stood there impotently watching her friend hack away at her clothes. Sloane walked back into the room in time to see Jaye pulling the last bits of torn t-shirt away from her wet body.

"What the hell is going on?"

"Why don't you go up to Moira's and get me a dry shirt instead of standing there like a dummy?" Jaye asked Sloane.

Moira looked at her sister and silently nodded her head. She didn't want Sloane to get into one of her moods and smart-ass her back. Fortunately her sister was quick on the uptake today and bounded out the backdoor and up the backstairs without a word.

Moira was about to open her mouth to speak again when Jaye heaved a heavy sigh.

"You have no idea how much this sucks." She said to her friend.

"I could try." Moira told her.

"No, I just have to deal with this myself. Sorry I made such a mess in the fridge, I really will clean it up."

"You don't have to," Moira said with a sudden twinkle in her eye, "I'll get Sloane to do it."

Jaye laughed, but Moira thought it sounded a little hollow. She opened her mouth to talk again but was interrupted by Rick arriving and charging in the back door.

"Jaye! You aren't supposed to drive with your concussion!" he reprimanded. "I didn't even know you left."

"Duh, you were in the shower. Most peace I've had since I got home."

"Let's get you home, you're supposed to be resting."

"I'm sick of resting."

Rick looked at Moira, then back at Jaye. "Where's your shirt?" he asked her.

Jaye pointed to the mess of cut up fabric on the floor. "There." She told him, pointing.

Moira stayed out of it. She left the room to give them their privacy.

Out in the shop, there were a few customers waiting to be served and she helped them, but she was only going through the motions.

Just a few months ago, Jaye had been her biggest supporter while she went through some tough personal times. Right there when she needed her, barging in and taking over when Moira had been so upset she could hardly see straight. Now it was her friend who needed the sustenance, and all she was doing was pushing her away. Moira knew her friend was tough, almost fiercely so, but she didn't know how to be a real friend to her if she wasn't being allowed.

The customers' cleared, Moira walked back into the kitchen to find Sloane helping Jaye get into a clean shirt. Rick was not there.

"He's getting the car." Jaye told her when she noticed Moira looking around. "And by the way, thanks a lot for calling him. Now you can relax, my babysitter is back on duty."

Before she could react to this sting, Jaye gathered up her jacket and purse and left.

"What the hell do I do now?" Moira asked her sister.

"The only thing you can do as her friend." Sloane said. "Wait."

Chapter Nine

Rebecca Lawson

Rebecca hated Fayette. When she had graduated from law school, she had been in the top ten in her class. Enough to be well placed in a firm if she so chose, but not in one of the most prestigious firms. Only the top three were sought out for those auspicious placements. Top ten got you your pick of the smaller firms where her first years of practice would be spent largely in doing research in the law library and writing endless arguments on behalf of the partners. Never to be recognized for her own legal prowess. The choice of assistant to the Crown Attorney for the small town of Fayette was an easy one. Cut her teeth on some actual law, or so she thought.

Small towns weren't much for legal battles to stir the mind. The old man who she was apprentice to, in a manner of speaking, was hardly able at all to construct a decent sentence anymore. She often found herself wondering how he had held his post for so long; probably more to do with the fact that the only judge in the area was his cousin.

Six years she had spent being the driving force behind his slow tenure in the courthouse. In that time, only three real trials, two of which were cut and dried, only one of which seemed like it might shape up to some real excitement but wound up in a mistrial due to misplaced evidence by the chief of police, who had since retired.

Then, two years ago, after slogging around in the dusty offices for six long years, a miracle happened. She met Daryn Stewart, the cocky, beautiful police officer, newly transferred from Toronto and maddeningly sure of himself.

Rebecca met him during one of the Mayor's many social gatherings. Generally an excuse to have the important people of the town gathered together in one room, get them drunk, and keep their votes in his pocket. So far, a successful enterprise.

Rebecca had sat in the corner of the spacious room and nursed her gin and tonic slowly. She found these events fairly dull. The only reason she came at all was out of duty and boredom. She scanned the familiar crowd and watched the players of the town congratulate one another on being so important.

The group had split, as they were apt to do. In one corner there was the chief of staff from the hospital holding court with several prominent doctors and a few other notables from town; the pharmacist and a couple of pretty nurses among them. Likewise, the rest of the crowd gathered in groupings of related professionals. Rebecca was on the outskirts of a rowdy bunch. The scant legal representatives of the town tended to mingle with the police force. She could see Martin, a handsome lawyer with a fairly large firm standing in a group that seemed to be having fun, but she just didn't want to make the effort to try and talk to him.

Just as she was starting to feel that enough time had passed for her to leave without seeming rude, she spotted him. Leaning on the back of a chair with a glass of beer in his hand and surveying the room with a cool look.

She was instantly attracted to him, against her better judgment. He was too fine, too chiseled and far too aware of himself. Her mind drifted away to the unfortunately good looking boys and men who had captured her attention in her teen years and early twenties. Always she felt the sharp tug in the pit of her stomach for the bad boys, yet always the well behaved safe ones that she allowed to her lips, and eventually her bed.

Rebecca was tired of being the good girl. Instantly she cursed herself for her appearance tonight. Dressed in the same clothes that she had worn to work that day, she looked gray and dowdy. Far too buttoned up, nothing that suggested womanliness, excitement or intrigue. She looked the very picture of what she was; a boring attorney, someone who played by the rules and towed the line. With a slightly shaky hand, she reached up and undid the clasp that bound her long dark hair.

As she had suspected, the mere act of shaking her hair out from its customary tightly wound knot attracted his attention. He was like a wolf, zeroing in on its prey. She was sure he could smell her in the dense air of the room, picking up her scent through the smell of bodies, booze and smoke.

It was as if the room crumbled around her. The noise fell away, the faces mulled into a sea of nothingness and colours. Rebecca watched him walk towards her purposefully. She bit her lip in an effort not to smile.

Perfunctory words were exchanged, but they meant little. Names were given, but the real conversation was taking place on an entirely different level. There was an unbroken contact in both of their eyes. Rebecca could literally feel the desire radiating from him. Within minutes, she knew where this night would end up and followed him without question to his car outside.

They drove through town quickly. Daryn lived in a small apartment complex near the west end. His ground floor rooms gave away the fact that he had not been long in town. There were a few boxes perched haphazardly around the room and a smell of takeout food. It was neither welcoming nor cold, it was just nakedly male.

They moved without pause to the bedroom. She was a little nervous, it had been a long time since she had known a man in this way, and yet she burned for him. They had not made physical contact at all in the short time of their acquaintance. Words had been short and meaningless, or at least they did not register in her mind. For all she knew, she could have talked to him of something as trivial as the weather or something as important as her family, but her memory was lost in a fog of lust and need. All she knew was that she had to have this man and for some reason he needed to have her.

They moved into the bedroom and Daryn reached up to remove her blouse. His hand fluttered for a moment at her buttons, and then made a sharp detour towards her face where he ran his thumb over her bottom lip.

She was trembling. She could feel her knees sweating and knew that when their bodies finally came together it would be nothing short of magnificent. Daryn gave her a crooked grin.

"Rebecca," He said. "Pretty name."

She responded by throwing her arms around him and kissing him almost violently on the lips. Oh yes, this was just what she had always fantasized about with the bad boys who consumed her thoughts always but never her body. This time she would not shy away, she would just take.

Daryn almost tore at her clothes, but she was beyond caring. She pulled at his own with an equal fervor and they fell onto the bed. In that moment, Rebecca shed years of doing the right thing and let herself fall into the abyss of physical pleasure. As she knew he would be, Daryn was an expert on her body within seconds. He bit at the little spot on the side of her neck that made shivers run the length of her body. He grabbed a handful of her hair and kissed her, letting his tongue trace the outside of her lower lip before slipping into her mouth wickedly. His large warm hands travelled the plateaus and peaks of her torso with ease, tweaking and teasing her in every place that made her gasp and moan with delight.

Together they writhed, almost wrestling at times, calm and focused at others. When he finally came to be inside her, she found herself straining to meet his hips with her own, and with the same intensity.

The next morning they awoke naked, tangled in the sheets and completely hungry. Rebecca gently extricated herself from the bed and tip toed to the bathroom before he stirred. She looked at herself in the mirror and smiled. It felt good to be bad for a change.

Their affair was strange though. Daryn was a difficult man to pin down. Not that she was trying to pin him to anything specific per se, but it seemed as though ever since that first night together, his time as the predator had effectively ended and she was the one who felt as though she was in constant pursuit. They exchanged emails, spoke occasionally on the phone or texted one another, but always with a hint of an ending to their tryst at hand. Daryn liked her, this she knew. He found her interesting and exciting, or so he told her on their rare actual dates. Their sexual chemistry was undeniable. He made it clear once that he was not looking for a relationship in the traditional sense of the word, but he enjoyed women, enjoyed her, and hoped that they could be friends. With occasional benefits. After that conversation, she knew she had found exactly the kind of man she didn't need in her life, but like a drug, she couldn't seem to make herself stay away from him. He made her laugh, he made her feel good in his company and, on their nights alone, he made her come like a demon. It wasn't hard to compromise her personal wants in the relationship department for this anomaly.

Every day when she got to work, she opened her email first to check if there was a message from him. If there was, she responded right away, and they would spend part of the day bantering back and forth electronically and playfully. If there was no message, she would find herself checking almost every half hour just to see his name in her inbox. Painfully holding herself back, to be patient and wait for his lead. She knew she was behaving irrationally and somewhat like a schoolgirl with a crush, but couldn't help herself.

This relationship, such as it was, continued for two years before there were subtle shifts in the status quo. Rebecca's mentor, and technical boss, died of a heart attack in the spring and she inherited his position, title and office space. Moving from assistant to full Crown Attorney for the county took up much of her time. Even though the case load was still small compared to the work she would be doing if she were in a city; she represented four towns in the county and the minutiae of the work was staggering. Daryn too moved up the ranks in the force and became a full investigative officer instead of just a beat cop.

After almost a year of having more space between them as they settled into their new roles, Rebecca began to notice little things. Sure, they still slept together on occasions when their schedules allowed, but every now and then she found evidence that there were other women in the man's life. Not that she had any kind of a claim on him, which had been clear from the beginning. It hurt though, knowing that there was always another conquest on his horizon, and none on hers. Slowly, she stopped answering the emails or returning the texts with the immediacy that she once had. Sometimes she would stare at his name in her inbox for days before writing a response. Daryn didn't seem to notice until one night when he showed up at her apartment a little after ten o'clock. Rebecca let him in, but did not take his hand and lead him to the bedroom, as she had been in the custom of doing.

He moved to kiss her and she stepped back, turning to seat herself on the sofa.

"What's going on babe?" he finally asked her.

"I can't see you like this anymore." She said.

Funny, the words were out of her mouth before she could stop them. She hadn't really meant to call a halt to the whole thing, but it must have been what her heart wanted. She didn't even feel too sad about it.

Daryn flopped down beside her and put his hand on her knee.

"Why, we're so good together?"

How like a little boy he was, pouting that his favourite toy had been taken away.

She explained to him that the time had simply come for her to stop pretending to herself that she didn't need any more than what he was prepared to offer.

Daryn sighed, "I thought this might come up at some point. It's your call, babe. And if you ever change your mind, you know where to find me." And he got up, put his jacket back on and left.

Rebecca had been in Fayette for nearly nine years when the biggest case she ever had was plunked on her desk one morning by the clerk. A local woman had been attacked outside a restaurant in town and very nearly raped. There were two men being tried for this, both of them with prior convictions. The arresting and investigating officer was Daryn.

Chapter Ten

Joshua Moody

It is cold and damp and smells bad, like pee or something else, maybe blood, maybe both. Don't like it here in this house, Frankie said that it would be okay here but I don't like it, don't like it here at all. Paint is peeling from the wall, looks like burnt skin sliding off a body, makes me think of the smell and makes me miss my mother. Don't know whether it's day or night or morning or whatever. Been so sleepy, so sleepy. Frankie says it will pass and the horse will make it all go away, run away on the horse. I don't care I never liked horses either they scare me I just want to make this feeling go away. Feels like my bones are creaking in my body. If I'm really quiet, I can even hear them moaning, like tree limbs in the forest under too much stress from the wind and the weight, just before they fall to the ground in crunching horror. My bones sound like that, feel like that. Like they're going to fall out of my body and crack onto the hard ground I'm sleeping on.

Frankie said this was a house, a real house. With furniture and food and everything. This is not a house at all, it's a shell. There are boards over some of the windows, but they don't keep out the wind the way glass does. Not that is matters, there's no heat in this place anyway. There's no food either…well, not much. Last night there were some chicken pieces in a bucket that were cold. I got one, Frankie got three. I don't mind that he got more than me; he's the one taking care of me after all. Frankie is really smart, and as horrible as it is here, at least it's not the street. At least we're not in Toronto. Frankie said once that we may have to go there, but I don't want to. I don't like big cities. I don't like lots of people around me. Frankie is the only one I trust right now.

We ran away together, four years ago, just before I turned sixteen and Frankie was already almost eighteen. Didn't want to stay in that foster house a second more than I had to. Frankie was the one that took care of me. Saved me from the beatings by taking so many of them on himself. Cleaned my skin for me whenever there was cigarette burns on it, or cuts from the leather of a belt biting into my skin. Brought me the weed that helped me to forget the pain. Together we spent the days trying to avoid beatings and abuse, getting stoned or drunk or both and exacting our revenge by stealing from the families to feed our cravings for drugs and booze.

Making our escape was easier than I thought it would be. We just left one night, with a bag each of clothes, a bottle each tucked away on the inside and some jewelry that we knew we could sell. We spent the first month sleeping in farmer's barns and places like that. It's always easier to plan this stuff in the summer. Frankie got us a job running pot for one of the locals. It got us free weed and access to a lot of houses. You wouldn't believe the kind of people who wanted to get their hands on it, and the kind of access you could get to a house when the buyers were already stoned.

In eight months the cops were on to us and we had to leave town. We robbed a store and got bus tickets to Waterton. Our clothes got dirty and the weather turned bitterly cold. Weed wasn't doing it for either of us anymore. Frankie got hooked up with a dealer from Toronto who gave us some crack. In just a year we went from smoking it, to injecting it. I was scared to at first. I don't like needles. But I had nightmares and I was scared to be outside at night. Crack was okay to smoke, but it just didn't help me forget after a while. I really needed to forget. Especially at night. I never told Frankie how hard it was for me to be out in the dark with all the sounds of the animals and insects all around us. My old coat that I had run away with was torn in a few places and didn't keep me warm. But Frankie never complained and I didn't want him to think that I was a baby. He was tough, so I tried to be tougher. I always tried to be tougher for Frankie. So I let him help me with that first needle, and I never looked back.

One night we were lucky to find a place where the owners were away. Frankie had been watching it for days and said that they must be on vacation. We waited until after midnight, when the neighborhood was silent, checked the windows for security stickers and broke in through the back door.

It was heaven. They had food in the fridge and in the cupboards. They had television and a shower with hot water. We made frozen pizza and French fries, ate ice cream and cookies, cheese and chips and anything else we found that looked good. We watched Much Music and took hot showers. I went into the bedroom of what had to be the parents of the house and found a bunch of new clothes. Frankie joined me and stole as much jewelry as he could find. He also found a playboy magazine and disappeared in the bathroom for a while. I didn't care; I had never really had a girlfriend before so I didn't miss anything like that. Especially since the only thing I knew about sex was stuff I learned from the smelly old man at that last house, and I didn't want to relive any of it. Frankie used to tell me sometimes that I needed to get with a woman and forget about the other stuff. Sometimes he would find a woman; they would find an alley or the backseat of a car someone had forgotten to lock. I just didn't want to. Not yet.

We spent two days and two nights in that house. It was the best time ever. We had money from the shit we pawned and we had drugs, booze and food. Warm blankets, new clothes and I even swapped out my old torn coat for a leather one.
After that Frankie tried to case a different neighborhood all the time. He found out when people left for the weekend, and we lived like kings. He found out who locked their cars and who didn't. He is the smartest person I know.

By the next winter we had moved on again. The police in Waterton started getting really mad at all the break- ins. One of our buddies was brought in and rolled over on us. Now they had our names. I started getting scared again, but I never told Frankie. We hitched a ride to Fayette and found the crack house on the outskirts of town. I never went to a real crack house before. I hated it. Frankie gave me heroin and for those awesome moments of sweet fog and delight, I didn't care about the smell or the floors that were bare or anything like that. Heroin was my favourite. At first.

It wasn't long until it took more and more of the drug to feel the same as that first time. And then I just needed it more and more often. Frankie started getting mad at me. We couldn't break into houses as much as we did in Waterton; the cops already had our names. For all we knew, they already had warrants out for us too. So, one night, when the weather turned bad and there was no way to hike out to the country and steal apples or anything from a farm and we were starving and cold, I robbed an old lady. Just stole her bag and brought it back to the house. It was enough to get us a couple of hits and enough for some food. I knew Frankie was proud of me.

The next weekend I hitched a ride to Cantabria and did it again. This time I got an older guy on his way out of an ATM at night. I scored seven hundred dollars. Who knew what he had planned for that money, but I needed it worse than he did. I couldn't wait to get back and show Frankie, but the buses weren't running this late at night. I tried to hitch but no one wanted to pick me up. My clothes were dirty and raggedy again, and I started to get scared that maybe I would get stuck here all night. I didn't want Frankie to think that something had happened to me or that I wasn't coming back. So I stole a car.

I had to hit the girl to get her out. I had never hit someone before. It felt good to be on the other side of that fist. When she fell down, I kicked her once for good measure. Right in the stomach. That felt good too. Then I got in her car and drove away.

I ditched the car outside of town and walked the rest of the way back to the house we were staying at.

This winter hasn't been as cold as the previous ones. But that doesn't mean that it wasn't still just as hard to stay warm or find something to eat. Most of Frankie's contacts in the drug world had dried up too, shying away from both of us after the heat we took from the break-ins. He was cranky and frustrated. I was just a plain old mess. The night after I got back from stealing that car, I had told Frankie about hitting and kicking that girl. How good it felt. He got it, he always gets it. The money didn't last us a week. I needed my fix more and more often these days, and the longer I went between the worse I felt. Frankie became quite interested in my story of beating on the girl with the car. He said that sometimes he too felt like he just wanted to hit someone. When we went out at night looking for a score, he started kicking at the old vagrants that lay huddled against the buildings in the dark alleys of the town.

Fayette may have been a picture-perfect little town, but scratch under any perfect looking service and you will find there is always something darker lurking underneath.

Since we had come here, we had found that there was a small group of homeless, mainly alcoholics and addicts, like us, and a fairly thriving drug trade. Fayette seemed to be quite the little trafficking depot. More drugs flowed in and out of this tiny place than, well, I never really was good with big city names, but I will say it was surprising. Not too many actual users here, but loads of people living the quiet high life on the proceeds.

One thing Fayette did have though was a really great old downtown. Because the town was old, there were great alley ways and back streets to wind through and hide in. If you stayed close to the restaurants, you could stay warm behind the dumpsters and sometimes one of the younger guys who worked the kitchen might slip you a little something through the back entrance.

This is where we were that night. Sitting in a back alley, coming down off our last high and getting drunk on a bottle of Jack we had bribed from the dishwasher of a fancy restaurant with some reefer. Frankie was in one of his terrible moods. He kept telling me to shut up all night. I hated it when Frankie was mad at me. He was like my big brother. I never wanted him to get mad.

We needed money. It had been weeks since we had been able to wash, and since the cops were onto us for the break-ins, we decided to get a cheap motel for the night. Somewhere with a hot running shower and a mattress instead of a dank floor. All we needed was one good score. Someone who looked like they might be carrying a decent amount of cash on them.

I took another long pull on the bottle and passed it back to Frankie. He scowled and swallowed a huge gulp. We could hear people coming out of and going into the restaurant. We heard a woman shouting something at someone and asking for keys. Frankie nudged me. We crept up to the front of the alley and saw that there was a car parked really close to us. A girl was standing near it and she was dressed fancy. Another nudge from Frankie. I knew what he was thinking. We were going to get this girl's purse. Frankie downed a big portion of the whiskey and gently set the bottle down on the pavement, wiping his lips on the back of his hand. He picked up a piece of wood from something that had broken and been thrown down. I didn't like that, it seemed too dangerous, but I didn't say anything. Someone tossed keys at the girl, and they fell down behind her. She bent to pick them up and Frankie clocked her once, hard, as she stood back up again. She dropped at once.

I grabbed her purse, wrenching it from her hand and heard a cracking sound. I started to leaf through it, but like I suspected there was next to nothing of value in it. Women who dressed up like that rarely carried much actual cash on them.

The guy would have been a better target. I threw the purse to the side and bent down to check her pockets. Frankie was staring at her with a look in his eye. He told me to kick her and I did. It felt so good that I kicked her again. Her body looked funny, it moved and shifted where my foot made contact, but it was like she was already dead. It scared me, and in my fear I kicked her hand and heard a cracking sound. Frankie got down on the ground with her and stared at her where her skirt had exposed her in the fall. I shrank back as I watched him rip off her underwear, leaving them torn to the side. He started fumbling with his pants.

From the entrance to the restaurant, I could hear people again. We weren't all that far away and I knew that whoever threw the keys was going to be back, and soon. I tapped Frankie on his shoulder, but he shrugged me off. I didn't know what to do, so I started rummaging through her stuff again, desperate for anything that would let us leave.

I looked up and saw a guy walking right over to us. I was scared. I didn't want to get caught and I didn't like what Frankie was obviously trying to do. I looked up again just as the guy came around to where we were and I saw his face. I knew that if the tables were turned, Frankie would save me, but I also knew that I would never have tried to have sex with that girl. And Frankie was definitely going to try. I ran with all my might away from the car, away from the girl and away from the only friend I have ever known in my life. The sounds of sirens filled

my ears as I bolted down under the bridge, near the river. I
slipped in the snow and scrambled my way up to the alcove where
the stony ground met the concrete of the road above and I curled
into the smallest ball I could. I fumbled through my pockets,
looking for anything to help the pain. A little baggie filled with
white, with weed, with anything. There was nothing left. I had a
crumpled five dollar bill and my kit with my needle, spoon and
lighter. I had no home, no money and no Frankie to watch over
me.

I put my hands over my ears and I cried like I hadn't
done in years. How do you fix your life when no one knows you
exist? I was a ghost now. I lay down on the freezing ground and
waited to die.

Chapter Eleven

A week after returning home from the hospital, Jaye was summoned to the police station for a late meeting with the officer, the one who had come to see her and that she had so disliked. The second guy from her assault still had not been found and they wanted her to go over police pictures. She didn't see the point, everyone knew she had been knocked out, but Rick thought it might be good for her to go. Therapeutic even. To show him that she didn't need his advice or his help, she went alone. Rick barely argued. He just cautioned her to be careful and reminded her to take one of her pain pills before driving.

The pain of her wounds was nothing compared to the pain of dealing with this frustration with the police. They kept her waiting for nearly an hour before she finally was shown into a room.

It got later and later and Jaye was still impatiently sitting at the station looking through old photos and mug shots. She didn't recognize even one of these guys, although it crossed her mind once or twice that either she or Moira had probably gone to school with a few of them. Hardened criminals, weekend peace disturbers and drug dealers were the order of the day. She could tell that the officer was getting annoyed with her, but honestly, what can you tell a guy about remembering an incident that had you out cold in the first few seconds? She barely remembered the night, let alone could find some buried vision in her mind of two guys she only had a chance to smell.

It didn't help matters that this cop was so annoying. He had a much chiseled, very symmetrical face. It was the kind of face that most women would usually go for, she assumed, judging by his airs. Not Jaye. She could see that he was not so much leading man than that guy whom everyone assumes is the good guy until his evilness is revealed. Maybe it was the icy blue-gray eyes. There was a hardness that glinted behind the façade of the warmth. Jaye could see it, could recognize it, and she wasn't about to be duped by his easy charm and flattery.

"I'm not going to tell you again. I have no effing clue what those guys looked like. You can show me these pictures all night if you want to, NOTHING is going to register."

She crossed her arms under her breasts and stared at him. It still hurt, but right now being in charge was more important than being comfortable. She wasn't going to give this ass an inch.

"You keep on with that 'can't do' attitude and we will be all night." He retorted. "I'm going to get some coffee and another photo book."

As he stormed out of the room, Jaye stood up to stretch. She was stiff and tired. They were using one of the interrogation rooms, by the look of it, and therefore she had no idea what time it was. No clock, one two way window, a door, a camera in the corner with the red light off, two chairs and a table. Bland walls, in other words, maximum dowdiness.

Her wrist still hurt and her head was throbbing from the time spent looking at grainy, black and white pictures of ugly men. It was hot in there too. She pulled off her sweater carefully and adjusted her shirt, which was already getting sweaty. Maybe they kept the room hot like this to make suspects uncomfortable, but surely they could have turned down the heat for her? She was no suspect; she was the victim for crying out loud! She lifted her hair from the back of her neck, arching to try and stretch her still sore ribs in the process. What she really wanted to do was to clasp her hands together and lift them over her head for a really good stretch, but she knew that neither her healing wrist nor her ribs would let her move like that just yet.

Goddammit, she thought to herself. Why did this have to happen to her? Life was going just fine.

Work was great, her relationship with Rick was….okay, it was great, but with the recent arguments, maybe not quite as wonderful as usual. She had been happy. She had been on a definite path and she was still so fucking pissed that it had all been snatched away from her.

Officer Stewart came back into the room. With a well practiced eye he took in the sight of Jaye, trying to relieve her sore muscles, slight sheen of sweat on her brow, shirt straining her breasts and look of pure hatred and defiance on her face. Jaye caught his look. His nostrils had flared. She knew that she could sometimes have an effect on men, and it didn't bother her in the least. It used to be something she relished. Right now she was just peeved. She dropped her arms back to her sides.

"Get a good enough look?" she asked him.

He reached behind himself to shut the door, never breaking eye contact.

"What if I said no?"

"Then I'd tell you that you're pretty shitty as a victims' advocate. You don't hit on the victim, asshole, you help them."

"One look hardly qualifies as 'hitting on'." He told her with a wry smile.

"That look did." She fired back.

She indicated the thick binder in his hands. "Won't do any good. I've told you and told you, I didn't see the guys."

He set it down on the table and lowered himself into the chair with a sigh. "I know. Believe me, I know. Your lawyer knows, your boyfriend knows and your doctor knows."

"Then why am I still here?"

"It's protocol. I have to show you these. My boss wants everything in the case to be by the book. It's the first time we've had an assault in this town in over seven years. Most of what we see is minor break-ins, theft and drug stuff. He's pissed that this happened and he doesn't want any loose ends that could mean one or both of these guys walks, okay."

Jaye thought about that for a minute. Possibly pretty boy understood how frustrated she was. It was true; a small town like Fayette rarely saw serious crime. Most of the people who lived here were long time residents, or children and grandchildren of long time residents. They didn't rock the boat, they were friendly and kind. Crime in Fayette usually had something to do with latent teen boys who were bored, drunk or high.

Sure, they had a couple of hardened characters around here and there, but there was hardly a town in

Ontario that didn't, whether it be city or hamlet. Mostly they kept to themselves to avoid trouble.

Already the local paper had run two stories on the event and Jaye knew that there had been one or two journalists from neighboring areas that had reported on it as well. She just hoped it didn't go any further than that. She was no poster child.

Officer Stewart must have noticed the look on her face, because he gently reached out and touched her arm. Jaye jumped a mile.

"Sorry, didn't mean to scare you, but you know, if we get through this bunch then you'll be able to go home. I just wanted to let you know that I'm sorry I have to make you do this."

"Why are you being all nice to me all of a sudden?" Jaye asked.

"You look like you're pretty much still in pain." He sheepishly admitted. "And call me Daryn. Officer Stewart is so formal."

"Don't waste any of your pity on me, I'm doing fine." She barked. That's all she needed, Officer Casanova to start feeling sorry for her.

She slid back into the other chair and leaned over him to get the newest book. Her breast brushed his forearm in the process. She could hear him inhale sharply through his nose.

Something clicked over in her head. There was a shift in the balance of power in the room. Sure, he kept her here for hours knowing that it wouldn't be any help to the investigation, but she was still a woman and an attractive one at that. Jaye slowly slid the book along the table and then scooted her chair a little closer to him. She let her legs relax and drop open at the knees, causing her thigh to rest ever so slightly against his.

Make no mistake; she knew exactly what she was doing. A part of her brain was reprimanding her for playing like this when Rick was sitting somewhere completely oblivious to her flirtations.

But there was a reason behind this, she kept telling herself. For the past week and a bit, nothing had been under her control. Rick was acting like some kind of stranger to her. He kept on treating her with kid gloves. He hardly talked to her except to ask if she was okay, if he could get anything, stuff like that. Sure, it was kind of nice and endearing the first day or two, but she wanted the old Rick back, the one who would talk to her plainly. Not to mention that since this whole thing had happened, he barely touched her either. Like he was afraid to hurt her, bruise her already beaten body or dredge up some kind of memory from the night itself and scare her. She needed contact, she craved it. If all her previous assessments of this guy had been right, then getting some positive male attention from him should be like taking candy from a baby.

Jaye dropped her gaze to the book in front of her. She flipped open the cover, let her eyes wash over the first set of prints and then looked up at Daryn from under her eyelashes.

"Nope, don't recognize any of them." She told him in a husky voice.

She slowed down the tempo of her breathing, slid her foot across the floor just enough to make her leg slide out as well.

Well, why the hell not?

Really, just like riding a bike, Jaye employed all her powers of seduction on him. It really hadn't been that long...four years wasn't that long. Besides, she often still used her flirtatiousness with Rick; at least, she did up until a few weeks ago.

All the pent up energy, pain and disappointment seemed to flow into her in a completely different direction now. She felt a heat building inside her, the kind that stems from purely selfish need, and a small amount of fear.

Daryn was having no trouble at all reading her signals. Jaye kept on flipping lightly through the pages, but was now staring straight ahead and letting her eyes burn into him.

There was a flicker of feeling happening in the pit of her stomach. She felt that old fear of being pulled into something dangerous despite herself.

Jaye finally closed the book and rose from her seat. She kept her gaze locked in. She knew he was hooked already.

"I'm going home." She said in a tone hardly above a whisper. She slid her hand over the back of the chair, picking up her sweater in the process and bent down to unhook her bag from where it had become tangled under the chair leg when she moved it.

He followed her every movement like a predator tracking its prey.

"I'll walk you to the garage." He muttered, "safety first."

Jaye let out a tinkle of laughter at that. There was parking under the building for the staff and the officers of the station, where they kept their squad cars and also where any impounded vehicles wound up, on the rare occasions that it happened. If there was any safer place in Fayette, she didn't yet know of it.

It was darker now then she thought it would be. Jaye walked through the office with Daryn following her. Most of the twelve or so desks were now dark and abandoned for the night. Only two people seemed to be still at work. Lord how she wished she had worn heels, or at least a sexy skirt, but what's the point of dressing like that when impressing a man is the last thing on your mind, as it had been for her....until tonight.

Jaye still wasn't sure what was compelling her to tease him like this. All she knew was that she had that feeling broiling under her skin, like an itch, and if she didn't scratch it, she might just go insane.

There was a small service elevator around one of the corners of the desks and such, probably for transporting criminals to their awaiting rides to prison. Or something along those lines.

Daryn had already pressed the button and was watching her with something approaching lust and curiosity. A strange mixture to wear on the face.

Jaye noticed that his eyes became even bluer. She thought for a fleeting moment of Rick. The last time he had touched her in any way; it had been to pat her on the hand. As if she was a child. Tonight she was no one's child. No one's victim, no one's project. Tonight she was a woman.

They reached the garage, still without another spoken word. The tension was palpable in the crisp

January air. Jaye walked with a slow purpose towards her car. She knew that he was walking just steps behind her. She could practically feel the heat radiating from him. The scent of her jasmine perfume was in the air.

Jaye reached her car and leaned back against the driver side door. She stared at him, practically daring him with her eyes to make the first move, any move. Her stomach was rolling and pitching but she ignored it. Her head hurt from the hours of staring and squinting, but she didn't pay it any heed. Her heart was pounding out of her chest, like it did when she was a little girl, like it did the first time she had ever been on a motorcycle. It was a fantastic feeling.

He leaned in to her; put one of his hands on her hip.

"You okay to get yourself home tonight?" he asked her.

"I'll be fine." She replied.

And then it happened. He leaned in and brushed his lips on hers. Jaye didn't want to be anyone's damsel in distress tonight. She lifted her good hand and grabbed hold of a bunch of his hair, pressing her lips hard against his. His mouth opened and she responded by sliding her hot tongue into it. Jaye could feel his hand scrunching up her shirt into the ball of his fist. She pressed against him harder.

Probably unaccustomed to a woman taking the lead in such a situation, Jaye could feel Daryn trying to control the tempo of the kiss. He eased off, tried letting go of her clothing and fluttered his hand upwards.

Jaye broke off and snapped her head back. She slapped him hard in the face, so hard that her hand stung. Instantly, the cold air brought up finger imprints in an angry red on Daryn's cheek.

"What the fuck was that for?" he demanded.

"I don't need rescuing. I'm not a princess. Either fucking kiss me or go back to your little desk like a pussy." She replied.

He tried to kiss her again, but she laughed at him. "Too late. I'm going home now. Don't bug me with any of those pictures again. Tell your boss I won't do anymore."

She turned her back on him, unlocked the car door, got in and slammed it shut, leaving Officer Stewart looking at her with total bewilderment. Power was an incredible thing, and it felt good to be the one holding it again.

Chapter Twelve

Daryn

Daryn was sitting at home on a blustery Wednesday afternoon fiddling with his cell phone while staring at his computer. While he was grateful to have a day off to recoup after the whirlwind of activity that had been his life the past two weeks, he was feeling restless. If this had been a year or so ago, he would have texted Rebecca, gotten some banter going and maybe had her come over to ease some of his stress. As it was, he was consoling himself by splitting his computer into two screens, one for porn and one for reading through the old emails he used to write back and forth with her. With his left hand, he was absently flipping his phone open and closed, debating on whether or not to send her a quick text anyway. It's not like it would be totally inappropriate, they were working together, in a sense, on this case. But he knew that nothing he would contact her about today would have anything to do with work.

Probably, he mused, and in fact very likely, she had deleted all copies of their emails ages ago. She didn't seem the kind that would hang on to them, especially as the subject matter of so many were heavily laden in sexual content. That was her style after all. Very organized. He was willing to be that if someone had gone through her computer during their time together, they would find a folder just for their emails. He was equally sure that the folder would have been sent to the recycle bin and deleted the day it ended.

Daryn had been so pleasantly surprised, the more time they had spent together, to see that the bedroom was the one place where she let her hair down. Everything else about Rebecca was centered on control. She was a neat freak, she was precise to a deadly sharp point professionally, and she was organized to a fault. But in the bedroom, all bets were off. Grinning at the memories, Daryn found himself getting hard just remembering how her hair tumbled over her shoulders and the way sweat had glistened from her skin. He glanced at the movie playing silently on the right side of his computer screen and then turned it off. The movie was doing nothing for him, at least nothing that his own memory and reading the old emails wasn't doing better.

He chuckled to himself as he scrolled down through some of the earlier ones, to the ones where she had finally started to learn how to play his kind of game. She had eventually gotten nearly as adventurous in the oblivion of cyber space as she had in the bedroom. His only regret was that he had never quite gotten her to the point of sending him anything...inspirational and video, over email. Oh sure, she had allowed him to take a few pictures of her in her underwear (which he had promptly downloaded onto his computer after promising her that he would delete them) and there was the odd topless shot of her taken unawares as she had slept in tangled sheets. Perhaps he should have played the attentive boyfriend a little while longer.

Sighing, he skipped to his favourite email. During the height of their affair, Daryn had gotten Rebecca to talk about fantasies. This particular email had some pretty great details about the idea of a threesome. Something she had once told him in the light of day that she would never actually consider. Daryn's eyes skipped lightly over the words and he closed his eyes for a second and pictured her long fingers dancing over the keys while as she typed.

Normally, he did not get so hung up on a woman. No matter what she looked like, Daryn was one who enjoyed the chase, most definitely enjoyed the conquest, but usually got bored shortly thereafter. With Rebecca, it had been just the opposite. Oh sure, he had certainly enjoyed the chase, even though it hadn't been much of a challenge. Rebecca had practically thrown herself at him that first time. It was the weeks following that first night where he had actually had to work to keep her coming back. She seemed to regret sleeping with him before she even really knew his full name. Daryn thought that was one of the things that had made it so hot.

At first, he thought she was just playing an elaborate game of cat and mouse. She would peep her head out of her little buttoned up mouse hole, only to disappear back inside just as quickly. There were days when he had been so frustrated that she toyed with him. Of course, he soon realized that she was fighting a losing battle with herself. It was fun watching her trying to decide whether or not to let her hair down and embrace the bad boy that she so desperately wanted, but keep on denying herself. Little by little, he wore her down. He spent what seemed like endless hours with her in his, or more often her apartment talking over food and wine. His voice getting deeper and huskier as he moved topics of conversation from work and such to more…interesting fare.

Late at night he would slip over to her on the couch and whisper into her ear, his voice low the way she loved. Even now thinking about how she shuddered as she finally found ways to tell him exactly where to put his fingers, how hard to squeeze her flesh, how softly to kiss her skin. He had loved making her feel as though she was in charge, when all the while he was guiding everything about their sex life.

Daryn's hand had made its way into his comfy sweat pants and was working silently within.

There was one particular night, well into their second year of being more than friends and less than a couple, Rebecca had finally given in to one of Daryn's biggest fantasies. She had consented to a public tryst. Daryn knew that it went against every fiber of her very law abiding being to do this, and that turned him on all the more. They had set a date for a late night picnic in the local conservation area, picked out a spot near the back of the park, away from the most travelled routes, but certainly still within the realm of possible discovery.

It had been a warm and sultry night. Daryn could barely remember the food they ate or what they drank; he only remembered the sensations of Rebecca's body on the blanket under the stars, with cool breezes flitting past the warm ones and the smell of the earth and the trees all around them.

It was shortly after that night that he found himself trying to put distance between them. In trying so hard to bring Rebecca out of her shell, he found himself getting more and more attached to her. He stopped emailing her every day, several times a day. He stopped calling so often. He even started seeing other women again. He couldn't stand seeing that look in her eyes when they did see one another that said she knew he was sleeping with other women, but since they had never made any declarations of exclusivity, she was never the one to bring it up.

Daryn opened his eyes again on the couch and flipped the video back on his computer screen, now entering into the fevered pitch of the movie. He didn't want to be thinking about how he hurt someone else; he only wanted to think about the fun times. The naked fun times.

He closed his email and opened the video up to full screen. That was better.

He had just gotten comfortable with his position on the couch again and his hand very neatly occupied when the sound of his cell phone jarred him out of his sex-fogged thoughts.

"Dammit!" he grumbled. "One fricken night off and they gotta call me." He hastily withdrew his hand and shut off the video. Then he grabbed his phone and pressed the button to answer it.

"Officer Stewart" he barked.

"Daryn, we need you to come in." said the voice on the line. It was Darlene from administration. "We got him." She said.

"Ten minutes, tops." He said and then hung up the phone.

All earlier thoughts had jumped straight out of his head. They had located and brought in the other suspect in the attack. Daryn dressed at speed and tore from outside and into his car. He crossed town in mere minutes and pulled into his spot at the station in what must have been record time.

Entering through staff entrance in the parking garage, the very one that he had walked Jaye into just days ago; he seemed to pick up speed once he entered the office. The beautiful tension was pulsing through the office and the faces of the staff were bright with excitement. Fayette's most violent crime in years, the most dramatic arrest and search, and finally the other half of the puzzle was sitting in a holding room at this very moment waiting for Daryn to talk to him.

Tapping his foot with impatience, Daryn could barely hold himself still through the inevitable debriefing before interrogation.

"Suspect was apprehended at 15:45 this afternoon at 16675 RR # 7 Fayette. Suspect had several syringes on his person, as well as evidence of crack cocaine. Arresting officers are McCurdy and Jensen. Jensen still on scene with two other dispatched officers searching premises for further evidence as per warrant obtained this afternoon at 16:25. Suspect's name is Joshua Moody. Suspect is approximately 5'7", 135 lbs, aged 20 years. Residence unknown…."

More details were trotted out, but Daryn wasn't really listening. What he heard was that he had a drugged up kid, scrawny as hell, sitting in a holding room and waiting for someone to get his side of the story.

Daryn loved this part of his job. The other kid, Francis, was a real piece of work. Spitting out smart ass reply's to the questions, demands for alcohol, for a lawyer at outrageous times. There was nothing Daryn loved better than knocking a smart ass kid like this down a peg or two.

As much as he was known for being the 'go-to guy' when it came to women, Daryn knew that his real strength when it came to policing was in handling the rough young ones who thought they were the cock of the walk.

Daryn spent a minute looking at the kid through the window before he went in. Nothing he had built up in his head about him was the reality. He had pictured a swanky, swaggering toughie slouched in his seat, handcuffed hands on the table, smirk on the face-practically daring you to call him on his bullshit.

This kid was the complete opposite. He couldn't have been more than five and a half feet tall, at the most. He was scrawny and filthy. He looked like he would jump at the slightest sound. But what really got to Daryn were his eyes. For someone so young, he must have really been through some tough times. This kid's eyes were as round as saucers. He looked like an animal that had been caught in the headlights of a car at night. He looked like he might pass out if he was spoken to too harshly.

Daryn grinned. This was going to be a piece of cake.

Throwing the door open with a bang, he smiled when he saw the kid jump in his chair. There were handcuffs holding him to the seat and a pungent scent of urine in the room. The kid took one look at him and started to cry. Daryn didn't try to hide his disgust. Like tears were going to garner him any sympathy. He had seen too many punks like this in his time, crocodile tears poured from them the minute those handcuffs clicked shut and they realized that they were now in serious trouble, especially the young ones.

Sitting down, he stared at the kid for a few minutes and waited for the water works to stop. The smell was burning into his nostrils. They would have to find this kid some pants before putting him in the holding cell that night. No matter what he did, at least he could have some clean pants. Otherwise the public defender would be crawling down their collective asses with shouts of rights and humane treatment. Just another damn thing to worry about.

It took a full seven minutes for this kid Joshua to compose himself. Even then, he kept his head down and did not speak. Daryn had started out with the tough sounding questions, but after about twenty minutes of no response, he started to soften up a bit. After all, the kid was only twenty.

Two hours later and the kid had not uttered a single word. Daryn had left the room twice for coffee and a bite to eat and to confer with his boss. They had decided that he was in fact, capable of speech, since there had been noises coming from him when he had been arrested and when he had sat crying. But for whatever reason, he just wouldn't give anything up now.

They had explained to him that he would have a lawyer coming to see him in the morning, that he and Francis had been assigned council. At the mention of his accomplices' name, the kid finally looked up and made eye contact.

"Frankie?" was all he said.

Daryn left the room again at this and shook his head. Either this kid was retarded or he had a serious father-type complex going on with his partner in crime. He left the other officers to get him squared away for the night and went to grab the kid's rap sheet. He wanted to know as much about him as possible. Even if it took him all night.

Chapter Thirteen

Jaye had decided, after a lot of discussion, that she wanted to go to her meeting with Ms. Lawson, the Crown Attorney, by herself. There was no need for Rick to sit idly by while she talked with this woman, and quite frankly, Jaye felt that she might have a slightly easier time talking to her without a man, even her man, in the room.

She dressed carefully for her appointment, trying to look put together, but at the same time like herself.

Jaye found herself getting irritated at the slightest things. Just Rick's suggestion this morning that she might want to wear something conservative to the appointment made her angry. Why should she change something simple about herself to please another person? Finding no good reason for that she threw on her favourite pair of loose jeans, a pogues t-shirt and a fairly decent looking sweater. It was clean, but it was in no way dressy.

At quarter to ten and Jaye was out the door. Rick had left over two hours ago to go to work, seeing as she had told him not to take another day off on her account.

First stop was to the Bean Post, where she picked up a large cup of dark roasted coffee. She also grabbed one of their muffins for something to munch on. It was nowhere near as good as the ones she and Moira made in the shop, but she didn't think she could face going in there right now without getting into a huge scene with Moira playing the sad and concerned friend and Jaye wanting to pull her hair out at the treatment.

Finally, Jaye brought her car to the back of the large old courthouse in the upper part of downtown. It had once been a mansion belonging to one of the founders of Fayette, but now (with a garishly ugly new addition on the back) it housed the courtroom, several legal offices, the Mayor's office and the municipal offices. Jaye, who had lived in Fayette for so very long, had never set foot in the place before. On her only other opportunity to see the inside of the historic building, which was during a high school civics class, she had skipped off in order to go smoke behind the library with a couple of friends.

There was a rear entrance near the parking lot at the back of the building, and Jaye chose to go in this way as opposed to walking all the way around to the main entrance on the other side. She stepped out onto the snowy sidewalk and bustled towards the door.

Inside there was a glass fronted sign that posted the directions to the various parts of the building. She found the one pointing towards the Crown Attorney's office and quickly headed in that direction.

Down the hallway, turning a couple of times, Jaye finally found herself standing outside of a door marked Rebecca Lawson, Crown Attorney. She pushed the heavy door open and stepped inside.

There was a pair of desks in the large room, as well as a couch, a small table, several lamps, a much larger table and three walls completely covered in bookshelves and books. Jaye assumed that the room itself must have, at one time, been some kind of drawing room or living room. It was pretty impressive in size.

A woman sat behind the larger of the two desks and rose when Jaye entered, moving swiftly over to her and holding out her hand to be shaken. She was tall, taller than Jaye, with a very conservative looking chocolate brown suit on and her hair twisted up into a bun. Jaye ignored the proffered hand and sank down into the plush leather couch, ripping into her bag and taking a big bite of the muffin. She took immeasurable pleasure in watching the unavoidable crumbs roll down from her front and disappear into the cracks of the couch.

"Good morning, you must be Jaye. I'm Rebecca."

Jaye nodded at her with her mouth full. She was slightly disappointed that her lack of manners didn't seem to rile this Rebecca at all.

"Please, stay there and get comfortable, I haven't really had much breakfast myself yet, either." Rebecca told her.

She watched as her new lawyer walked over to her desk, opened a drawer and took out an apple, then grabbed a bunch of papers from a folder on her desk, tucked them under her arm and finally picked up a mug and crossed back over to the couch. She sat down near Jaye and dropped the paperwork on the small table, set down her coffee and took a huge bite of her apple.

Jaye swallowed her bite and took a sip of her coffee.

"Sorry," she said, dusting off her hands, "I haven't exactly liked any of this process so far, I guess I've been getting a little rude." She held out her hand. "I am Jaye, thanks for having me here and thanks for representing me."

Rebecca took her proffered hand and shook it, swallowing some of her apple in the process.

"It's good to meet you." She said with a still slightly full mouth.

Jaye laughed a little. She had thought that this woman would be every bit as uptight as she looked, but clearly there must be some redeeming quality to her if she could get past the iciness she came in with.

"You're hardly older than I am," Jaye observed, taking a closer look at the woman who would be fighting her battles, legally speaking.

"Only a couple of years, judging by your file." She said. "I hope that doesn't bother you?"

Jaye shrugged.

"Okay, let's get down to it." Rebecca said, taking another bite of her apple. "I have here your police and medical reports. It says that you refused to be informed on the complete and detailed nature of your attack, is that correct?"

Jaye nodded and pulled off another piece of her muffin, which she stuffed in her mouth. Maybe this Ms. Lawson was close to her age and not as stuffy as she assumed, but she in no way was going to go for the whole 'girlfriend' approach and win any points with Jaye.

"Do you mind if I ask why?"

"Sure, if you must know, I didn't much care for the cop they sent in to talk to me. He looked like he was far more interested in my tits than in telling me what had happened. I don't trust guys like that." Jaye told her.

Rebecca then did the one thing that Jaye would never have thought she would do. She threw back her head and laughed loud and long. Jaye crossed her arms over her chest, but the lingering ache from the broken bones made her think better of it. She uncrossed them again and stared at Rebecca, who was now dabbing at her eyes.

"Glad you think that's so funny." She said.

"Oh no! It's just that I know that officer and I'd say you pegged him exactly to perfection. They keep on sending him when there's a girl involved because most women can't help being put at ease by his looks. Unfortunately, he knows that."

Jaye raised her eyebrow. "So, you know him well, huh?"

"Yeah. Sad but true. Let's not talk about Officer Stewart though. Would you like me to tell you what happened?"

"No. I still don't think I want to know the whole thing." Jaye told her.

"Okay, then let's move on. We have one suspect in custody…a Francis Moody, the one your husband…"

"Boyfriend…Rick is not my husband." Jaye corrected her mid-sentence. "And we're not talking so much these days right now anyway."

"Okay, boyfriend. The one he caught at the scene." Rebecca studied her for a minute, making Jaye uncomfortable. "Did you want to talk about it? It's pretty common in relationships where one person has been through something traumatic. The other one either goes into denial mode or else they go into protective, mothering mode. Neither one seems to be particularly helpful to the victims. I could recommend a good therapist if you want."

Jaye shook her head. "It's nothing. I don't really want to talk about it."

"Okay, back to business then. The police apprehended a second person last night, though I won't get the details on him until probably later on today."

"Fine. Then what happens?" Jaye didn't so much care about what had already transpired, she just wanted to know what came next. It's not like any of them could go back and undo the attack, but she was almost desperate to know how or when or for how long these guys would be punished.

"Okay, there will be a preliminary hearing, which will probably be pretty quick. I should have mentioned that they both already have prior records and a warrant out for arrests in Cantabria and Waterton. There's no way any judge will let them go on bail. You with me so far?"

Again, Jaye shrugged, but she leaned in a little closer so as not to miss anything.

"After the preliminary, a court date will be set for the trial. Normally, if we lived in one of the bigger cities, this process would take quite a long time. Luckily for us, our courthouse here only serves the county and we should be able to get in there really fast." She reached out and put her hand on Jaye's knee. "I am talking about a matter of days or weeks, not months." She said.

Jaye stood up. "That's fine. The sooner the better in fact." She didn't like that this woman had touched her, as if they were sisters or close friends or something.

"If there's nothing else today then…" she gestured towards the door.

Rebecca stood up as well and walked over to her.

"Look Jaye, I understand you're angry right now. So, we won't go over anything else for the time being. But I want you to call me if you remember anything that you think might be helpful or if you just want to talk. I know how irritating Daryn…I mean

Officer Stewart can be, so if he gets under your skin, you can just call me and I'll be present for anything that you have to talk to him about, okay?"

"Sure, fine whatever." Jaye grabbed her coffee cup from the table and threw the rest of her gross muffin in the garbage. "Just don't try and act like we're friends or anything. I don't know you any better than I know that creepy cop."

Jaye left then, without giving her new lawyer a chance to say anything else. She felt antsy. She didn't want to be cooped up in anyone's office hearing the gory details of how some low life's had broken her world apart just because they thought she might have a couple of bucks in her purse.

*****

The meeting with Ms. Lawson had been a bust, as far as Jaye was concerned. She didn't particularly care for the woman, no matter what nice things Sloane had had to say about her. Sloane didn't know jack about people anyway. She was just a sheltered little princess. And this lawyer? Well, as far as Jaye could tell, she was a stuffed shirt buttoned up goody two shoes. What the hell did she know about getting bashed around? Nothing. What could she possibly know about her relationship with Rick? Even less. Jaye was still kicking herself for letting her guard down for even those few minutes and talking about him, how hard it had been to be around him lately.

And what was up with the way she got all flustered when talking about Detective Stewart? Probably had the hots for him and no guts to do anything about it. If Jaye had to venture a guess, the woman hardly, if ever went on dates and if she did, the guys were probably about as interesting as cottage cheese.

She clicked open her cell and checked her messages. There were two from Rick. She didn't feel like calling him back. He was being insufferable. Kept trying to keep tabs on her like a toddler. She was in no mood for his patronizing tone right now, asking for the millionth time if she was okay. Jaye decided to go talk to Moira, maybe she could convince her friend to go and do something exciting. She had always found tattoos fascinating; they should go and check some out. Fayette may be a small town, but they still had a tattoo and piercing parlour on the less trendy side of the downtown area. It even had a strip club that had only been up and running for the last two years but had done banner business since then. Of course, it was almost on the way out of town. No way would the old residents allow such a place to be built within the town proper.

She jumped back into her car and wound her way from the courthouse which was located on the top of the hill in the newer part of the downtown core to the lower half of the shops, which were all trendy and quaint.

Making the short drive, Jaye found herself marveling, as she often did, about the nature of the town. Once upon a time it had been a sleepy little hamlet of only five thousand residents, but in just ten years it had doubled to ten thousand. The industrial section of town was constantly growing and expanding. Being in close enough proximity to Toronto meant that it was becoming quite the little commuter town, with all the amenities of the city slowly setting up shop and attracting ever more growth and trade. Where once there had only been a few buildings across the river, such as the hospice and a few large offices, now there was an entire industrial boom of offices, depots and the like. On this side of the river the quaint lower downtown area kept on expanding as big old houses were converted into commercial space and restaurants.

More business in the area meant more business for Moira, and consequently herself. They had talked about needing to bring on more staff, as well as Sloane, because it was becoming clear that they would need another set of hands in the kitchen. Especially now that she was so limited in what she could do in a day.

It pissed her off that she couldn't work at the same level yet, or indeed at all. It was bad enough to have missed so much work, but now even on the one day when she had gone in, she found that frustration or pain interrupted her from doing things, which made her angry, which in turn made her sloppy. Jaye had never been one to ask for help before, and she had no intention of starting now.

She swung around the corner and parked in the small lot at the end of the street near the store. Then she switched off the car and sat still for a minute. The last time she had come in, it had not gone well. She had been a little high on painkillers, and very angry, both at herself and at Rick. It wasn't fair that Moira had to bear the brunt of that. She hadn't meant to be like that with her. She actually felt a little nervous to go in.

Jaye told herself to shake it off. She got out of the car and walked to around to the back entrance of the shop, hesitating before going in. Finally, after a couple of deep breaths, she turned the handle, walked through the first door, took a quick look up the stairs that led to Moira's apartment, and walked through the second door to the kitchen.

Chapter Fourteen

Moira was sitting on her high stool at the counter icing a cake. By the looks of it, a wedding cake. It was already looking like a work of art, and Jaye took a second to admire her friend working. Sloane popped in from the front of the store and startled to see Jaye there.

"Oh, hi Jaye. When did you get here?" Sloane asked in her chipper way.

"Just now, I didn't want to startle Moira when she's working. Anything I can do to help today?"

Moira, who had stopped and turned towards her when Sloane started speaking, looked a little wary.

"I don't know Jaye; I think I have everything pretty much under control today. Mom was in last night and helped me finish a lot of the back logged stuff." She told her. "Besides, I thought you were going to take more time to recover."

"Recover, reshmuver. If you're nearly done there, and you're all caught up, why don't you come out with me for a bit? I was thinking of going down and checking out that tattoo place. I've always wanted one of those."

Moira snorted at her. "Tattoo, me? You must be joking."

Sloane was smiling, "Omigod! I would sooo go with you, Jaye, that sounds like so much fun. I'll bet Martin would love it, but you know, can't do it pregnant."

"Why don't you go with her though, Sloane, I can't leave." Moira said. "There's some stuff I need to finish, like this cake, and I can watch the front. It's been a while since I've done that anyway." She looked at Jaye carefully. "You're not really going to get a tattoo, are you?"

"Why not? I've always found them fascinating. Besides, you only go around once." Jaye looked between the two. "You don't really have to come with me, Sloane." She said.

"No, it's okay, I kind of really want to. I'd be too scared to go into a place like that on my own."

Jaye shrugged at her. "Suit yourself. Let's go."

Jaye turned and left, not waiting for Sloane to keep up with her. Outside she silently fumed, why would Moira ditch me like that she wondered? Now she was stuck with Princess Sloane. Of all the people she would have picked never to go to a tattoo parlour with, Sloane was only second on the list to her own mother. Nonetheless, she could hear Sloane's trendy shoes slapping along behind her. Without a word and without turning around she went back to her car, unlocked it and climbed into the driver's seat. She clicked the lock so that Sloane could climb in. Hardly waiting for her to buckle her seatbelt, Jaye started the car and drove off.

The Ink Spot was in the upper portion of downtown, up the hill, towards the end of the business part of the strip and right beside a Laundromat. It looked a little shady from the outside, but Jaye knew the guy who owned it. They had been friends back in high school and had taken an art class together. While Jaye's artistic journey had led her on to decorating desserts, Levi's had taken him into the world of tattoos. She actually couldn't wait to see him.

Jaye got out of the car with a grin on her face. She was really going to do this. Sloane followed her like a puppy dog. They walked into the shop and Jaye plunked herself down on a chair, picked up a book of drawings and started to leaf through it. Sloane, not surprisingly, was drawn to the counter full of bright and sparkling looking piercings.

"These are so pretty! How come there's only one of each out here? Do they hide the mates so no one steals them?"

"They're for your bellybutton." Jaye told her, hiding her snicker.

"Oh…." Sloane said. "Wow."

Levi came out from a back room. He was still just as scrawny as Jaye remembered him and his hair still stood up in all directions. He still favoured Buddy Holly glasses, but now he had muscles bulging under the collection of pictures on his arms. Both of his whole arms were covered in spider webs, gothic looking art and a couple of renditions of pepe le pew, his favourite loony tunes character.

"How can I hel….Jaye! Holy shit I haven't seen you in years! How are you babe?" and he crossed the floor and pulled her into a huge bear hug that almost lifted her off her feet.

"I'm great, ouch, but a little sore." Levi released her and looked at her with a raised eyebrow. "It's nothing, couple of broken ribs and this bum wrist." She held up her wrapped wrist for inspection.

"Sorry sugar, didn't mean to hurt you. So, what are you doing in my dive? Gonna let me pierce your nipple?" he winked at her. Behind them, Jaye could hear Sloane gasp, and she fought not to giggle.

"No, no, I was thinking about getting a tattoo."

"Thinking about, or wanting one? You shouldn't get one unless it's something you really want."

"I want one. Just deciding what to get, and where to get it." She told him.

"How about on your ass?" He winked again.

"Stop trying to get peeks at my girly bits." She laughed.

"Hey, a guy's gotta take a chance when a cutie like you comes in here. What about your friend?" he nodded in Sloane's direction. "You game, honey? For you I'd do your butt for free."

"I'm pregnant." Sloane stated. She was probably going for a tone of righteous indignation, but just came off sounding petulant and very young.

"She's just here for support. Levi, this is Sloane, Moira's sister."

"I NEVER would have guessed that one." He said, but he shook her hand nonetheless.

They bantered back and forth for a little while. Jaye had forgotten how good it felt to flirt for the sake of flirting.

Levi had always teased her back in school and she had loved every minute of it, because there was never any question of anything happening between the two of them. It made it safe, and yet they could get away with the most outrageous suggestions. It made her feel like a girl again.

Sloane sat on her stool and flipped absently through the book of designs. After a half an hour of chatting, and periodically looking at one of the drawings that Sloane pointed out, Jaye finally made a decision. She decided to get a phoenix head with the word 'strength' wrapped around it. Levi promised to custom draw it for her and told her to give him half an hour.

Jaye and Sloane left the shop and walked to The Bean Post, Fayette's favourite coffee shop.

"You don't have to stay with me, you know." Jaye told her once they had their beverages and were sitting at a table near the window.

"I know. But, if it's okay with you, I'd kind of like to watch you get this." Sloane took a dainty sip of her hot tea. "Besides, I think Moira wants me to keep an eye on you, in case you do anything…weird."

Jaye laughed. Sloane may be a bit wishy washy, and she certainly was spoiled, but she was also very honest. This was one of the few things about Sloane she respected.

"So, what would be considered weird?" Jaye asked her.

"I don't know. Isn't getting a tattoo on a whim weird?"

"I guess it depends on who you ask."

"What's Rick going to think?" Sloane wondered.

"I don't care, really. It's my body. If I want to put art on it, then I will. I trust Levi; whatever he draws up will be beautiful. You'll see."

"How do you know him? And how does he know Moira?"

"We were in our final year of high school together. Levi is one of those guys who flirts with all the girls, makes them feel amazing, but then dates these real quiet types. He's an absolute sweetheart. I'm really happy he came back here to open his shop."

"Doesn't look like he's doing much business." Sloane mused.

"Probably because its mid week, I'll be he's hopping busy on the weekends."

Jaye checked her watch. "We should get back there." She said, and she got up from the table, finished the last of her coffee, and put the cup back on the counter at the far end so the girls in the store wouldn't have to come and get it.

As they walked back, something occurred to Jaye.

"Why is Moira asking you to watch me? Besides thinking I'll do something 'weird'. That doesn't seem like her."

"Well, you've been kinda different since the…you know," Sloane gestured helplessly in the direction of Jaye's body. "the accident."

"Honey, if that was an accident, I'd hate to see what attack looked like." Jaye snuffled at her.

They went back into The Ink Spot and Levi was waiting for them at the counter with a huge grin on his face. He held up his drawing, which was indeed breathtaking. The lines were so simple and beautiful and the script of the word flowed around the phoenix head as if it were a cloud of smoke billowing majestically from its own beak.

"I love it!" Jaye said honestly.

"Where are we putting it?" Levi asked.

"On my back, centre upper part of my back, between my shoulder blades."

"Well then, come on back and we'll get going."

The girls followed Levi into the back of the shop, where there was two tattoo stations set up, and Jaye removed her shirt and sat in her bra. She immediately became aware that there were still many bruises on her torso.

Levi paused in his set up of his station and looked right at her, then at Sloane, then back at Jaye. He raised his eyebrows at her.

"You want to talk about it?" he asked her. "Cause if that guy of yours is beating on you, the guy who works with me on the weekends is about six foot five and weighs about two fifty. He would take him out for you, no questions asked."

Jaye tried to snicker, but it came out sounding hollow. "No, Rick doesn't beat me up. This is from...something else."

"You read the paper?" Sloane asked.

"Sloane!" Jaye whipped around and shot her a look to shut up.

"Yeah, not much usually in it, except for that piece about those guys....that was YOU?" Levi was dumbstruck.

"Yeah, it was me, so what?" Jaye defenses were back up again. She didn't want to talk about this with Levi. She was just starting to feel like her old self again. He was one of the few people who treated her normally up until ten seconds ago. She didn't think she could take any more pity.

"I don't want to talk about it." She told him.

Levi shrugged and went back to setting up his inks and his tattoo gun and Jaye tried to relax again.

She could feel him wiping something cold over the spot where he would work.

"Ready babe?" he asked her.

"Go for it." She said.

Levi pressed the transfer onto her back and handed her a mirror. Then he held another one up so she could see the placement of the tattoo. It looked magnificent, and it was only the ink transfer. She smiled broadly and gave him the go ahead.

The gun buzzed loudly and Levi placed his hand lightly on her back. The first passes of the needle were a little jarring, but she soon became accustomed to the feeling of it dragging through the top layers of her skin. She could hear Sloane behind her making tiny little noises every once in a while, as if she was reacting to the pain that she imagined was happening.

Ironically, to Jaye it did not hurt at all. Perhaps it was because she had been living with far worse pain over the last little while, or perhaps her body had simply decided not to register anything else that might cause her to ache. She just let her mind carry her away as Levi worked.

A series of random occurrences drifted past her mind's eye. She saw that beautiful house, the one that had started the fight in the car with Rick. She saw the first wedding cake she had ever done and the tears of happiness in the bride's face when it had been delivered. She saw her brother David and herself playing among the waves of the ocean as children.

In just under three hours, Levi had finished and was cleaning her up for inspection. Sloane had drifted off to sleep in the chair where she had been watching. Once again, he handed her a mirror and lifted his second one to show her the work.

It was breathtaking. The phoenix head was majestic, with hues of deep red, burnt orange and shining gold picking out little intricate details. 'Strength' was slowly flowing around it as if it was an ethereal dream, instead of a word of power. Jaye loved it. It captured everything she wanted it to.

He covered it with a plasticky kind of medical gauze and taped it down. Then he handed her a bottle, telling her to use it to keep her tattoo healing properly, and no matter what she heard, NEVER to put polysporin or any other medicated ointment on it. He asked her to come back in a week when it was healed and show it off. She promised to with a careful hug.

They woke Sloane and walked back out to the front of the shop where his next client was waiting.

"What do I owe you?" she asked him, taking out her wallet and reaching for her card.

"Jaye, I can't charge you for this. You were the one who encouraged me to do something with my art. And, you know, it's an honor to give you something to help you get through, you know, your ordeal."

Again with the pity. Jaye bit her lip. She knew he was just trying to be helpful but it almost made her feel sick.

"I'll tell you what. We'll do a swap. You come to me for a cake, anytime, for anything, and I'll do one for you that will be so gorgeous you won't want to eat it. It'll be my treat."

"Cake that I don't want to eat? That'll be the day, but you're on." He hugged her carefully so as not to disturb her fresh work and kissed her near her ear.

"Don't be such a stranger." He whispered.

"I won't." she told him.

With that, she and Sloane left and Jaye drove her back to work.

"You won't have much to report, I guess. You slept through most of that." Jaye teased her.

"I know, sorry. Sometimes I get super tired for no reason." Sloane patted her belly. "Thanks for letting me tag along though. I can't believe I've actually been in a tattoo parlour! My friends will never believe me." She giggled and got out of the car.

Jaye shook her head. Never in a million years would she understand Moira's baby sister.

She turned her car around and drove aimlessly for a bit. She still didn't want to go home. Cranking up the tunes, Jaye turned her car away from town and headed south. The highway was not too far away, but it was already starting to get dark. Coming on to three o'clock in the afternoon but with the shorter days of winter and the dark snow clouds gathered overhead, it felt like six. Just as she was heading further away from the town, a bright neon sign with a picture of a girl on a pole came into view. She had almost forgotten this place was out here.

With a wicked grin, Jaye made a beeline for the gentlemen's hotspot.

Chapter Fifteen

Jaye swung her car along the twists and turns of the road that led out of town and towards the notorious club. She could remember with distinct clarity the amount of fuss and uproar that was caused when the owner petitioned for the location, his liquor license, the renovations he performed on the building itself. She and Moira had cracked many a joke about the type of place it must be on the inside. They had begged Rick at one point to go in on a spying mission for them and come back with reports on everything from the décor to the price of a drink. Rick had refused. He never really went in for that kind of stuff anyway.

Now, freshly tattooed and feeling bold, Jaye decided she was going to go in on her own.

She couldn't get over how dark the sky was already. It was only late afternoon. Probably there was a winter storm brewing up. Jaye had to think about the last time she had paid attention to something as mundane as the weather. She couldn't remember. It seemed like a lifetime ago that it mattered to her whether or not it was going to snow, or rain.

Finally, the glaring sign popped into view from behind a large tree and the driveway swung off to the left. Jaye maneuvered her car into it and sat behind the wheel for several minutes.

What on earth was she doing here?

Glancing down at her clothes, she shrugged her shoulders at the jeans and top she had on. They were no where near exotic, although she doubted very much that the clients who frequented the place were all that picky about attire. Hell, she was even willing to bet that there wasn't one of those "no shoes, no shirt, no service" signs anywhere to be found here. Especially considering most of the staff was sure to be without shirt at one point or another during the evening. And she could pretty much bet that they weren't all that picky about whom they 'serviced' either. She snorted to herself.

Jaye dug around in her purse. She located her phone and changed the ring to vibrate, sticking it in her jeans pocket. Then she found her bottle of Tylenol Three's and swallowed two of them with the last of a bottle of water that she had also found in her bag. Finally, grabbing just her bank card out of her wallet and sticking that in her pocket as well, Jaye tucked her purse under the seat and got out of the car. She locked it, stuck the keys in her other pocket, and walked with purpose towards the door.

The Club, even without the token cutesy name that she might have envisioned, lived up to what Jaye imagined any strip club would at the very moment that she entered the front door. The lighting was garish, and yet it still seemed dark inside. There weren't too many cars out front and likewise not too many customers inside either. It took a few minutes for her eyes to adjust to the variations in colours and lights and she blinked several times as she made her way from the entrance hall to the main room. There were patches of the wood floor that were stained and some that were sticky, probably with spilled liquor. Immediately, she felt both embarrassed and exhilarated to be there.

She sidled up to the bar and ordered herself a cosmopolitan, a drink she hadn't had in ages. The bartender was a busty woman who looked as though she was heading into her mid years with gusto. She had probably been a dancer once upon a time, too.

Jaye picked up her drink and headed over to a small table in the corner near the entrance to the 'stage' area. The whole place was dark and the lighting for the stage just made the outlying tables seem like they were shadowy hiding places.

On the stage there was a girl swinging around a pole to the tune of a song by Pink. She was wearing a cowboy hat and boots and not a whole lot else.

Jaye studied her. She was fascinated by her. This woman was only a few years younger than herself. She was wearing glitter almost everywhere, on her face, in her hair and on her body. Probably to make it look like sweat glistening off her skin, Jaye figured. The expression on the girls' face was what got to her the most. There was a look in her eyes as if she was somewhere far away and it was obvious that she enjoyed what she was doing, the dancing anyway. Jaye had seen that exact expression come over Moira's delicate features while she was working on a particularly complex and beautiful cake. It was a concentrated effort to take the beauty inside your head and transform it into something tangible. Whatever it was, the girl was obviously in her mind somewhere very far from this tiny little bar outside of Fayette.

Jaye sipped at her drink and glanced around the room. She was the only woman in whole place not working. There were a few girls in tiny little nighties wandering around the floor amid the few patrons. Jaye could only imagine how busy this place must be by the late hours of the evenings.

The cold cosmo was going down so smoothly, probably amplified by the painkillers she had downed just before coming in. There were a handful of men dotted around the room. Jaye raised her glass again and surveyed them over the rim, trying to look nonchalant. Some of the men she recognized from around the town. It wasn't even that late in the day yet, so the sight of a few prominent business men was a bit of a surprise. So were the farmers. Didn't they have chores to do?

She finished her cocktail and settled down lower in her seat, trying to find a comfort zone that didn't affect either her bruises or her newly tattooed skin. It wasn't easy.

A tall brunette came gliding over to her table.

"Another drink, sweetie?" she asked as she leaned down to provide a not too subtle glimpse down into the depths of her cleavage.

"Oh, sure. You don't have to do the lean thing with me. I'm not a lesbian." Jaye told her.

The brunette straightened up. "I didn't think so. So, what are you drinking?"

"Cosmopolitan."

"Ha ha, Sex and the City fan, right?"

Jaye laughed with her. "I suppose so. Actually, I just felt like having a drink that really made me feel like a girl again, you know?"

The brunette winked at her and took off for the bar. She came back a minute later with a fresh glass and handed it to Jaye.

"So, do you mind if I ask you a question?"

"I don't mind at all." Jaye told her after a sip.

"You're not a lesbian, it's…" she checked the clock on the wall, "quarter to five on a week day, what in the hell are you doing here?"

"What's your name?" Jaye asked.

"I'm Dynasty!" she exclaimed with her arms thrown up over her head for effect, causing a few men to look their way. She slid into the chair beside Jaye.

"Actually, my real name is Donna. We all have really lame stage names. That girl up there," she pointed to the woman on the stage who was down to nothing but a g-string, "her stage name is Sax….like saxophone, but her real name is Susan." She giggled.

"Nice, do you guys get to come up with your own names?"

"Hell no! You think I would have named myself after a cheesy TV show that ended more than a decade ago? The owner comes up with something that has the same first letter as our real first names. So, you still didn't tell me why you're here."

"I'm deciding whether to chuck my career and apply here. You girls make pretty good money, right?" Jaye held her face still, trying to see if Donna would realize that she was kidding.

It took a minute, but Donna's face broke into a huge grin. "I really hope you're not making fun of me. Cause I was starting to like you." She giggled.

Jaye pushed out the chair beside her. "Will you get in shit if you sit down for a minute?"

"Naw. It's only Stella in right now. The boss and the bouncers don't come in until later, when we get really busy." She indicated the barmaid as she spoke and sank gratefully into the chair.

"So really, why are you here?" she asked again.

"It's a great question. I guess I just wanted to be somewhere where the women hold all the power. You know?"

"What in this dump? Actually, you're right; we do pretty much have the power here. Well, when the boss isn't around anyway." She lifted up her foot and rubbed tucked her fingers in through the side and rubbed the arch of her foot. "Gawd, it feels good to sit for a minute. These things are murder on your feet."

Jaye looked down at the five inch platform shoes and laughed. "Hazard of the job, huh?"

"You have no idea. I nearly broke my ankle about a month ago."

"I'm Jaye, by the way. Nice to meet you." She held out her hand.

Donna shook it, grinning widely. "So, are you a writer or something?"

"No, actually, I'm a baker, but I'm currently not working."

"You should find out if that little place down on the Main St is hiring. The Cake-something. They have the best stuff in there."

"I'm a partner there, actually, but thanks."

Donna turned her head on a quizzical angle. "If you're a partner there, then why aren't your working right now?"

Jaye held up her wrist with the wrappings on it. "Kind of hard to ice cakes when you're wrist is fucked up." She chuckled. "Do you read the paper?"

"Sure, of course I do."

"Read about those guys caught attacking a woman outside a restaurant a little while back?"

"Um, yeah. Dirty bastards. I just hope they hadn't been in here. We get all kinds of whackos."

"Yeah, well, I'm the one they attacked." Jaye stared her in the eye, defying her to look sympathetic.

"So, now you're out for a drink in a place where male contact is really controlled. Makes sense to me." She said, without a trace of anything but kindness. Jaye sighed. Finally, someone who got what was going on her head.

"Exactly."

"I kept on thinking that you looked familiar though. Did they put a picture of you in the paper?"

"No way. I don't want to be a poster child."

"Hmm. It will come to me later I guess. I have to go, it's my turn on the stage soon. It was really nice to meet you, Jaye."

"You too, Donna."

Jaye spent the next two hours drinking her cosmopolitans slower. The first two had hit her pretty hard, and she was determined to keep her mind clear.

The place changed the closer they got to night. With the clock creeping around to seven…and then eventually eight, the tables filled with the men of area trickling in. The music on the system was louder and faster and the girls danced for shorter periods of time, most of them now circulating on the floor in between numbers. Jaye was fascinated with the whole thing. She watched Donna and her co workers dance away on the stage, a look of fiery independence in their eyes. Knowing that every man in the place was watching them and was thinking about them and knowing that they likely wouldn't give any of them the time of day, that was real power. Jaye wanted a taste of it. It felt to her like the night she had kissed that smarmy cop. She was the one calling all the shots. No one would dare try and force her into something. Like a superhero.

Okay, maybe not a superhero, because who ever heard of one in a g-string and pasties? And generally they don't get money stuffed in the tops of their stockings. Generally, they didn't wear stockings.

The night marched on and Jaye's earlier resolve to sip slowly at her cocktails waned. Donna had told some of the girls she was there and soon she found that a complimentary bottle of champagne was sitting in an ice bucket at her side. These were some pretty incredible girls.

By ten o'clock, Jaye was well and truly drunk. Drunker than she had been in a long time. She got up to go to the bathroom and some random man pinched her ass as she walked by the table.

She rounded on him in a fury, but was stymied from an actual physical reaction by a bouncer who had seen it happen and was at the table in a wink. He threw the guy out, stating that not only was it not allowed to touch the women, but he couldn't touch the other patrons either. Fascinated she watched him get escorted out while his table of buddies laughed at him. She stumbled her way into the bathroom and then back out.

On the way back to her table, Jaye nearly fell. Strong arms reached out to grab her and hold her steady.

"Hi Dynasty…" she slurred. "You came back to talk to me!"

"Lord you're wrecked. Why don't you come in the back and lie down? We have a couch back there."

"I don't wanna lie down. I wanna dance." She told her.

Donna righted her on her feet and went to the bar. Jaye could hear her asking the barmaid for coffee…strong coffee. Taking advantage of being let go, Jaye climbed up onto the stage. Huge cat calls erupted from the table of men whose friend had just been ejected.

She began to attempt to take off her shirt but the lingering wounds and the alcohol made it virtually impossible. Strong hands took a hold of her and guided her to a back room.

Jaye awoke about two hours later to find Rick and Donna standing over her.

"I went through your phone, honey, I hope you don't mind." Donna looked sad.

Great, another person who saw her as someone to take care of, and right when she had thought that this woman might have possibly understood her more than anyone else had lately. She didn't care anymore. The champagne and the earlier drinks were wearing off and she just wanted to go home away from all these eyes and pitying stares. It didn't seem that there was anywhere she could go anymore that someone didn't feel a need to rescue her. She sat up, brushed aside Rick and grabbed her coat from Donna.

"I'm going home." She said.

"You can't drive…you've been drinking all night." Rick replied.

"I'm fine. You can follow me if you're so worried."

Before he could protest again, she threw her coat over her shoulders, grabbed her phone back from Donna and headed out the door with Rick hot on her heels. As she stormed through the club, absolutely no on paid her any attention at all.

Rick took one long hard look at her as she got into her car.

"When we get home, we have to talk."

Chapter Sixteen

"I'm trying really hard to understand what's going on with you, Jaye. You barely seem interested in what's going on with the police and these two guys, you don't want to hear about what happened after you were knocked out and yet you tell me that all your crazy behaviour lately is some kind of attempt to get back your 'power'?"

"I knew you wouldn't understand. I knew you'd call me crazy."

They were standing in the bedroom of the apartment, staring each other down like old west bandits about to have a dual.

"Maybe I am calling you crazy, 'cause you sure aren't acting normal!" Rick yelled.

Jaye knew he hated confrontation. She didn't like fighting with him either, but even more she couldn't find the words to tell him about all the wicked thoughts going through her head lately and she couldn't seem to stop her behaviour.

"What the hell were you doing in a place like that, anyway?" He wanted to know.

"I don't see what the big deal is! Those girls are just making a living the only way they know how.

Besides, I think it's beautiful. It's only guys like you that make it all seedy and dirty."

Rick shook his head at her, which made Jaye want to scream and tear at his hair.

"STOP THAT!" she bellowed.

"Stop what?"

"Making that face at me all the time. You keep treating me like some kind of broken doll that you're afraid to break. You're treating me like one of your kids with a missing arm that you have to fix. I HATE it!"

That one had hit home. Rick looked as though she had slapped him in the face. There were tears in his eyes. Good, she thought.

He kept quiet and so she continued her assault on him.

"You never treat me normal anymore, so how else do you expect me to act? You don't talk to me normally; you call me all the time just to check up on me. You don't touch me at all, unless you're trying to help me do something. I'm not some old lady you have to walk to the bathroom. I'm your fucking girlfriend for crying out loud!"

She began taking off her clothes. Despite the weeks that had gone by and the healing she had done, it was still hard to do it on her own, but she bit her inner cheek hard in an effort not to wince. She saw Rick's hand flutter for a moment by his side. He wanted to help her, she could tell. But enough was enough. She yanked the rest of her shirt off and pulled off her jeans. Then she carefully unhooked her bra and stepped out of her underwear.

"You never touch me....you never even kiss me like you used to. Kiss me now, Rick." She pleaded. "Kiss me now."

Jaye ran her good hand down her body seductively. She let her fingers linger on her breasts, the tips grazing her nipples, before dropping her hand down further and further.

Angry as he was, Rick was still a man. She could tell that he was fighting some kind of battle in his head, but she was done with trying to fight it out. She wanted him, right now, and by god she meant to have him.

Sinking back onto their bed, Jaye did the one thing that she knew would send him over the edge and pull him into her own urgent purpose. She lifted her hand once again and slipped a finger into her mouth, turning it slowly around and sucking on it hard.

Rick's resolve crumpled and he crossed to her in only two steps, pulling off his own clothes in the process. Naked in record time, he stretched out next to her on the bed and pulled her in for a deep kiss.

Jaye could feel his body shaking. It had been a long time for them both, just over half a month, which seemed like an eternity to her. She kissed him back hungrily, scratching at his back with her fingernails. It was as if she couldn't get enough of his mouth and she drove her tongue into him with a ferocity she had never before shown. Rick tried to roll her so that he was on top, but she surprised him by swinging a leg over his torso and forcing him down instead.

Letting go with her lips, Jaye let her mouth travel lower and took one of his nipples in between her teeth. At first she was playfully nipping at him, but suddenly she bit down on him harder. Rick let out a small yelp, but she reached down and cupped his balls with her hand and he ignored the pain she had just dealt.

Jaye felt drunk. Her mind was swirling and soaring off into a place of its own. She began to tug and stroke at him harder, biting his other nipple-this time with no playful nibbles to lead up to it. She could hear Rick making sounds, but they sounded like they were coming from far away.

She shifted her position and sat astride him, sinking down onto his hardness with a sigh. It felt so good to have him again. With an exaltation that radiated through her being, she began to move on him. No slow preamble for her tonight, her actions were furious and she clawed her nails across his chest as she rode him.

Thunder pounded in her ears and the world fell away and shattered into a thousand pieces. She wanted more of this intoxication. From her mind's eye, she saw Rick's arms reaching for her hands and she snatched him at the wrists, guiding him to her breasts. With her hands over his, she helped him grope her harder than ever before.

"Grab my hair." She whispered with a rasp. But when she let go of his hands, he merely slipped them down to her waist. It felt like he was trying to hold her harder, or push her and she could hear his voice through her fog, but had no idea what he was saying.

"Do it, grab my hair." She commanded.

Rick's hands rose up and gathered a bunch of her hair in them, but it was much too soft. Jaye ground herself down on him harder. "No...no, do it harder." She urged.

She could feel him trying to move. Maybe he wanted to be on top, but this was her night, and they would do it her way. She bent down suddenly so that she was practically lying flat over him and bit his neck hard.

"I want you to fuck me. I want you to hurt me..." she whispered.

Suddenly Rick's strong hands threw her off to the side where she hit the mattress with a thump.

"Goddammit Rick!" she shouted, "What the hell?"

She sat up and turned to him. He was sweating like crazy and there were red marks all over his torso. He looked both furious and completely crushed.

"What? Am I too repulsive for you to touch now?" she asked him, her voice dripping with scorn. "You can't even make love to me anymore?"

Rick choked; a look of pure fear and sadness in his eyes. "Make love? Is that what you called that? Jaye, you were hurting me. You were scaring me. That's not you." He shook his head and swiped at his face with his arm.

"This isn't you anymore. I don't even know who you are. And I definitely can't do this."

He got up off the bed and began dressing.

Jaye watched him go into the closet and come out with a suitcase.

"What are you doing?" she asked, suddenly worried.

"I'm leaving. I've tried everything I can think of with you, but you're not YOU anymore. You're some kind of angry creature that I don't recognize." He started throwing clothes into the bag, not really paying attention to what he was taking. Then he disappeared into the bathroom and came back out with a handful of toiletries.

"I know you're hurting, and you've been through something terrible." He said sadly. "Lord knows I was trying to be there for you, Jaye. But you keep pushing me away. You're acting like some crazy person on a mission to destroy herself. And then you do this...this..." he swallowed hard and looked at her. "This isn't you. You aren't the Jaye I know and love anymore. Call me when you find her."

With that, he zipped up the bag and marched out of the apartment without looking back even once.

Jaye looked down at her nakedness and punched the bed, hard. How dare he? She got up and went into the kitchen where she got out the bottle of whiskey. Then she went into the top cupboard above the fridge and pulled out her emergency cigarettes. She tore the kitchen apart trying to find matches, finally finding some in the bowl where they kept miscellaneous things like magnets and store coupons. Then she grabbed a bowl and headed back into the bedroom. She sat down, lit a stale cigarette, coughing at the dry taste of it, and opened the bottle, tipping a large swallow into her mouth. She tapped the ashes into the bowl and took another long swallow.

Fine, he wanted to bail on her? She was better off alone anyway. She didn't cry, not once. Instead she drank herself back into a stupor and finished off the pack of smokes. Then she curled into a ball on her bed, throwing a sheet across her middle, and let the alcohol still raging through her system carry her off into oblivion.

*****

Rick arrived at the back door entrance to the apartment above the Cakery at just after one in the morning. He had already called Jack on his cell phone. Lately Jack had been spending most of his nights with Moira and after a brief conversation; he had agreed to let Rick have the keys to his apartment for a while.

Knocking only once before the door was opened, Rick stepped into the foyer.

"Come up for a sec?" Jack asked him.

Rick nodded and followed his friend up the stairs.

Inside, Moira was in the kitchen making tea. She wordlessly set out some cups, milk and sugar on her coffee table and sat down beside Jack on the couch. Rick dropped himself into a chair.

"You know, I think this is the second time I've ever been up here." He said, trying to make polite conversation.

Then he dropped his head and started to sob. He was grateful that Moira and Jack let him have a moment to fall apart. He never was much for sappy emotional scenes.

When he composed himself and lifted his head again, Moira was holding out a tissue. He took it and dried his face.

"What happened?" Jack asked gently, eyeing the red and raised bite mark on Rick's neck.

"I can't...I can't even say. She's seriously losing it though. I had to drag her home from a strip club tonight. I don't even know what she was thinking..." he rambled out.

Moira shook her head. "She won't really talk to me either. She's shown up at work a couple of times, but she just gets mad and leaves. I wish we could help her."

Moira poured tea into the mugs she had brought out and handed one to Rick, which he took gratefully and blew on before taking a sip. Somehow he felt just a little better from it.

"There has to be something we can do." He said.

"I'm sure leaving her isn't the answer, but I do understand why you can't be there right now. I'm just worried she'll do something even more drastic without you there to keep her grounded. Valentine's Day is just around the corner and lord knows I'd like the old Jaye back before then." Moira mused.

"Maybe we should all talk to her together." Rick said. Then, warming to the idea, he expanded on it. "You know how they do those interventions for addicts and stuff, to tell them how much they love them and get them help? We should do that for her."

"I don't know. I mean, your heart is in the right place, but I'm not sure that would go over so well. She might get even madder." Jack interjected.

"Why don't we sit on that idea for a while? I'm not saying it's a bad one, but let's talk to her doctor first. She might have some insight or advice." Moira added.

"Okay. Thanks again you guys. And thanks for letting me use the apartment, Jack. I appreciate it. I'll probably wind up just going home again tomorrow. I hate being away from her when she's hurting like this."

"It's no problem. We're here for you, too." Moira said, getting up to hug him.

Rick let himself out and drove back across town to Jack's apartment. This night had been horrible. He just hoped that Jaye's doctor would be able to shed some light on how to help her without driving her further away. Because, God, he missed her like crazy.

Chapter Seventeen

It was the first full night Rick had spent voluntarily away from Jaye in so long, he couldn't even remember. Jack's apartment was nice, but it wasn't home. He spent time wandering around, even though it was late and he needed sleep, but his brain was too busy.

Rick decided that he didn't want to sleep in Jack's bed. Something about it just didn't feel right. All he could smell was the faint scent of vanilla, which was probably from when Moira spent the night, but it just made him think of Jaye and it was far too distracting.

He finally settled down on the couch. It was older, slightly battered and very comfortable. The kind of couch where you could easily slip into a deep sleep but that wasn't going to happen for Rick, not tonight anyway. In fact, he hadn't been sleeping well at all since the attack.

Ever since that fateful night, all he could think about was rounding the corner of the car and seeing that…that disgusting man trying to violate and hurt his love. The soundtrack of his mind played their fight over and over in his brain with this image, so the pain of his guilt became nearly unbearable.

If sleep did somehow manage to come to him, the same scenes just played out over and over, augmented by his imagination. He imagined seeing much worse happening to Jaye as that bastard crouched over her. He imagined himself being held down and forced to watch the assault.

Rick twisted on the couch, trying to expel the thoughts from his brain. He punched the pillows down and pulled up the blanket that he had brought in. He thought about Jaye at home, taking her medication and the sleeping aid that she had been using since she came home from the hospital. Then she would lie down on the bed and be sound asleep within minutes. The kind of drug augmented sleep that didn't allow for dreams. The only way she seemed to be able to get through a night.

It was a fairly still night for late in January. There were no blowing winds, no snow falling and the air was still. Of course Fayette rarely got some of the harshness of winter that the rest of Ontario seemed to suffer from. Something about being located in a 'snow belt' area. Which sounded like it meant they should get more snow, not less, but Rick didn't care about the term, he never really liked winter to begin with. Go an hour in any direction though, he often noticed, and winter was in abundance. From where he had propped his head on the couch, Rick could see the slight glitter of frost on the window and the biting way the light from the street lamp seemed to cut through the still atmosphere. He closed his eyes and tried to will himself to sleep, but it wasn't happening.

Frustrated, he got out his blackberry and went through the emails he had accrued. There were several from work, a few from his mother and father and one from his sister in Alberta. With a wry smile, he thanked his lucky stars that he didn't live there. It was minus 40 degrees there tonight. Here in Fayette it was only about minus five; cold enough, if you asked him.

No, Rick was not one for winter. If you asked him, it was nothing but trouble. Except for those who were born without limbs, the majority of his clients were victims of accidents, eighty percent of which happened in the winter. Snow blower accidents, skiing accidents, there were a myriad of ways to slice off an arm or a leg on an icy, snowy hill. Then there were the car accidents where people became careless on the snowy roads and forgot how to handle themselves. It made Rick sick to his stomach to think of how often this kind of thing was avoidable. Once, he had to fit a guy for a prosthetic foot after he had put his foot from the ankle down into a fishing hole on a drunken dare and left it there for ten minutes. The frostbite had been so severe that removing the foot was the only option. The stupid guy was proud of it. It didn't bear thinking what some people would do with enough whiskey or beer in their systems. Rick himself was not a big drinker, but he just couldn't picture a scenario where he would intentionally harm himself just based on the amount of alcohol he consumed and what his companions thought.

He punched the buttons on his phone and exited the screen. He didn't want to waste anymore time tonight dwelling on people like that. Instead he decided to just lie as still as possible, close his eyes and make himself fall asleep.

He was standing in that same alley, again. It is the place where all his inner hatred now gathers. He can't see what's going on yet, everything is too dark. Somewhere in the black corners of his mind he can hear Jaye asking him why he doesn't want a house, why he doesn't want to think about a future with her in it. There is a scratching noise coming from somewhere behind him and he tries to turn to see what it is, but his body won't cooperate. Slowly his eyes adjust to the darkness. Jaye is lying on the ground, exactly as he found her on that fateful night. The men who assaulted her are nowhere to be found. The scratching noise gets louder and louder and Rick tries desperately to move anything, his head, his limbs, even his eyes but his whole being is glued to Jaye and her broken body.

He sees a large creature...no, two creatures, creeping out of the shadows towards her body. One of them is dripping saliva from its ugly maw; the other has razor sharp claws that it's twitching towards her, as if just waiting to get close enough to break through her delicate skin at first opportunity. He tries to scream, but the sound won't come out of his mouth. Its agony, seeing Jaye helplessly lying there with no idea that her body is about to be torn into shreds.

Rick startled awake. The nightmares were getting progressively worse. It was so incredibly difficult to sleep here. But he had to make a point. Jaye was in such a dark and twisted place and she seemed to be hell bent on doing things to make those around her suffer. Half of him wanted to run screaming away from her, from even this town, and go and start over somewhere else. But a stronger urge was churning in his gut and there was no doubt which was going to be the one to win out.

Rick jumped into Jack's shower and quickly washed away the sweat and churlish thoughts dredged up by the nightmare. He was careful to hang the towel up afterwards and re-dressed quickly. Then he left the pillow and blanket neatly on the bed and grabbed the rest of his things.

Racing back outside in the cold, he stowed his bag in the backseat of his car and drove quickly through the quiet town back to his own apartment.

He was terrified to wake her up, so he turned the key in the lock oh so carefully and guided the door shut so that the click would be quiet. Rick tiptoed in, sliding his shoes off his feet and leaving them near the door.

In the bedroom, Jaye was curled up on her side of the bed. There was an empty bottle near her and the room smelled like smoke. Rick twisted his mouth. She only smoked when she was really stressed out about something. The drinking was a bad sign too, lord only knows how much she had had at the club before he had dragged her back home. He crouched down on the floor by her side and listened to her breathe for a bit. When he was sure that she was sleeping okay and that she hadn't consumed enough to warrant a call to emergency, he slipped back over to his own side of the bed.

His clothes he hung carefully on the back of the chair. Then he set the alarm on his blackberry for six thirty, knowing full well that there was no way she'd be up that early.

Rick got into bed more slowly than he ever had. Every rustle of the blankets, every bit of his weight on the mattress and he was sure she would awaken. He didn't want her to know he was here, but he needed the sleep, and there was no way he was going to get any sleeping at Jack's, or anywhere else for that matter. The only place he could truly relax was in his own bed, next to Jaye. Finally, sometime after one thirty in the morning, sleep came.

The alarm roused him far before he was ready. As angry and confused as he was with her, there was no way he wanted her to know that he had come back home and spent the night. Again, it took what felt like ages for him to get out; again he worried about rousing Jaye and having to face another confrontation with her. He eased into his clothes and for a second, debated leaving out a glass of water and some aspirins, since he knew that she would be waking up with the mother of all hangovers in a matter of hours, but decided against it.

Like a thief, he crept out of his own place and went back to Jack's to get himself ready for the day. He didn't call, he didn't text, he didn't even email. As far as Jaye's behaviour was concerned, well, it was something he couldn't deal with right now. But he still needed her. No matter how hard she tried to push him away, he needed her in those dark midnight hours, and if it meant sneaking in to his own home in the middle of night, well, so be it. Feeling like some kind of sneak thief was better than feeling like he couldn't do anything at all. It was better than the feeling of watching his only love slowly turn into someone he didn't even know.

Chapter Eighteen

The next day, Jaye came home exhausted from the physiotherapy to improve her wrist function and the endless conversations with the prosecutor and her doctor. She sank into a bubble bath with a clenched jaw. She still felt annoyed. Rick wouldn't be home for ages yet, if he came back home tonight at all, and she was restless. She didn't want one more person to mollycoddle her or talk to her like a two year old. She was a grown woman dammit.

Leaning over to soap her legs, Jaye grabbed a razor from the side of the tub and began shaving. It had been at least two weeks since she had shaved her legs, she realized. Not since the night of the anniversary dinner. There were generously long hairs sprouting from her skin like little insect legs poking out. She was slightly amused by them. She dragged the razor over them, severing them like little appendages and imagining tiny bugs under her skin writhing in pain. It brought a wicked grin to her face. She liked the idea. As she finished with her legs, Jaye looked down at her body in the water. There were still bruises, albeit more jaundiced looking now then they were earlier. Jaye hated them. Fading they just looked worse. She had stopped looking in the mirror lately to avoid seeing her banged up face, which still had stitches above her eye. Probably the rest of her face looked like hell, but right now she was beyond caring.

She just wanted to have fun again, to feel like the old Jaye again; the one who still laughed and cracked jokes. Unfortunately that side of her just seemed to be drifting farther and farther away.

The bath still felt heavenly though. It was hard to ignore the itching on her back from the tattoo she had gotten from Levi and it was hard not to keep staring down in between the suds and burn her gaze into the wounds on her body. Jaye could feel an anger burning in her brain. She still hadn't told her family about what had happened. Not that her parents would be able to do anything, or her brother for that matter. She just didn't want to go through the pain of speaking the words to them out loud. In fact, aside from fights with Rick or Moira or anyone else who was close to her where the subject matter was obvious, Jaye hadn't spoken the words out loud at all. The thought startled her. She had never even said it to Levi, just asked him if he read the paper. It was easy to let people know what had happened without actually letting them know. It was a relief not to have to talk about it if she didn't want to.

She took an enormous gulp of breath and sank down under the water. The sounds of her fingers clicking on the side of the tub were like being in a submarine, she imagined. All thuds and pings, not like real sounds at all. It was soothing. All you had to do was submerge yourself and reality completely changed; like being swept away into a parallel universe. She wished she could stay like this for hours, but her lungs wouldn't let her hold the amount of air she used to be able to. The longer she stayed under, the more her ribs screamed at her to go back up to the surface.

She burst back up, too fast, ribs aching and shaking a little from the exertion. Another thing to piss her off, it seemed. Oh sure, her doctor had told her how lucky she was not to have really serious injuries, how much worse it all might have gone, but all she could think about was the new limitations she had. Can't work with a broken wrist, can't dunk her head under water for a measly twenty seconds, hell, and can't even sleep with her man! It was all so maddening!

Jaye took a few slow breaths, trying to see how much she could get into her lungs before her ribs fought her. She let them out slowly and tried to control the tempo. In…out….in…….out. One more big breath in and she slipped under the water again. Keeping her eyes squeezed shut, she focused on the sounds of the pipes, the drip of the tap hitting the water, the feel of her hair fanned out around her. It felt like everything was burning the longer she stayed, but she gritted her teeth and silently ordered her body to obey her commands.

Finally she surfaced again, panting, almost sweating and triumphant. Her body ached with effort and her head pounded but she felt like she had achieved something important. The longer submersion was proof that she could take back the command of little things. Really that was what she wanted more than anything. Buoyed by the efforts, she sank down once more under the water.

The trial was coming up so soon and all she could think about was how angry she still was, how lost she still felt. Rebecca wanted her to read a victim's impact statement, but she didn't see how she could possibly do that, considering there was absolutely nothing she remembered about the night at all. She found herself wondering if Rebecca had approached Rick for anything to that effect. She wondered too if it had just been her imagination playing tricks on her or had Rick really crept home last night and into bed with her. She could have sworn she felt his body pressed against hers in the small hours of the night. Of course, she had also drunk herself into a black out state after their fight and on top of all the alcohol she had consumed earlier at the club, it was a wonder if she could clearly remember anything.

She resurfaced, frowning. It was one thing to lose the events of a night from being hit on the head, it was quite another to do it voluntarily with drink. That was stupid, classic stupid. How many times had she and Moira sat up talking about Sloane's ridiculous friend who got drunk all the time, who drank to such excesses? How many times had they lamented her behaviour, or simply made fun of it? The last thing she wanted was to turn into some kind of drinker, oblivion that was not what she craved. It just got so hard sometimes. It was hard to talk to Rick; she hadn't even really tried to talk to Moira. Hell, she didn't need the alcohol to feel like things were spinning out of control, things already were. Her whole world was shot to hell.

Maybe she should call her. Jaye climbed out of the bath and toweled herself off with care. She avoided looking in the mirror. Maybe she and Moira could go out and grab some dinner together and just talk the way they used to. The more she thought about it, the more she smiled. It was a great idea. Besides, something told her Rick wouldn't be coming home again tonight. He was so mad. He hadn't talked to her or texted her all day.

Jaye went into the bedroom and dressed in some comfortable clothes. A little over two weeks past the attack and already she was starting to heal a little. Her wrist was still bound up, but she was finding it easier now to work with it in its bindings, now that she had gotten used to it. Her ribs were still sore and it still hurt to breathe too deeply, but it was getting easier with them too, to dress herself and move her arms around. She was even wearing bras again. Her concussion had been mild, so the after effects weren't all that severe and she had no problem driving or reading or anything like that. She just got a little dizzy when she saw flashes or sudden movements. As for the rest of her injuries, well, she was avoiding looking at them but she could still feel the bruising under her skin. Her stitches were starting to dissolve, but at least her head no longer looked scary.

Finally clothed, Jaye picked up the phone and dialed Moira's number.

There was no answer.

She called Moira's cell phone.

On the third ring she picked up.

"Hello, Jaye? Is that you?"

Call display. Was there no surprising anyone anymore?

"Hey Moira. Um…" suddenly all the earlier thoughts of spending time with her best friend seemed lame. She was at a loss for words.

"You okay, sweetie?" Moira asked.

"Yeah, yeah, I'm fine. I was, uh, just wondering what you were doing tonight. Like, did you have dinner plans or anything?" She chewed on her lip, trying to figure out why she so suddenly felt self conscious.

"Well, actually, I hadn't even thought of dinner yet. I'm still at the store."

"Really? What are you still doing there? It should have been closed up hours ago." Jaye glanced at her clock. It was now creeping up to seven o'clock.

"It's nothing. Just, um…I've, I mean we've, had a lot of orders this week and I'm a little behind at getting to them. So, I've been staying later to finish stuff up."

"Oh." Jaye felt a little let down. It was partly her business too and here her best friend couldn't even pick up a phone and tell her that things weren't going so well. She swallowed hard. "Do you need any help?" It was a shot in the dark. She knew that the last time she had been in, she had behaved a little poorly.

"That'd be great. If nothing else, I'd appreciate the company. Can you bring pizza?" Moira asked her.

Jaye smiled a slow grin. "I can bring anything you want." She said.

Inside of half an hour Jaye was standing once again at the familiar rear entrance to The Cakery. Once a daily trek for her, she had only been twice in the last two weeks and both times had not been extremely successful. Now, all she wanted was to go in, get to work with her best friend and feel normal. No rolled eyes, no pity. Pizza was a good sign. She couldn't wait to get back to the way things were.

"Hey stranger!" Moira greeted her as she walked in the door. "Long time. Sloane says you got a tattoo from some 'scary guy we know from school'. So…what did you get and whose the scary guy?"

Jaye plopped the pizza box down on the counter and hopped up to sit on it. She flipped open the box and grabbed a hot slice, biting down with a sigh. "Mmmm, veggie and feta cheese."

"My favourite!" Moira exclaimed.

"I know." Jaye winked.

"So…the guy, the tattoo. Spill it."

"Remember Levi? From art class?" Jaye asked, her mouth full.

"No way!" Moira looked up from her work. "I love that guy! What'd you get?"

"Come and see." Jaye told her. She put down her slice on the lid of the pizza box and waited for Moira to get over to her. Then she twisted a little and raised her good arm up over her head and reached to the back of her shirt. She started to pull it up slowly. Moira must of noticed that it was a little tricky, so she carefully reached up and helped her.

"Oh!" she gasped. "It's so beautiful. Does it hurt?"

"No, it kind of feels like a strong sunburn. OH!"

"What??" Moira jumped a bit.

"Here," she fished in her purse and came up with a bottle of moisturizer that Levi had given her. "I can't get this on by myself and Rick...well, he's been working a lot. Can you help me? It's supposed to help it heal better."

"Sure." Moira smoothed the cream on Jaye's back and kept silent.

Another awkward pause, lord but Jaye was getting sick of them.

As Moira washed her hands after, Jaye started eating again. She rattled the box at her friend and finally Moira came over to help herself.

"So, what are you working on? Looks like a wedding cake, nice."

"Actually, it's a sweet sixteen cake, if you can believe it."

Jaye did a double take at the cake on the counter. It was three tiers and quite intricate. It looked exactly like a wedding cake.

"You must be shitting me." She said.

"Nope. She's having some kind of Winter Princess themed wedding and she wanted three tiers, white on white, with edible glitter and all the sconces and scallops I could fit on it. Can you fucking believe it?"

Jaye snorted. "Looks like something Sloane will wind up picking out for her perfect little girl someday."

"That's what I thought." Moira agreed with a wicked grin.

They laughed and ate and Jaye began to settle into a feeling of relief. This was what she had been missing. She should've come here so much sooner. Poor Moira was drowning trying to do all the food by herself. And Jaye had never felt more like her old self than she had just this last half hour. She polished off her slice and hopped down, heading straight over to the computer.

"Now, if I can't help too much with the actual baking, the least I can do is organize things a little better. Are you keeping up with the electronic inventory?"

"Jack's been doing it whenever I can't get to it. It should all be up to date on there." Moira told her, going back to the cake.

"Good." She scanned the files of the computer. "Holy shit! Did we open a branch while I was away? This is enough work for two stores!"

"I know, it's pretty great, huh? You know, I was thinking that it's really time for us to start accepting resumes for some full time help back here. My mom's been taking up some of the slack, but my nana hasn't been too well this winter. Mom can't be here as much as I need her to be. Any idea when…"she trailed off for a second and then cleared her throat. "when you're coming back? What does your doctor say?"

Jaye swallowed again. She kept her gaze on the computer. "Well, my doctor says that I shouldn't plan on doing anything until after the trial. He thinks the stress will be too much for me."

"And…how is that going? The stress stuff I mean." Moira asked her.

"Why? Rick been talking to you?" Jaye could feel that old familiar heat rising in her face.

"He was here last night. What the hell happened with you guys?"

"We had a bit of a fight."

"Duh."

"Okay, we had a pretty big fight. Why do you want to know about it?"

"I don't know, because you always used to tell me when you guys fought? I haven't talked to you much lately."

Moira shrugged her shoulders and Jaye could tell that she was trying to look nonchalant, but this was obviously a fishing trip, trying to get Jaye to talk about things she didn't want to talk about.

"Look, how about you focus on that cake and I'll get this stuff caught up and we leave the rest alone, okay?"

"If that's what you want."

"That's what I want."

"Fine."

"Fine."

They went back to work but the Jaye felt like the first fist had already been thrown. Five minutes of silence and it all came bubbling out.

"We had a fight about sex, okay." She blurted.

"I thought it was about…" Moira bit off her sentence.

"What, you thought it was about what?" Jaye demanded.

"Well, you being angry all the time. We just want to help you know."

"Save your help for someone who asks for it. I was doing just fine last night on my own."

"So then why did Rick borrow Jack's apartment? That doesn't sound like the actions of a guy who is doing 'fine' in his relationship."

Jaye stood up and turned around to face Moira. She was already standing, staring at Jaye with her hands on her hips.

"What the hell do you know about anything? You've only been dating Jack for three and a half months! Get back to me when you've been together for three and a half years!!"

Moira looked as if Jaye had slapped her.

"Hey, calm down! I was only trying to make sure you're okay. I love you, you stubborn bitch!"

"Really? Then why are you talking to my boyfriend about me behind my back, instead of calling me and talking to me directly?"

"You told me to leave you alone!"

"SO DO IT THEN!"

"I think you should go." Moira said.

"Fine. Don't bother calling me. I'll be back in a few days to update the system again, but I'll use my key so I don't 'disturb' you."

She threw her coat back on biting hard on the inside of her lip to keep from shouting anymore. She hated fighting with Moira. If she had just left her alone, they could have avoided the whole thing. Her eyes burned with tears that she refused to shed and her head throbbed. It seemed like there was no topic of conversation that didn't make her raging mad. She hurried her leave so that she wouldn't say anything else she regretted.

Just as she was almost out the door, she heard Moira speak.

"Jaye, get some help."

Chapter Nineteen

Joshua Moody

It's cold in here. Not as cold as the old house had been and certainly not as cold as it was lying out on the streets for so long trying to avoid the police, but it is still cold. I hate being cold. Hate being stuck in here and not being able to talk to Frankie, except for the times when our lawyer comes in. But it is all a blur.

They won't let me have anything in here. They took all my stuff, all my stash when I came in. They even took my clothes. Oh, how scary that moment was. I remembered back to the last time a man made me take off my clothes. Couldn't stop shaking. Someone kept on talking about withdrawal. Probably mean my fix. I haven't had a fix in so long my skin is crawling all the time and the cold only makes it worse. I'm so itchy.

I wish I could remember more from when they brought me in but my mind is playing tricks on me these days. I can't concentrate. I can't even think straight. I wish they'd let me stay with Frankie, but somebody told me he hit one of the cops when they brought him in.

This place is horrible. Everyone here talks all the time. At night when it's supposed to be dark, the lights are never fully out, but I don't mind that so much, I never did like the dark. I don't like hearing the other people here talking all the time. They call each other names. They're mean. At least one of the big guys got me a little weed to take the edge off. Not that it helped. It wasn't very good and I had to hide it so that I wouldn't get caught smoking it and I got nervous and dropped half of it in a puddle outside in the yard.

Our lawyer says they know who we are. Me and Frankie. They know about the times we stayed in houses to keep warm and they know about the girl whose car I stole and they know all about that girl we beat up that night. I don't like him. He's supposed to be helping us but he won't hardly ever let me and Frankie talk and he says that we have to plead guilty since Frankie got caught still trying to get with that girl. I don't know why he did that. I don't get it. There's always at least one girl in that house where we were staying who would get with Frankie if he wanted. But he told me he was getting tired of those girls. Don't know where they've been, he kept telling me. But you can't just get with a girl because she's passed out. I don't know much about girls, but I know that's wrong. I know, because how many times did I wake up in those foster houses with someone who thought I was passed out. It's wrong. Frankie shouldn't have done that.

The lawyer, he looks at me sometimes like he's expecting me to say something. I don't like to talk to people I don't know. Frankie keeps trying to tell him that, whenever we're together, but he don't want to listen. He thinks I know something. I can tell by his eyes like little black holes in his face, trying to get to me, *but I ain't going to let him. I learned early, the less you say, the less they can hit you with. People like that got a way of taking your words and using them against you.*

At least it's getting easier to get through the day without a fix. I thought I'd never start to feel better. It may be cold, but I'm getting food everyday and there's a shower. Makes it easier in the night when I know that at least my belly is full.

I know what that lawyer means when he tells us we have to plead guilty. I don't even care. Jail used to scare me but after the last two weeks by myself nothing seems as scary as that. I hope he doesn't think I'm going to get up and talk though. Right now anything would be better than that. I don't even talk to the guys in here. Not even the one who scored me the stash. He just walked on over and said "looks like you're hurtin' kid" and handed it to me. I took it. He walked away. Why can't the lawyer be like that? Why can't he just come in and say what he has to say and then leave? No, he lets Frankie talk and talk and he just stares at me with those shitty eyes. He don't like us much, me and Frankie. We should at least have a lawyer that likes us, shouldn't we?

I feel bad about what we did. We shouldn't have been so hard on that girl. But we just needed the money. It all comes down to the money, doesn't it? I wonder how much they're paying that lawyer to talk for us. Can't be that much, or else he might like us more.

I know if I just stay quiet and take what the judge gives me one day I'll be out again. I'll be older. I won't have to stay in dirty old houses with creepy people. I won't have to ever go back and stay with a family that I don't know who don't know me and don't like me and don't want me. I'll get a job somewhere warm. Maybe Florida. Maybe working on a boat somewhere. I'll tell Frankie where I am and we'll get a boat and live on the ocean and never have to be around people ever again. It sounds pretty good, in my head. But it's hard to think about it when I'm lying here on my own with nothing to do but count the bars on my cell.

I remember one time, right after we ran away. I was having trouble sleeping outside and Frankie would tell me stories about what we'd do when we were rich. He'd talk for hours if that's what I needed. How we'd move to Hollywood someday and probably be the kind of guys who invested in movies and made all the money when they did good. Frankie was always full of all the good ideas. Sometimes I wished I could be more like him. I wish I could talk to people as easy as he does and I wish I was strong like him. But I've never been strong. I'm still not.

Still cold. Even though I have a blanket and a pillow, they don't like to use the heat in here. I see guys walking around with their shirts tucked into their pants and I wonder how they don't have goose bumps everywhere. It's worse at night, and it's worse when my skin crawls and I itch and I just want to be back in that house again, the first one we stayed in when we finally got hot showers and hot food. I know it wasn't our house, but for those couple of days, I pretended it was.

Now I'm here in this cold and terrible place where everyone talks tough like Frankie does and no body sees me. I can't stop getting the shakes and all I want to do is sink down into the floor and disappear.

My head has been aching for days and days. Sometimes the guys in here make noise at night on purpose to bug the guards. Sometimes they talk about stuff they're gonna do to the first woman they see when they get out. They all talk about how they miss women. I don't miss them at all. Only two women I've seen in years I've hurt. Maybe if I knew my mother, it would be different.

Tonight it's one of those nights where the noises are getting to me. I'm aching so bad for a fix. I can almost taste it in my mouth. I can almost feel the cold needle poking into my skin. The only thing I can't feel is that sweet sweet heaven when the stuff hits my blood and everything goes pink and yellow and wonderful. The ache in my head goes away and cold goes away and everything goes away.

I want to go away on that ride again. I want it so bad.

The guys in here keep talking to the new fish. New fish…new fish…

Makes my brain hurt to listen to them. They been talking about him all day. He's younger than even me. Just turned eighteen if you listen to what's being said. I always listen.

You can't help it in here. Even if you're trying to tune 'em all out and get some sleep, you can't help but listen to every little noise. I listened when they talked about him coming in. They don't like him. They say he did something bad to a little girl. They keep telling him to off himself, or they'll find a way to do it for him. Put him out of his misery. Hey, we all got misery. Why should he get to get out of his? I had a way out of mine, I had Frankie and my brown sugar.

This kid isn't going to last in here. I can tell. He's already crying. Men in here don't cry loud but you can still hear them. You can hear the way their breathing changes and how others will make a lot of noise to cover it up if they like you and how it will get all quiet real fast if they don't. They don't like this guy. They've all shut up. It's extra humiliating to get heard crying in here. If they shut up for you, they want everyone to know you're crying. It means you'll get no respect from anyone.

Aw man, he ain't even trying to cry quiet. I learned fast, if you gotta cry, you stay quiet. The first couple of nights in here when I was hurtin' so hard and I was scared and I just wanted to go home go away I cried. I mashed that crappy pillow down into my mouth as far as I could, anything to make the sounds go away. The guys all talked loud but I could hear the sounds of my own sobs in my ears and it just made me hurt worse. I tossed and turned on my tiny bed, clawed at my skin tried to jam my thumbs into my eyes, make the pain go away make the ache go away scratch it all off scratch my skin OFF! I shook and shook all night and cried and through it all I could hear the guys talking to each other. It don't matter what they were saying, they were giving me my peace to get through it. I haven't cried once since then.

But this guy. He's wailing. The sound is beating on my ears and making me want to hit him. We all have to listen to it. Even the guards aren't telling him to shut up.

There's a sound like running water, but it's not hitting metal. I know what that means. Our sinks and toilets are metal and if you can hear water and not the sound it makes on the cold steel, someone is catchin' their piss, someone is going to toss it right at this kid. It happened once before, since I got here. It makes the whole place stink and it lets you know damn fast that you are in some pretty big danger.

I hear snickering. It's gonna happen soon. I brace myself. There is a sloshing sound and then a wail from the kid. Must have been someone right across from him that threw it. Loud laughter is going on as the kid screams bloody murder. A guard comes down to see what all the fuss is about, but he does nothing. I guess if you hurt a kid, even the guards don't care about you. I'm glad that never happened to me.

The next morning I hear that the kid is dead. I am sitting in the dining room and I'm at a table all by myself because they separated me and Frankie in here so we aren't allowed to talk or anything. All anyone is talking about is that new fish kid from last night. They found him this morning in his cell, his throat

213

was all cut up. Someone must have thrown him something sharp to do it with. The old guys in here can get anything. They said that the skin was hanging all jagged on him cause the knife or whatever it was he used was sharpened wrong and it had bad edges on it.

I shoot a look over at the table far away from me where Frankie is sitting. He is watching me. He knows I don't like to hear about stuff like that. I can tell by his face that he making sure I'm okay.

A guy comes and sits down with me. I don't know him. He's usually over in Frankie's area. He tells me:

"You hear about the fish?"

I nodded at him.

"You got a friend in here, eh?"

I nodded again.

"Okay, listen up then, cause I ain't going to tell you this ever again. Your lawyer, he gonna come at you and offer you something to talk about your friend. He's gonna promise you all kinds of shit, less time, maybe no time, just so you can tell it was all your friends idea. You with me?" he looks around the room carefully.

I nod at him again.

"You're lucky right now, kid. You got people in here watching your back. You roll over and that won't happen no more. Get it? You talk, it all goes away and maybe you find

yourself down there in the morgue covered in piss next. Get it?"
he nudges me, "Get it?"

There's eyes' everywhere watching me. I look up and see
Frankie studying his food like it's the most interesting thing he's
ever seen. I'm getting a warning. I nod at this guy who's talking
to me and he grabs my piece of shitty burnt toast from my tray
and puts it all in his mouth at once.

"You're a smart kid." He tells me, spitting little bits of
toast out of his mouth as he talks. Then he leaves and heads
back over to where Frankie and his boys are sitting.

I put my head down, keep on eating. Shiver a little.
It's cold in here.

Chapter Twenty

Rebecca sat in her office trying hard not to sweat. Daryn was due in any minute to drop off the police reports for her. Sure, he could have had them messengered over, or even emailed them, as he no doubt did for the opposing side. She knew exactly why he wanted to deliver hers personally. They had not seen each other in a very long time. Not since the night she had shown him the door of her apartment. There had been no phone calls, no text messages, nothing to indicate years of a sort of relationship between them. She couldn't walk down to the ladies room, there was not enough time. Instead she pulled a small mirror from her purse and checked out her reflection.

Her cheeks were flushed. Not a good sign. There were also a few strands of hair that had fallen loose and were orbiting her face in not the most flattering way. Rebecca licked her fingertips and tried to smooth them back, but it was a difficult task with one of her hands trying to hold up the mirror so she could see.

Of course she could just let her hair down, that would solve the problem, but that was what she always did with Daryn in the past, let her hair down just in time for him to run his fingers through it.

She moistened her fingers a little more and tried to tame the last piece of unruly hair just as her door swung open. There he stood, looking every bit as dangerous and daring as she remembered him. Against her better judgment, she smiled at him, and then cursed herself. Couldn't she just for once be the cool and aloof one?

"Am I disturbing you, counselor?"

Was he ever.

"Hi there Daryn, did you want to have a seat?" she asked, trying to keep her voice on an even keel.

Daryn sat down in one of the two chairs she had in front of her desk and pulled out a manila folder with a thick sheaf of papers in it. He tossed them onto her desk.

"Here you go, doll. Everything we have on the case so far, but I don't imagine we missed much. Now what do you say we blow out of here and go grab a coffee on the taxpayers' time?" he grinned at her.

"Sorry, I'm too busy." She retorted.

"Aww, watsa matter? You don't play anymore now that you're the top dog? It's just coffee. It's not like I asked you into the back of my cruiser." He winked at her.

It was infuriating how he could still get to her. Rebecca found herself responding physically against her will. What was worse was that she was sure Daryn noticed. He had learned to read her body very well and quite early on in their affair. Obviously, he had not forgotten how. A rather slow and impish smile spread across his features as he stared her down. Rebecca took a measured deep breath to calm her nerves.

"I don't go out when I'm working unless it's for legitimate business. And now that you've brought me all this work to do, I'm afraid I'm going to be far too busy." She told him.

Daryn got up from his chair and swung his body over so that he was half perched on the edge of her desk.

"Come on baby, the whole reason I brought these over in person was so I could kidnap you. It's been far too long." He intoned; his voice now settling into the deep husky register that he knew from history drove her mad.

Rebecca tried so hard to be in control, but she knew she was fighting a losing battle. In spite of the personal armour she had resigned to keep in place, she smiled at him.

"Really I can't. This is a big case; I really have to devote my time to it."

"All work and no play…" Daryn said. "When was the last time you played? I'll be willing to bet a week's salary that it was the last time you were with me, wasn't it?"

Well, now she was damned if she answered and damned if she didn't. If she lied, she knew Daryn would see right through her, if she kept her mouth shut, he'd take it as being correct…which he was. It was maddening that men could go out and pick up a random girl and just get laid when they wanted and women couldn't do the same without suffering some serious defamation to their character. And as much as she hated it here in this stupid small town, she would be buggered if she'd let her reputation stop her from getting a bigger and better job in another city. She wanted to leave at the top of her game, not feel like she'd been run out of town with a scarlet letter on her chest.

"So, I'm right then, huh?" Daryn chuckled softly at her.

"What? Sorry, I was thinking about something else."

"Sure you were. Come on, babe. Tell me why you stopped spending time with me."

Rebecca sighed. "Because, work just got too busy and I'm getting too old to waste my time with someone who doesn't want the same things I want. You," she pointed at him, "don't want any of the same things I want."

"That's bullshit. We both hate being here, we both hate this town and we're both trying desperately to pad our careers so that we can move on to bigger and brighter things. Tell me what's not the same about that?"

"You don't want a real relationship. I do."

"No you don't." Daryn said with a wink.

"What?!"

"You don't. You just think you do because that would be the next logical part of your checklist."

"What the hell are you talking about?" Rebecca was starting to fume. She should have just taken the papers and showed him the door…again.

"You know, your checklist. You're a checklist kind of girl, Becks. Graduate with honours, check. Get into law school, check. Graduate in top ten percentile, check, get job with maximum allowance for advancement, yadda yadda yadda. You and I both know the drill. Living in this small town is no picnic, but it's a means to an end. In a small town, you can climb the ladder faster and eventually move on to Toronto or Montreal or some other big city where you'll be able to pick your way into a high powered job five years faster than you would have otherwise. I get exactly where you're coming from. You just think you need the equally high powered mate to go with it, and I'm telling you that that is a load of bullshit. You women are just hardwired to think that none of this success will mean anything if you don't have the man to go with it." He paused for effect. "Check mate."

"Quite the speech." Rebecca said drily.

"Yeah, but it's true. I don't know why you spend so much time fixating on this. We had it so perfect. No ties, no expectations, great sex."

"Maybe I had expectations that you never could live up to. Maybe that's why I ended it."

Daryn leaned in even closer. She could smell him now, and god, he smelled good. "I don't think so." He said.

He bent his head down and kissed her. Rebecca felt herself melt completely, every trace of an argument flying from her head as she responded with vigor.

Daryn wrapped his arms around her and pulled her to her feet, never breaking the kiss. He twisted her so that her back was to her desk and hoisted her up so that she was sitting on it.

With her mind screaming at her that this was the worst possible idea, her body ran leaps ahead of her brain and began pumping the blood through her veins like an athlete. She could feel the heat rising and her pulse pounding. She quickly did a mental check, Daryn had closed her door when he came in, there were meetings going on all over the building so not too many people would be roaming the halls. She had cleared her own schedule to work on the case so no one would be popping into her office unannounced. Still, sex in her office was a wild and dangerous idea, and she couldn't believe how wholeheartedly she was about to embrace it.

Rebecca reached up and undid her hair. She heard the moan escape from Daryn as his lips trawled their way down her neck and she smiled to herself. Oh yes, she could still affect him as well. She let his hands coax her legs apart and cursed herself for wearing tights under her skirt.

Daryn's hands were re-discovering the landscape of her body. She could feel them on her breasts, first over her blouse, then, roughly untucking it from her skirt and under it. She reached around and started to undo the buttons, as he had been known to pop them off some of her best work clothes in the past. As her fingers fumbled and trembled to open her clothes, she felt Daryn's hands under her skirt. His mouth went back on hers and he kissed her hard, then ripped her tights open and drove his fingers in under her panties.

Rebecca left her shirt open and went to work on Daryn's clothes. She pulled his shirt out, quickly undid the top three buttons and then pulled it over his head. One of her shoes dropped from her foot as she wrapped her legs up and around Daryn's waist. She bit her lip hard to keep from moaning out loud when he dipped his head down and took her already stiff nipple into his mouth. She could practically feel him smiling at her reactions.

It was both maddening and exhilarating that he knew exactly how to play her body. Rebecca undid the buckle on his pants, popped open the button and slid down the zipper, letting them pool around his ankles in one beautiful drop. She dug her fingers into the taut skin of his backside and threw her head back as soon as she felt him unlatch from her skin and drop to his knees in front of her. Ever conscious of the fact that at any second her door could swing open, Rebecca leaned back with one hand on the desk and bit down on the fingers of her other hand to keep from crying out at the exquisite pleasure being brought forth by his tongue. He was always such a master at that particular trick. She could feel the sensations burning through from her toes all the way to the tips of her fingers. Releasing her hand from her teeth, she reached down and grabbed the back of Daryn's head, holding him oh so close in just the right spot.

An orgasm ripped through her quickly, almost violently. She could feel Daryn moving, rising up from his position and fumbling with a packet. Trust him to always have a condom nearby. She braced herself for his entry, which was swift and hard. His strong hands grabbed her ass and slid her forward a little bit on the edge of the desk so that she was almost teetering off.

It was perfectly rough, exactly what she needed, what she wanted. Exactly the kind of sex she had fantasized about every time she found herself dating the 'good boy' and dreaming about the 'bad' one. It was raw and animal and just plain good. Rebecca hadn't had sex of any kind in so long, she had worried on the few dates she had had since she had sent Daryn packing, whether or not she would be any good anymore. Maybe it was just Daryn, or maybe it was her enthusiasm, but it seemed that she hadn't lost the touch after all.

Her thoughts were interrupted as he pulled back from her suddenly and pulled her down from her perch. He turned her around bent her over the desk, pausing to give her a playful slap. She didn't even bother to shush him. As they started into the rhythm once again, she completely forgot about being quiet. Once again the urge to orgasm boiled beneath the surface of her skin and she started to cry out. Daryn whipped his hand over her mouth quickly. His pace became more urgent and they moved together in a fury.

The second Rebecca's heat subsided; practicality took over her brain once more. There was no way he was going to pull the old 'love 'em and leave 'em routine' with her this time. She straightened her skirt, kicked off the torn tights and sank into her chair, fishing out a clean pair of tights still in the packaging from her bottom drawer.

"I'm impressed. You feel a certain need to keep a spare pair of those in your office?" Daryn smirked at her as he put himself back together.

"Well, can't go into court with a run in my hose, now can I? Always be prepared. I have a clean new blouse in there too, in case of coffee accidents."

"Ah, the perpetual girl scout." He said, saluting her.

Rebecca watched him laugh softly at his own joke as he gathered himself back into his clothes. She fixed her own, quickly and then walked to the door of her office.

"You have to go. I have work to do." She told him, opening the door and waiting patiently beside it.

The urge to tuck her head out into the hallway and look around for possible eavesdroppers was strong, but she fought it off. She wanted to prove something, both to Daryn and herself. She wasn't some wimpy little girl; she was a strong and powerful woman.

"What, still won't come out with me for a coffee, at least?" Daryn was finishing up with the buttons on his shirt, smiling at her with a cockeyed grin. He looked like the cat that just swallowed the canary.

OH! She wanted to scream out loud. She knew that look on his face and knew it well. He thought that he had just come in and played her and with that little bit of sexual satisfaction, she would just blindly follow along at whatever he wanted. And in the past, it had so worked. But not today.

"No. I haven't changed my mind, Daryn. Now, if you'll just get going…"

He strode over to her and went to pull her in, probably for a kiss, but she put her hand out against his chest and pushed him firmly away.

"I don't think that's appropriate, Office Stewart. Thank you for the paperwork, I'll call you if I find any holes in your investigation."

She smiled at him and ushered him out the door. Not to be shown up by a woman, Daryn left.

But just as he got into the hall, Rebecca saw him turn, like he was going to say something else to her.

She closed the door.

Chapter Twenty One

It had been a whole week since the fight that had seen Rick walk out of the house. Things were not going well between them, either. Every time Jaye picked up her phone to talk to him or text him, she put it down again. There just didn't seem to be the right things to say to him. Judging by the lack of activity on her phone, he was feeling pretty much the same way. She had had a brief conversation about it with Dr. Spiers, but had shied away from getting into too much detail. As much as it was nice to have her to talk to, she still didn't fully trust her.

Her physical scars and wounds were healing well, but Jaye hadn't gone back in to work since the last time, fearing another fight with Moira. In fact, besides trying to avoid getting too personal with her doctor or her lawyer, fighting seemed to be the one thing she was able to do lately. The first part of the trial was set to begin in the morning and Jaye was getting antsy. In her earlier session with Dr. Spiers, she had confirmed that she would not be taking the stand at all. There was little to no point; she remembered nothing about the event at all; a fact which had been stated with much increasing frustration to the police, her doctors and her lawyer. It drove her crazy, but it was even worse that everyone else involved seemed to expect some miracle to place a memory in her head that was never there to begin with.

She skulked into the kitchen in search of something to eat. Certain thoughts had been creeping into her mind lately. Like, why was it so important that someone tell her of the exact details of the crime? Did she really have to know? It was hard to know why.

There was almost no food in the house at all. Not surprising, since she had been at home on her own a lot with not much to do but eat. Jaye glanced at the clock. It was already past six in the evening. Still no sign of Rick. The sky outside was dark and depressing. Faced with the option of going shopping for groceries without Rick by her side to banter about what they might be in the mood to eat as the weeks wore on, Jaye decided to go out. It was no good just staying cooped up by herself staring out at a dark sky and wondering if Rick would come home or if Moira would talk to her or just basically driving herself crazy.

She went back into the bedroom and changed her clothes, opting for some low slung jeans and a soft pink sweater with a wide neck that always hung from her shoulders. Tonight she was going to have some fun.

One hour later Jaye was seated at a table in the back corner of the club. It felt good to come back here. She liked how the room was mostly dark. She liked the girls, especially Dynasty/Donna, who had come over right away to say hello and to promise not to send her anything to drink. Jaye was on ginger ale tonight. She'd had enough of drinking for a while. It was so empowering to be in this place. The women here were beautiful and strong and funny and they had such complete control when it came to the men around them. It was so refreshing. Never mind that the other patrons dotted around the place were sneaking her leering looks, she paid them little to no attention, except to people watch.

"Having fun yet?" Donna asked her when she sat down to join her for a break.

"I love this place." Jaye told her.

"What? Why? It's such a shit hole." Donna laughed at her. She took a pack of cigarettes out from the tiny clutch handbag she carried. "Want one?" she asked as she shook one out.

"Isn't that illegal? We're indoors." Jaye asked, though she picked one out for herself anyway and lit it.

"Of course it is! You can't smoke in bars anymore, even adult ones. But the local P.D. gives us a break in return for preferential treatment. You'll see."

Jaye took a nice long drag and leaned forward in her seat. "You mean you sleep with the cops and they don't report you for allowing this?"

Donna snorted, "Hell no! Well, I don't know about the other girls, but not me, and certainly not in here! No sex in the club, number one rule. You want to sleep with a guy you do it on your own time. Never in here. We don't even have a backroom, unless you count the dressing room."

"Well, what do you mean then?"

"You'll see. One or two of them always manage to come in sometime around ten or so." She glanced down at Jaye's wrist. "You don't wear a watch?"

"No, why?"

"We don't keep a clock out here. It's like a casino, if they don't know what time it is…"

"They'll stay and keep spending money." Jaye finished for her, nodding. She pulled out her cell phone. "Wow, it's already almost ten."

"Well then, I gotta go. I'm due back on the stage soon. You like Pink? I'm dancing to one of her songs next."

Donna bent down and gave Jaye a big hug. "It's good to see you sweetie. You're welcome here anytime." She stood back up and adjusted her bra.

"And keep an eye out. I'll bet the tips from my next dance that there will be at least two cops in here within the next couple of minutes."

Jaye laughed at her. "I would never take your tips. You work too hard for them."

Donna blew her a kiss, which received a nice little holler from one of the guys at a nearby table. She winked at him and Jaye chuckled to herself. Of all the unexpected places to make a new friend.

True to her words, within about half an hour three guys sauntered in and strode right up to the bar. They weren't in uniforms, but Jaye recognized one of them right away. His oh so perfect hair, his slick charm, even the way he carried himself. It was that Officer Stewart. The one she had spent all that frustrating time with, kissed and then blew off in the parking lot. Well well well. She immediately turned her head away from the trio. Undoubtedly, he would suss her out of the crowd sooner than later and would come up to say something. It was just a matter of when. Actually, considering how much he had irritated her from the moment he first entered her hospital room, he was turning into a rather amusing man to toy with. This could be a little bit of fun.

The next time the busty little waitress came back to her table, Jaye ordered a cranberry juice, but she asked for it to be served in a martini glass with a slice of orange. She wanted it to look like she was drinking.

The waitress laughed. "Oh sure honey. You got an ex in here tonight?"

"Not exactly, but I am planning to mess with a guy's head."

She twinkled at her and hurried off to order the drink with the bartender. Returning moments later, she placed the drink on the table with a flourish.

"Enjoy!"

"Oh, I will." Jaye said drily.

She kept her gaze forward, looking only towards the stage. There was a girl dancing on it right now whom Donna had pointed out as 'Fantasia' but whose real name was something like Fay.

She could hear the drone of men's voices as they oohed and ahhed her performance, making every kind of unimaginative suggestive phrase you could think of. Jaye found herself chewing on her lip to keep from snorting at them.

She felt his presence before he spoke a word. What was it with guys like that, the ones that actually seemed to leak testosterone in a cloud around them? Jaye picked up her faux drink and took a sip.

"Jaye?" his voice was rich and deep.

She turned slowly in her chair and cast a slow gaze up towards his face. Oh yes, this would be like shooting fish in a barrel. She wasn't remotely interested in this guy, but the idea that she could strike on back for all the women that he had probably effortlessly charmed in his life was intoxicating.

"Oh, hello Officer, off duty tonight? No helpless women to defend and protect?" she let the charm slide from her throat like silk.

"Hmm, you're very funny. Yes, I'm off duty. You can call me Daryn."

"Okay, Daryn." She kept her gaze unbroken.

He shifted his weight from one foot to the other but did not look at all put out.

"Mind if I join you?" he finally asked, pulling out a chair right away and plunking himself into it.

"I guess not. Won't your friends mind, though?"

Daryn shot a look back to the bar where the other two were standing with beer in their hands and their gazes thoroughly locked on the stage.

"I doubt they'll notice." He laughed. "I only came because they asked me to. This isn't exactly my cup of tea. I'd rather take in a movie."

"Sure you would."

He raised his eyebrow at her. "Should I even bother asking what you mean by that?"

"I'm friends with a couple of the girls here. They mentioned that you would be stopping in."

"By name?"

"Maybe."

He laughed again. "Well what can I say? I guess I'm busted. But I'll have you know, they have excellent chicken wings here."

"If that's what you fellas are calling them these days." Jaye retorted, as one of the girls on the stage removed her bra and tipped upside down on the pole.

Daryn followed her gaze and erupted loudly. Jaye kept her gaze neutral. This guy was simply too easy to play. She could practically see his brain whirring with the possibilities of chatting her up and where that might lead. Especially coupled with the fact that she was 'drinking' and was sitting right now in a nudie bar. She must look like the lame antelope in the herd to his lion.

"So, how are you holding up? Okay?" he had a look of appropriate concern on his face.

"I'm doing just fine thanks." Jaye sipped at her drink again.

"How many of those have you had tonight?"

"Oh, this must be around number six or so."

"You sure that's such a good idea?"

"I don't see why not. I'm a grown woman. I can drink this if I want to." She retorted.

"Yeah, but how are you going to get home?"

"Same way I got here, I imagine."

"Hmm. Maybe you should slow down."

Jaye shrugged and took a large gulp. The juice was still nice and cold and she had to admit, even as a virgin drink, cranberry juice went really well with orange. She ran the tip of her tongue over the corner of her lip, getting every bit of sweetness from her mouth. Ever aware of the attention from her new table mate, she made sure to drag her tongue slowly to the other side as well, running it along her lip line suggestively. If Rick saw her right now, he'd probably break up with her on the spot. But then again, she hadn't seen or spoken to him in days, so who knew where his mind was at.

"Taste good?" he asked her.

"Mmmm Hmmm." Jaye murmured, lowering her eyes and peering out at him from under her lashes.

"So, I wanted to ask you about the other night." He said, leaning in towards her. "You know, the last time I saw you. I figured this is as good a place as any, seeing as I'm not here in official capacity."

"What about it?"

"Why did you kiss me?"

"Because," Jaye said, looking him straight in the eye, "I could."

"You don't like too much bullshit, do you?" he asked.

"I don't like any bullshit."

"What if I told you then, no bullshit, that I find you very sexy and attractive?" Daryn shuffled his chair so that he was a little closer to her.

"I'd say that's nice, thanks."

"That's all you have to say to that?"

"What did you want me to say?"

"Well, don't you find me attractive at all?"

Jaye cocked her head to one side and pretended to study him. In truth, if it wasn't for the overwhelming stench of his bravado and ego, she might have found him attractive. But right now, he wasn't Rick. He might as well have been a stray dog licking at her shoe.

"Now that you mention it, I suppose you are the kind of guy most women would find good looking." He beamed at her, "But not me. Sorry." She grinned right back, but let a little of her iciness show through and watched the wide smile drop from his features. Ah, clearly someone was not used to being sloughed off so easily.

"Well, you were right about one thing." He sounded rather like a petulant child. "Most women do find me attractive."

"I'm sure they do."

"So, if you're soooo not interested, why the kiss?"

"I felt like it." She shrugged and then downed the last of her drink. A waitress was over to their table within seconds.

"One more of the same?" she asked Jaye.

"You really think you should still be serving her?" Daryn inquired.

"She can handle it."

"Bring me a real martini, please. Not one of those fruity ones. And," he turned again to give Jaye a pointed look, "some chicken wings, medium. Thanks love."

"Sure thing Daryn." The waitress winked at Jaye and sauntered off.

"Not the kind of place you frequent, eh?" Jaye couldn't help but laugh.

Daryn threw his hands in the air. "Okay, okay, truce!"

They were quiet while their drinks were replenished and while Daryn ate. Jaye kept her eyes on the stage and on Donna whenever she was roaming around the floor.

"Are you a lesbian?" Daryn blurted after watching her for a while.

"I really don't think you can ask me that." She said.

"Why not? This isn't the army, and I'm not asking 'officially' I'm just curious."

"Well, I don't think it's any of your business, really."

"Wait, you have a boyfriend, I remember him from the hospital. So, what's with you eye humping the girls?"

"Eye Humping? That's a new one." Jaye laughed loudly. "God, I'm going to use that, I really am."

"You are an expert at avoiding pointed questions about yourself." Daryn sounded smug.

"And you are an expert at crossing personal boundaries."

"I haven't yet heard you ask me to stop asking questions." He pointed out.

"Daryn," she reached over and put her hand over his on the table. "I'm not gay, Donna is my friend, and I want you to stop asking me those kinds of questions."

"Fair enough. How about you give me another chance at that kissing thing, then?"

Jaye opened her mouth to answer him, but he was too quick for her. Within seconds, he had leaned in and covered her lips with his own, kissing her much rougher than the first time they had ever locked lips. In her mind, she celebrated a small victory. Thinking quickly, Jaye kissed him back with fervor. It had been so long since she had been kissed with intention. She could feel his hands traversing her body, sliding along her thigh. Jaye cracked one eye open and tilted her head so that she could look down. Ah yes, the most telling of all male reactions. This guy had the response time of a race car driver, and Jaye was about to pour cold water all over him, figuratively speaking.

Pushing thoughts of Rick from her mind, Jaye let Daryn get comfortable with his seduction. He wasn't a bad kisser really, and it was fairly obvious that he knew what he was doing with his hands, and that he wasn't shy about being as forward as he could get away with. She was doing mental math about where she would draw the line, while still giving enough away to make him think he stood a chance with her.

Finally, he broke the lip lock and buried his face in her neck, sloppily kissing and licking her skin. His hand ran up and down her arm, but she felt the distinct brush of his thumb on her nipple. She could feel his hot breath on her, and she knew he was hooked.

"Why don't you let me take you home?" he whispered into her ear. "You've been drinking. Wouldn't want you to get hurt."

"Hmmm." She whispered back. "Like last time?"

"What?" he extricated himself from her neck and pulled back.

"You know, like last time. Except that I wasn't drinking then, and I'm not now." She stood up and straightened her sweater over her shoulders.

"But, I…" Daryn looked down at her martini glass.

"Juice." She informed him. "And I thought you might be kind of fun to mess around with, but I usually prefer a real man, not some guy with an act down pat."

She grabbed her handbag and turned around to see Donna and two of the other girls watching her. Daryn's friends from the bar also appeared to be watching. Probably getting ready to shake their heads when he left with a conquest, their mouths were now agape at the sight of Jaye blowing him off so easily.

"You see, you were right about one thing tonight…I do have a boyfriend. And he's ten times the kisser you are and one hundred times the man. But thanks for the laughs."

She strode away from him with an unsuppressed smile of triumph on her face. At the door, she turned back once more.

"Hey Daryn!" she shouted, causing several heads to turn and face them. "See you in court."

Chapter Twenty Two

After days and days of barely talking, Jaye was surprised when she came home to find Rick sitting in the living room of the apartment on the couch. Out of nervousness and guilt, her hand immediately went towards her lips. What in the hell had she been thinking letting that creepy cop kiss her?

"Hey. What are you doing here?" she asked him.

"I thought I'd stay with you tonight, you know, so I could come with you tomorrow."

"Oh. Okay." she went into the kitchen and poured herself a glass of water.

"Where were you?"

"Out. What does it matter?"

"Out where?" he sounded frustrated.

"At the club, if you must know. I have friends there. You know, people who don't judge you and accept you for who you are."

Rick harrumphed. "Oh, yeah, I'm sure you have none of those around here. No wonder you have to go and hang out with low lifes."

"Hey, fuck you Rick. You have no idea about any of those people."

"And I suppose you're an expert on them after, what, two nights there?"

"God, I can't say anything to you, can I?"

Rick sighed and stood up. He came over and wrapped his arms around Jaye, but she remained stiff in his embrace. As he straightened back up, Rick sniffed loudly. "I don't suppose one of those girls is a transvestite or something, are they?"

"Why?"

"Because you smell like men's cologne," he sniffed again. "Cheap men's cologne."

Jaye pushed him away and walked towards the bedroom. "Officer Stewart was there."

Rick followed her in. Jaye noticed that his bag was on the floor in the corner. She sat down on the bed.

"Strange place for a meeting with the police," he pointed out, his face twisted in anger. "Did he happen to fall into your neck or something? Because I don't understand two things. One, why you would even be talking to that guy...in a STRIP CLUB and two, why in the hell you would smell like his crappy cologne."

"If you must know, I kissed him." Suddenly the whole 'gaining power' aspect of that little incident seemed ridiculous to her. She was ashamed. She kept her head down and wouldn't look Rick in the eye. Expecting him to get mad, it caught her completely off guard when she finally looked up to see Rick studying her with the most pained expression on his face.

"Jaye, what in the hell are you trying to prove?" he asked her quietly.

"You wouldn't understand," she replied. "I barely understand. I'm sorry."

He shook his head.

"You want to leave again?" she whispered.

"No, but...I think I'll stay on the couch."

Jaye felt terrible. Here she was thinking that she was proving something by using Daryn to further some idea in her mind of what she was still capable of as a woman, and he wasn't even worth anything to her. And there was Rick, the man who meant more to her than anything in her life and she couldn't seem to help but push him further and further away. She took off her clothes and went to get into bed.

Rick came through the room to go to the bathroom and saw Jaye climbing under the covers. "What the hell is that?" he asked, noticing her back for the first time.

"Oh, it's a tattoo. I just got it a little while ago."

"Can I see it?" he asked gently.

Jaye shrugged. "I guess."

He came over and knelt down on the bed as Jaye turned to sit with her back to him. She could feel his fingers tracing the outlines of the artwork tenderly. She could hear him breathing and practically feel the heat radiating from his skin. When she felt him get up off the bed again, she turned and faced the bathroom door. "Do you like it?" she asked.

"Do you?"

"I love it."

Rick kept on going until he was out of her view. She heard water running, but through the distortion of that sound she heard Rick say, "It's beautiful."

*****

As Rebecca had told her it would be, the court dates were set very quickly. In a town like Fayette where very little, if any, violent crime happened, the case was ushered to the front of the proverbial line. There was a bail hearing set for almost immediately after the second guy was found. Jaye was told his name but in all honesty, she had a hard time remembering what it was. Or perhaps it was just that she didn't care to know. Both Rebecca and Rick did most of the talking that morning anyway. Jaye just let their words wash over her as she sat in a haze. She had taken two of her pain pills that morning, instead of one, so she was feeling a pleasant disconnection from the activities in the courthouse. In fact, she intended to spend the entire time sitting on one of the chairs in Rebecca's office, as she wasn't needed for this part of the process anyway.

*****

Rebecca sat at her appointed desk and shuffled through her papers. In the short time she had had to prepare for this, she had managed to dig up quite a lot of information on the two accused. The elder one, Francis, had a long rap sheet and the younger one, Joshua, was catching up to him quickly. There were outstanding warrants for their arrest in the neighbouring town of Waterton and there was evidence to suggest that they had been involved in some similar break-ins in Kincaid and Cantabria as well. As well as the break and enter and theft charges, both boys had records from the county of their time spent in foster homes, were known to the drug rings in the area, and Francis was wanted on trafficking charges. There was a missing person's report filed for Joshua with the clerk's office a few years ago by his foster family. She had spent enough of her legal career chasing after some of the rats who took in children like strays and then spent the better part of their formative years destroying their innocence. It made her shudder to think about it.

No matter what the background of these two boys was though, this was an open and shut case. There were witnesses and plenty of physical evidence.

When the familiar "All Rise" sounded from the mouth of the bailiff, Rebecca stood along with the public defender, a man she did not recognize, and waited for the Justice to arrive from Chambers.

The Honourable Jon Howard was the justice assigned to their case. Rebecca stifled a smirk. There were only a handful of judges in the area that might have been assigned this case, and Judge Howard was probably the one that she would have picked had she been given the choice. He was notoriously hard on violent offenders. In fact, the rumour mill in the legal world was that he only moved to Fayette to escape the city and the never-ending stream of violent criminals. He was close to retiring and had no patience any more for lawbreakers in general.

Rebecca stole a glance across the way and saw that the public defender seemed to be muttering something under his breath. She was sure that it wasn't anything positive.

The room was not terribly full that morning. It wasn't really surprising. Not too many people were going to show up for this part of the proceedings. But when the trial itself got underway, well, there would be plenty of people out then. Rebecca had been around Fayette long enough to know that there was a certain crowd of people who wouldn't miss out on the chance to watch what would happen to these two boys who had messed with their idyllic and beloved hometown.

She turned and smiled at Rick who was seated directly behind her. She had been informed that the boys would be pleading guilty. Well, they would be crazy not to under the circumstances, and their lawyer would be doing them a disservice had he advised them otherwise. It was nice for Rick that he could be here from the get-go. He would not be testifying, so he could be present for any part of the events in the court. As court was called into session, Rebecca patiently waited to see how the morning would go.

The other lawyer was a man named Barry Simms. When prompted, after the reading of the charges against the accused, he stood up and informed the Justice that his clients would be pleading guilty. Rebecca tried to hide her smirk as she concurred with this. Even the Judge Howard seemed slightly amused. Something about the one boy had made Rebecca fairly certain they would plead not guilty in order to necessitate a jury trial, but perhaps they were just anxious to get this over and done with, especially with the outstanding warrants. Certainly, if she had been their representation, she would have pushed for this option as well, if only to garner some small favour with the judge and hope for reduced or dropped charges on their other crimes.

Rebecca looked over to the boys sitting by their lawyer. One of them, she guessed the older one, looked cocky and self assured. He even looked a little brazen. Not a good sign. It would no doubt be noticed by the judge and not appreciated. The other one looked terrible. If she wasn't so intimately acquainted with what had transpired the night of the attack, she might even have felt sorry for him. He was pale and fidgety. His hair stood on end and he was wearing ill-fitting clothing. He looked terrified. Once or twice, it looked like he was leaning over as if to say something to his companion, but an ever-so-subtle shake of the head stopped him cold.

Interesting. If she had to wager a guess based on the information she had from his history and from his behaviour here in court, she would lay good money down on the fact that he had been a mere accomplice, that the other, arrogant-looking boy had been the ringleader of all their criminal history together. The scared one reeked of the being the product of a flawed system and exposure to too much turmoil in a short life.

Rebecca snapped her attention back to the proceedings. They were wrapping up. Well, this was of course going to be a short day. The real action would start tomorrow. With nothing going on that took any kind of precedence over this, the trial, now that there was no need to seek out a jury, would commence in the morning. The boys would remain in jail tonight.

She gathered together her papers, snapped them closed in her briefcase and turned to smile at Rick, who was staring at the boys being escorted out with nothing short of pure hatred.

"Keep up your strength, and your patience," she told him. "We're off and running now."

They exited the courtroom together and headed back to her office to talk to Jaye. There was an ever-so-slight bounce to Rebecca's step. This was indeed going to be open and shut. She just hoped Mr. Simms wasn't expecting any miracles.

Chapter Twenty Three

Jaye sat up a little taller in her seat when she saw the door open and Rick and Rebecca come back in.

"Well, what happened?" she asked.

She watched Rick sink down on the couch and waited while Rebecca settled herself in the chair behind her desk.

"It's all going to go very smoothly for us. They've pled guilty, and they've elected for trial by judge."

"What does that mean?"

"It means, we don't have to wait to have jury selections, we're going to go ahead with trial first thing tomorrow. Ten o'clock. They are being held again tonight, no bail is even being discussed. The fact that they're pleading guilty means that they will absolutely get jail time. With both of them having previous warrants out, there's no way this judge isn't going to lock them up for at least some period of time."

Jaye had thought that this news would have made her feel better, but instead, it just made her tired. She wanted this whole thing to be over, now. She didn't want to have to wait for a whole trial.

"Okay, so we go home then, and tomorrow we come back at...what time?" she asked.

"Meet me here in my office at nine-thirty. We can go over the type of things you can expect and that way you'll be prepared and not shocked by any of the proceedings."

"I guess. Fine, okay. I'll be back then." She stood up.

"Wait, do you have any questions for me?" Rebecca asked her.

"No. I just want to go home." With Rick following after her, Jaye started to leave the court house.

There was a feeling of impending doom creeping up from her stomach. She could feel bile rising in her throat and fought to keep it down. She was aware that she was walking at a fair clip along the corridors and to the doors to the outside, but couldn't feel the actual sensations of her feet touching the ground. Exiting from the rear of the building, she saw something happening off to the side that made her turn her head.

It was Daryn, she was sure of that. He and another couple of officers were escorting two men in hand and foot cuffs towards a police car. She knew that these were the guys. The guys. The ones that had been sitting in a court room just moments ago, getting ready to stand trial for hurting her. She couldn't seem to tear her eyes away from them. They had to be at least thirty feet from her, and yet, it was as if she was standing right beside them. They were walking with their heads down, being shoved along the shovelled sidewalk and to the car, which was the first one in the parking lot. Jaye watched as the first one had his head pushed down while being ushered in. Then, just before he was equally escorted into the car's back seat, the second man looked up for just a second. Jaye took in a sharp breath. He looked so young, so scared. Her eyes and his seemed to lock on each other for an eternity before his head finally disappeared under the strong hand of an officer and that door was slammed shut. She couldn't make herself look away.

"Jaye...your coat," Rick huffed up from behind her and tried to hand her the warm coat she had thrown on that morning.

"I don't want it. You take it home for me. I'm going for a walk," she said.

"Are you crazy, it's minus seven out here! You'll freeze," he told her, pointing to her flimsy but dressy blouse that she had worn for court.

"I don't care," she tossed from over her shoulder and she took off down the road without even looking back once.

The courthouse was at the top of the hill which separated the 'old' downtown from the 'new' downtown. From here, Jaye could head to the left where the bulk food store, the Bean Post coffee shop or the grocery store and post office were. There was also the Laundromat and Levi's shop as well as a few restaurants. Down the hill were the trendier places of the town. The Cakery was located right on the river, just a few doors down from the bridge to the industrial sector. She didn't want to be anywhere near the uptown. Too many clouds swirled in her head when she power-walked down the hill, past the little alleyways that separated some of the store fronts. There was an alleyway beside the Cakery too, but she had never ever felt threatened or in danger there. Now, it seemed, there were shadows lurking from every one.

Probably from habit, her feet led her to the Cakery; although this time she entered from the store front. Sloane was standing behind the counter placing brownies into a box for a woman who was wearing a baby on a sling over her shoulder and gesturing at her own swollen belly. She looked up when Jaye entered and smiled.

Jaye didn't even smile back. She just walked straight back into the kitchen.

"Am I losing my mind?" she asked a very startled Moira, who had her hands buried in a large lump of dough.

"Hi Jaye, you done with court already?"

"Yes, yes, we're done. The real thing starts tomorrow." She waved away the importance of the statement with her hand. "Am I losing my mind?"

"You are if you drove down here without a coat. Are you trying to get pneumonia?" Moira asked.

"Give me something to do, I haven't worked in weeks. I need to do something to get my mind off all this," Jaye pleaded.

"What about your wrist?"

"Fuck my wrist. It was just a sprain anyway. It's loads better now."

"Nice Jaye. Okay, you need to keep busy, we need some of those truffles made and we've had an order for rum balls. You can do either one of those."

Jaye nodded at her friend and gathered together the chocolate, rum and other ingredients she needed to make the rum balls. Always, after the holidays, they would get at least one late winter order for the treat, especially if someone from town had served them and an out-of-town guest had inquired where they were from.

With her wrist still a little on the tricky side, Jaye made sure to work with extreme care. She didn't want to spill or drop anything on the floor this time.

She carefully measured out the chocolate, drinking in the rich aroma and trying to slow down her breathing. Her heart was still racing. She kept on darting her eyes back and forth to the entrance to the store and the back door of the kitchen. She couldn't shake the feeling that someone was going to bust in on them at any second.

"Don't be ridiculous," she murmured to herself from under her breath.

"What was that?" Moira asked her.

Jaye couldn't even bring herself to look her own best friend in the eye. She shook her head that it was nothing and tried to concentrate on her work.

"Here, I'll get the lid for you." She felt Moira reach over towards her and lift up the bottle of rum from the counter beside her. Just being aware of Moira's hand reaching around her nearly made her jump a mile.

"Are you okay?" Moira asked, gently.

"I'm fine," Jaye muttered.

As Moira twisted the lid from the bottle and placed it back on the counter, the smell hit Jaye and she panicked.

"NO!" she screamed.

"Jaye, what's wrong?"

"NO!!!!" she swiped her arm across the counter top and knocked the bottle to the floor. Staring wildly from side to side, Jaye reached her arm up to cover her head. In her mind's eye she could see someone reaching out with something, ready to hit her. She turned sharply to strike out before she could be hurt again. Her arm connected with something hard.

"OUCH!" the sound came from Sloane. "I was only trying to…" she trailed off.

Jaye was completely freaked out. She couldn't focus, she couldn't breathe, she could only feel. It was an absolutely terrifying feeling. She had to get out.

Without even uttering one word of apology or explanation, Jaye tore from the shop, shoving into one of the customers as she bolted through the front and out to the street. She hit the sidewalk, which was slushy with pedestrian traffic and fought to keep from sliding off onto her side. She scrambled towards the bridge and started running across it. Every sound of every car made her feel like she was being followed.

The bridge was no good, she decided. She would have to get somewhere else, somewhere they couldn't find her. She didn't want to go home, she couldn't show her face back at work, and there was no way she was going to going to go back to that courthouse. She had been doing just fine until she went in there today. Now the face of that boy just kept swimming in front of her vision and she couldn't shake him. Couldn't out-run him.

> The sound of a car coming up from behind her was maddening. Jaye reached the far end of the bridge and turned sharply to the right, almost losing her footing and falling over, but managing at the last second to stay upright. She could hear the car slowing to a stop and the sound of a door opening and closing. Covering her ears with her hands, Jaye began to speed up. She felt hands wrapping around her and trying to pull her in.

"Get your hands off, get your hands OFF!" she yelled, kicking out her legs.

"Jaye, calm down. It's me, it's Rick. Calm down, I'm not going to hurt you."

She stopped kicking out and struggling and turned to face him.

Her face broke and her jagged breathing making saliva slide out from the corner of her mouth. Her nose was running with the effects of trying to get away so quickly in the cold. She started to shiver and shake uncontrollably. She let Rick guide her to the car and drive her home, not speaking a single word.

Once they were back in the apartment and Jaye was starting to feel normal again, or at least breathe normally again, she retired to the bedroom where she pulled the covers over her head and tried to block out the day.

*****

Rick didn't bother trying to talk to Jaye. She was clearly starting to lose her marbles, or at least, she would by the time this whole thing wrapped up if she didn't get any help. He called Moira.

"Thanks for letting me know she had taken off," he said.

"Did you find her?"

"Yeah, she was down by the bridge. Good thing you got me on my cell. I wasn't that far away." He took a deep breath. "I think we're going to have to confront this. Whatever it is that's going through her mind, Jaye is clearly not handling it well."

"Do you need my help? You know I'll do anything for her, I just can't watch her freak out like this anymore."

"I'm going to get in touch with her psychologist first. If that doesn't work, then maybe we'll try that intervention thing we were talking about before. One way or another, we have to bring her back. This isn't Jaye, not at all."

"I know."

Rick took a couple of deep breaths. "You wouldn't believe how spooked she seemed, she was running and practically slipping through the snow and when I tried to get her, she practically attacked me."

"I know, in the shop, she seemed really weird and jumpy, but as soon as I opened that bottle, she just bolted."

"I don't get it, lord knows she's had a few drinks since the accident, and they didn't seem to bother her. I can't imagine it's the smell of the alcohol; otherwise she would have panicked like that before. I think it has something to do with being in court this morning," Rick said.

"Did she go in?"

"No, she sat in Ms. Lawson's office. I went in though."

"So, what did the guys look like?"

"Honestly, they looked like a couple of punk kids. One of them is so scrawny he looks like a strong wind would blow him over."

Moira was quiet for a minute on her end of the line. Rick could hear her breathing slowly.

"I wonder why they went for her," she mused sadly.

"I know exactly why. Because she was a woman, dressed up and looking nice, and she was alone." His voice wavered for a moment. "I left her alone."

"Rick, it's not your fault," Moira told him.

"I know it's not, but it feels like it is. I just wish my head would explain it to my heart. Then maybe it wouldn't hurt so badly to watch her go through all this turmoil and I wouldn't have to keep feeling like I was the root cause of it all."

"Rick, I've known you for four years. Hell, even in your job you help people. It's not in you to be hurtful to someone on purpose. You go look yourself in the mirror and remind yourself of that."

"Thanks Moira. I'll try."

Rick hung up the phone and went into the bedroom to check on Jaye. She had fallen soundly asleep, even though it was only mid-afternoon. He shuddered to think, if this was how she handled today, how on earth she would get through the next morning.

Chapter Twenty Four

Jaye slept straight through the afternoon and night until her alarm went off the next morning at eight. When she sat up in bed, she noticed that Rick had already gotten up and could hear him off in the kitchen making noise, probably making breakfast. It was nice that he was giving her some space. She went into the bathroom and sat on the toilet, thinking back to about three weeks ago when she had been so broken and in so much pain that she had peed on herself just trying to do this on her own. It was a relief to know that she no longer needed help of that kind.

Getting up, Jaye turned to flush the toilet and went to the sink to wash her hands. She looked in the mirror, something she had been avoiding for some time. The stitches had dissolved in the cut on her forehead but from the look of things she would probably have a light scar there for a very long time. She ran her fingers over the gash. It just felt like a bit of raised skin, a little bumpy and unnatural, but kind of cool at the same time.

She began to remove the rumpled clothes she had slept in and bent to turn on the shower. Her ribs still felt sore, but the movements were getting easier and easier with each passing day. The sprained wrist was also healing though it still had very little strength, she could at least do simple things again, like wash her hair.

After the shower, Jaye dried off carefully and went back into the bedroom to dress. She felt nervous, like preparing for a first date, or for giving a speech in high school. She picked out some dark-coloured pants and a dark blouse that she hadn't worn since her cousin's funeral back when she was still in college. It felt like a bit of a funeral anyway. There was something very sad about going to your own court case for assault. She could feel her heart rate starting to creep up again, much like it had yesterday, but she fought it back down. Today, just today, she was bound and determined to be normal.

Rick was already sitting on the couch with a plate of pancakes on his lap. She smiled at him.

"You made my favourite."

He shrugged, but she could see the edges of a smile dancing on his lips. "Well, it's a big day."

She picked up the plate on the counter and poured syrup all over the still-steaming pancakes. Then she took a seat next to Rick on the couch and began to eat.

"How are you feeling this morning?" he asked tentatively.

"Okay. Actually, I can't wait to get started on this."

Rick put down his fork. "I talked to Moira last night. She was really freaked out. I also talked to Dr. Spiers. She wants to see you later today."

Jaye heaved out a loud sigh. "I'll talk to Moira. I didn't mean to scare her. But honestly, it was a one-time thing. I'm fine now. I just want to get through this."

Rick took another huge bite and chewed thoughtfully. "I don't think you're fine at all. I think you're in denial," he told her.

"Well, I didn't ask you." She kept her voice measured. She didn't want to start a fight today.

"Moira's not the only one you scared, you know."

Jaye didn't answer him. Instead she took another large bite of pancake and chewed it. Just breathe, she told herself. You can get through this if you just breathe.

"Jaye?"

"What?"

"Are you ever going to talk about this? I mean, really talk about it."

"No, I'm not. I've decided that I don't want to talk about any of this today. I just want to go and find out what's going to happen next. There's nothing that can be done about what's already happened, it's better just to move on and try and deal with what's to come."

"Wonderful attitude," Rick said wryly. "Refusal to deal with what got you here. I'm sure that will go miles towards dealing with how to handle what's next."

Jaye got up in a huff. She strode into the kitchen and put her plate in the sink. Then she turned back towards Rick.

"That's how I want to handle it, okay? How about you stop trying to be Mr. Fixit and just be here for me with what I need?"

"You don't even know what you want, let alone what you need," he told her. She shot him a dirty look. "But I'll back off and keep my mouth shut about that if it makes it any easier for you...for today at least. Sooner or later you're going to have to deal with this, whether you like it or not."

"Yeah, well, today's not that day," she told him.

They finished cleaning up and getting ready for court side by side, but they didn't speak again. Jaye could feel the butterflies building in her stomach, but again, she pushed the feeling aside.

Gritting her teeth, she left the apartment with Rick, got into the car and headed for the courthouse.

*****

The first thing Jaye noticed about the courtroom was how there was absolutely no warmth to it whatsoever. It was in the high-ceilinged room at the front left side of the building; probably back in its time it had been a ballroom or something of the like; now it was full of cold, polished wood furniture.

She and Rick had met Rebecca in her office first. There had been a little small talk, and Rebecca had asked her if she had any questions about, well, anything. Jaye had just shaken her head. She was feeling the same kinds of things as yesterday when she had left. She was jumpy, she saw shadows everywhere and she couldn't feel her hands. Her eyes constantly darted around the office, the corridor and up and down every single doorway they passed. This time though, she was fighting that urge to run like a demon. She made herself think of all the things she had done in the last few weeks. She had gotten a tattoo; she had gone to the club and met real strippers, even befriending one of them. She had used that ridiculous and misogynistic cop and humiliated him in front of his co-workers. She was a tough bitch, dammit. But, she realized, she was going to have to stop grinding her teeth so hard or she'd have no teeth left.

Now, seated at the table next to Rebecca, her heart was finally starting to stay put in her chest again. Jaye made herself focus on the details of the room. There were high windows along one wall, with a half circle window topping it off. The main parts of the window had blinds covering them. The arched parts had wood that had been cut to fit them, blocking any natural light from getting into the room. Behind her was the seating for the general public. The long benches of seats reminded her of back when her parents used to take the family to church. When you thought about it, court wasn't all that different. You sat in the hard wooden seats and listened to the judge. You didn't speak unless prompted. There was a set protocol for how the time would be spent. In the end, someone's fate would be decided; someone's soul would be saved or lost.

She herself was seated with Rebecca at one of the two long desks just on the other side from the low fence that separated the 'visitors' seating from the rest of the court room. Each desk had several chairs behind it and a podium beside it. There was a riser in between the desks, also 'fenced' in with a single chair in it, probably from back in the days when the accused had to sit alone, maybe even before there were handcuffs to keep them immobile. It looked bleak and terrifying just sitting there by itself, a truly horrible seat to find yourself in.

In front of her was yet another riser, more desks. The court clerk was seated at one talking to, Jaye assumed, a bailiff. They were discussing methods for quitting smoking. The bailiff seemed to be warning the clerk, a woman, on how the nicotine gum was a waste of money. He was telling her that the taste was terrible and the consistency was that of wet cardboard. Jaye tore her attention away from their conversation and back to the details of the room. It was astonishing that anyone could talk about anything as mundane as smoking cessation when this huge event was about to take place.

Sitting up on yet another riser was the judge's desk. The chair was high-backed and the desk had beautifully ornate woodwork adorning it. There was a pitcher of water and glass sitting on it. Behind it on the wall was a picture of Queen Elizabeth, and on each side there was a flag, one of Canada, one of Ontario. Jaye stared hard at the flags hanging flaccid from their posts. She wondered, since they were attached to poles, which were attached to the wall, if it was against the law for them to touch the floor. She had heard of such things in the States, that a flag could never touch the ground. She wondered too about the point of having a flag indoors where it could never get caught up in a playful breeze. What a sad type of servitude that had to be.

Beside her, Rebecca was shuffling some papers around. She was wearing a long black robe over her clothes with an inverted V collar sticking out of the neck. The other lawyer, it seemed, had yet to arrive. Rebecca flagged down an older gentleman who was wearing a blue blazer and seemed to be doing little other than crossing the room intermittently.

She looked at her watch as he approached their table. "Hey Gar, what's going on? Shouldn't we be getting ready to start by now?"

"The illustrious Mr. Simms is not here yet. We've got a message out to his phone, but he hasn't answered. His secretary says that he's stuck in the snow," he chuckled.

"Oh, yeah, that entire humongous one half foot of snow on the ground? I'm sure that's really dangerous for him to drive in!" Rebecca smiled but Jaye actually snorted at the thought of someone using the scant snowfall as a reason to be late, especially if this guy was from town. Even in the worst weather, the town never took more than twelve minutes to cross from one side to the other. This probably wouldn't go over well with the judge, a fact which Jaye relished. They hadn't even officially started yet, and already the defence was shooting itself in the foot. What a moment to savour. It did wonders towards calming her down from the earlier feeling of a jackrabbit invading her chest.

"Don't worry," Rebecca leaned down and whispered to her, "they won't bring in the guys until their lawyer is here. You won't have to see them until then. Just stay calm and breathe."

"I'm trying." She whispered back. "You know, I think I saw them yesterday. Da…Officer Stewart and another officer were taking them into a squad car out the back"

Rebecca looked at her. "Young-ish boys? About my height, one of them really skinny?"

"Yeah."

"That's the guys."

Jaye noticed that Rebecca was looking at her rather intently.

"What?"

"You called Daryn by his first name, or were about to. Is everything okay?"

"Everything's fine. Why?"

"It's just that…when people get that look on their face about Daryn, or start being aware of only using his professional title, it usually means he's been up to no good. He's not hitting on you, is he?" She sounded appalled.

"No, he's not. Or isn't…" Jaye shook her head. "It's kind of complicated. I may have used him a little when I was having a bad night and he just happened to be there." A terrifying thought struck her. "That won't affect the case, will it?"

"No, don't worry, you're not on trial here. You're the one we're defending…though I must say, the idea of you using him, it's highly amusing. I doubt he's been used by a woman…well, ever. Oh, hey, does Rick know about this? You didn't sleep with him, did you?"

Jaye laughed out loud for a second, forgetting where she was. She quickly slapped a hand over her mouth and took a quick peek around the room. A few people had looked her way at the sound of her laughter, but most of them went back to their conversations.

"No way! I just kind of kissed him a bit and then basically told him to bugger off."

It was funny to watch Rebecca's reaction to this. She seemed to be stunned, surprised and relieved.

"Oh my god," Jaye hissed. "Are you sleeping with him?"

"Not anymore," Rebecca grimaced. "It's a long story."

"I'll bet."

The rest of their conversation was cut short by the appearance of the clerk.

"He's here," he said, referring to the late Mr. Simms.

Immediately the sick feeling returned to Jaye's stomach. "Okay, now," she said, leaning back towards Rebecca and whispering at her.

"Now what?"

"Now I want to know what they did. I don't know if I can handle this if I hear about it during the process. Tell me right now."

A shuffling from the side door made her look over just in time to see those boys being shuffled in. They were just being escorted to their chairs when another man rushed in from the door on Jaye's side wearing a robe like Rebecca's and hastened to sit down with them quickly.

Jaye looked quickly back at her lawyer. "Now," she mouthed at her.

Rebecca's mouth opened to answer, but it was cut short by the sight of the Court Clerk standing up to deliver her speech.

"All rise…"

Jaye stood shakily.   It was time to hear the truth.

Chapter Twenty Five

As the opening words were read out to the courtroom, Jaye tried to focus on keeping her stance steady and her jaw from quivering. She didn't dare look behind her for Rick, but could almost feel his gaze locked onto the back of her neck.

"Oh yay, oh yay, oh yay"

Jaye was only catching snippets of the opening statement being read out.

"…Honourable Judge….presiding…."

The thunder was roaring in her ears and she was cursing herself for wearing heels, no matter what Rebecca had told her about presentation and appearances. Mechanically, she and Rebecca took their seats while the charges were read out to the defendants and their lawyer.

"…that on the 17th day of January…Joshua Moody…..did wilfully…"

She tried to tune out the voice listing off the series of injuries she incurred. She tried to bite down hard with her teeth, anything that would make her concentrate on something else.

"…on the 17th day of January….Francis Archer….did wilfully….with sexual intent…"

A single tear slipped unbidden from her eye. So, there was something else. She always thought so, in the back of her mind. The times it had been insinuated, the shock from her doctor, her psychologist, Rick, at not wanting to know the full details right from the get-go. Details she hadn't wanted to know, but on some level must have suspected.

Jaye heard a few final words slip from the judge at the end of the reading of the charges.

"How do you plead?"

A tiny laugh hiccupped out of her mouth, so small, not even Rebecca heard her. How do you plead? How ironic that this was the question that was asked to the perpetrators of a crime. In Jaye's case, she hadn't had a chance to plead at all. Not for her safety, not for her virtue, not for her life.

*****

Rick sat in his seat in the gallery absently shaking his leg up and down. His nerves were frazzled just watching Jaye trying to cope with this new information. He never told her what he had caught that guy, that Francis, doing to her. Hell, she hadn't even wanted to hear it. He knew that she had told both of her doctors and that cop that she didn't want to know. He was questioning it now though. Maybe in doing what she had asked, they had caused her the greatest damage. How is someone supposed to heal from wounds they don't even know they have? Sure there were probably people out there who would argue that someone couldn't be traumatized by things they weren't aware of, but in this case, where it was all going to come out in the court room, she really should have been kept in the know.

Rick started to question whether or not some of her more recent and self-destructing behaviours weren't more than a little bit his own fault. On some level, she must have been aware that she had been violated. He didn't tell her. He didn't protect her enough, and now she was just falling to pieces.

With a critical eye, he surveyed the opposing table. The lawyer there was being bawled out by the judge for being late.

" Excuses are insignificant," the judge told him, "when you know you're expected in the courtroom, for a fairly high-profile case," he added, "you make sure to give yourself enough time for unexpected circumstances. You don't leave your clients in limbo and a judge waiting."

Rick hid a chuckle. If there was any way to sway this whole thing even more in Jaye's favour before it had even started, this Simms guy had certainly found the way to do it. His stare swung again like a pendulum and back to the two boys who were sitting at the table in the poorly selected, crappy clothes. As the lawyers started in on their speeches full of impressively large words, he began to tune them out and focus on smaller details.

Around him there were a few random people dotted throughout the courtroom. They looked so bored he wondered why they even bothered to come out at all. They looked exactly like the kind of people who showed up at every bingo night, every open house and every free event in the town. People with no, or at least no local, families. People who just wanted to be in some way connected with the goings on around them, if not through any actual personal contact. It was sad that this whole trial would probably be the closest they would get to feeling like they were connected with something big and important. At least, that's how they all appeared to Rick. One of them wasn't even paying attention. He was an older man, probably somewhere in his late sixties, and looking every second of his age. He was sitting at the end of the long row of seats on Jaye and Rick's side of the courtroom and had spread out his coat, hat and gloves on the seats beside him to deter anyone from getting too close. From somewhere, probably the depths of his deep coat pockets, he had produced a folded up newspaper and was filling in the crossword puzzle. Every so often he would put the end of the pen he was using in his mouth and turn his face upwards, his eyes squinched in concentration. It drove Rick crazy to watch him. Didn't he even care that there was something far more important going on? He had to force himself to drag his gaze away.

Up at the front, Rebecca was standing at her little podium talking to the judge. Rick shot some quick looks at Jaye to see how she was holding up. She had her head down and he could tell from her body language that she was feeling the stress but trying not to show it. He yearned to reach out and hold her. He wanted to jump that barrier and sink his fist into the two boys sitting there.

A crinkling sound startled him. The old lady to the left of him was opening a candy of some kind. Rick shot her a dirty look and then turned back to the boys.

The smaller of the two was staring back at him. Likely he had heard the wrapper as well, not surprisingly, annoying sounds always carry in serious settings, and now he was looking right at Rick. This was not the one he had caught and pummelled, that guy's face was permanently etched in his mind. This was the one that ran. Rick wondered how much of his face this kid had seen. He wondered if the kid had seen him here the day before and knew that he was here with Jaye, not just as some crappy spectator.

The kid turned back to face the judge again, but not before the lawyer shot a look over his shoulder to see who he had been watching. Rick met his gaze with his chin up. The lawyer raised his eyebrow and turned back as well. With the absence of a jury, it seemed peering at the gallery was part of the game. Rick would have bet good money that had there been twelve other people involved in the outcome of this trial, neither the kid nor his lawyer would have looked back at all. The smaller the audience, the less an act seems required.

Someone had sidled up to him during the exchange but Rick barely noticed until he felt his arm being nudged. Seated beside him now was a small dark haired man with a notepad and a pen. As he turned towards him, the man nudged him one more time.

"So," he whispered, "you know the guy?"

"What guy?" Rick whispered back.

"You know, that kid who beat up that lady. You were looking at him. You know him?"

"Nope." Rick turned back to face the front of the room again.

The guy leaned in a little closer. He reeked of cigars. Rick wrinkled his nose.

"Come on buddy, no one has ever heard of these kids and one of them turns to look right at you? Tell me you know 'im. Come on buddy. It'll be a great scoop. I'll give you a full page for an interview."

Ah, that explained it. This guy was a reporter. A quick scan of the back of the courtroom and Rick identified at least two other people who looked like they might also be reporters. One of them was a woman with very shiny hair and a very shiny blouse. She was chewing on the end of a pencil. The other one was another man, looking only slightly cleaner than the one beside him and much younger, probably not older than Rick, and very likely still in his twenties. Rick had noticed him in one or two spots around town lately. He was staring at Jaye's back. Rick didn't care for the way he looked at her at all. If the man on his side was still waiting for some nugget of information to drop from his mouth, it was going to be a long wait. He narrowed his gaze at the young reporter in the back. He was still staring at Jaye. It made Rick grind his teeth.

"You're thinking about it, I can tell. Come on, I'll even put your picture in if you're interested in your fifteen minutes of fame." The guy nudged him again.

Rick turned to face him with fire burning in his eyes. He clamped his hand down hard on the guy's knee and squeezed, enough to let him know that he meant business.

"Listen buddy, I don't know those guys, and even if I did, I wouldn't give any information to you," he hissed out.

The cigar smelling reporter backed off immediately. As he started to shuffle away from him to another seat towards the back with his peers, Rick noticed that he darted a look at Jaye and Rebecca. A slow, not too cheerful smile played at the corners of his lips.

Great he thought, now this guy knows I'm here with her and that I'm angry about it. Just peachy, he's probably going to write that I manhandled him in the courtroom.

He was sorry that he had let his temper get the better of him. Perhaps he was beginning to understand where all of Jaye's fury had been coming from. After all, wasn't she living in a glass bubble right now? And what else was a courtroom if not the ultimate classifier of right and wrong?

Rick tried to refocus on the activities in front of him. Rebecca was standing up right now and talking to the judge, but he just couldn't focus on the words. Jaye still had her head down. She looked to be writing something on the legal pad in front of her. He wished he knew what she was doing. It was maddening to sit here and try and focus on all the legal jargon being tossed around and not to be bothered by Jaye's appearance of being beaten. Deciding he needed some air, Rick stood up and carefully inched his way out the back door of the court and into the hallway. He did not notice someone slipping out behind him.

The old building was full of neat little corridors and over-sized rooms. The large addition that had been built years ago housed a myriad of tiny offices for matters of the town and the county. Rick ducked down a few familiar hallways and slipped out the door to the outside, at the rear of the building.

"Damn," he swore to himself. It was a very cold day. The temperature was somewhere around minus four but the wind cut straight through him like a knife and he had forgotten his coat in Rebecca's office. The air felt sharp and harsh in his lungs and yet it was helping him get jolted back into the right frame of mind. He took a few minutes to try and gather his thoughts before heading back in. He didn't want Jaye to turn around and think that he had abandoned her.

"Got a light?" asked a male voice.

Rick turned around to see the younger-looking reporter from the courtroom had come out of the doors behind him. He was holding a cigarette in his mouth and fishing through his pockets.

"I don't smoke. Excuse me."

He went to push past the man, but an outstretched arm stopped him.

"Look, I didn't talk to that other guy and I'm not going to talk to you, okay?"

The man threw his hands up in a gesture of surrender. "Hey, no problem. This is off the record anyway," he said as Rick tried to go back inside. "I wouldn't want to exploit Jaye."

Rick turned slowly on his heel. "What, you know her?"

"I used to." He stopped fumbling with his pockets and pulled out and lighter. "Ah, eureka!" Lighting his cigarette with a flourish, he took a deep puff and blew the smoke out the side of his mouth, away from Rick.

"How did you know her?" Rick didn't trust this guy.

"My name's Colin. I used to live here. I went to school with Moira and Jaye. I've been in Calgary for the last twelve years or so, but I'm back in the area now. This is my first big story."

"Lucky you." The sarcasm was biting. "Just because you used to know her, I'm still not going to give you anything for a story. She doesn't need that."

"Hey, I get it. No worries dude. I'll just give the facts. Maybe lean a bit on the other side for holding up the start of the trial. That kind of thing. Jaye's a decent girl. She doesn't need any shit."

"You mean she doesn't need any more," Rick muttered.

"Ain't that the truth." He agreed, flicking his cigarette butt into the bushes. "Hey, she's not still friends with Moira…or Sloane, is she?"

"They run a business together. Sloane works for them….why?"

"No reason. Just thought it might be nice to look them up, you know, once all this is over. I don't want to overstep my bounds."

"Good thing," Rick told him. He hustled back inside out of the cold and hurried back to the court, not even waiting for Colin to catch up.

Sitting back down again, he smiled when Jaye turned to look at him. She didn't smile back. She must have noticed that he left.

Feeling like a first class shit, Rick looked towards the back of the room again. Sure enough, the three reporters were still sitting there, still darting their eyes between people and paper. Well, he thought to himself, if nothing else, at least I'm not the one splashing this out for the whole world to see. At least I can give Jaye her dignity.

He frowned at the thought. Was he giving her any dignity? It felt like he was just watching her as she faded away.

Chapter Twenty Six

That night when Rick and Jaye came home she went straight into the bathroom and ran a bath while Rick ordered pizza. They were barely speaking a word to one another. Jaye didn't know what to say. It had been a long and tiring day, full of legalese she didn't understand and it had been really hard to sit at the bench with Rebecca for all those hours. Rick had left at one point in the morning, doing god knows what and they hadn't really spoken over lunch.

Jaye got into the hot bath gratefully and sank down as low as she could beneath the water. It was hot, really hot. It was probably going to turn her skin pink. She didn't care. She closed her eyes and tried to block out all the sounds around her.

So, one of the guys had gotten a little too close for comfort. 'Touching for sexual purposes' was how it was put. When the details started to come out, she thought she would faint, or maybe even fall over, but she somehow managed to keep it together. Then bloody Rick had taken off. It didn't make any sense to her. He already knew what happened, why would he have to leave the room? It was her skin that felt like it was crawling now with a thousand unwanted fingers.

She just wanted to find a way to get rid of the sensations. She squeezed her eyes tighter and started to hum to herself under her breath.

She lost track of time, hunched down in the silky hot water with her eyes closed. At one point, she wondered what would happen if she fell asleep. Would she drown? Would she finally be a victim in the ultimate sense of the word? She started to let her head slip down under the water line again when a sharp smell made her sit straight up again.

"Oh thank god," she said, sliding back up in the tub to see Rick sitting on the side of the tub with a plate of pizza in his hand. "That smells so good. I didn't realize how hungry I was."

"Not surprising, since you barely touched lunch," he muttered. "Look, I think we need to talk about some stuff."

"Like what?" Jaye bit down on the steaming hot piece of pizza and smiled. Oh, it was like heaven. She watched Rick grab the other piece from the plate and take a bite of his own. His face was serious, like it was when he was thinking hard about something. Jaye had seen this look on his face many a time when he was carrying around some particularly stressful baggage from work. "Are you worried about missing more work? Because you know, you don't have to be there every day for this." She took another large bite.

"It's not work. Listen," he lowered himself to the floor beside the tub and reached out to hold her hand. "I called David tonight."

"You what?"

"Look, you haven't talked to anyone in your family, your parents are away and you need someone here with you in your corner."

"I thought you were in my corner."

"I am. And Moira is too, and Sloane and everyone else but…" he paused, Jaye studied his face as he searched for the right words. "I think you need someone from your family here. I think it's important."

"Well. I don't know what to say."

She took another bite and tried to chew. It was so hard to know where Rick's head was. They had spent so much time talking about her lately, when they were talking, that is, that she had no idea the kinds of things that were going through his mind. He must have sensed that she needed a moment and so he got back up off the floor and left the room.

Jaye tried to collect her thoughts, an increasingly difficult task as time went by. Nearly a month had passed since their anniversary, the trial was actually going and she still didn't feel like herself at all. She was angry, frustrated, confused, jumpy and sad. She couldn't seem to stop herself from fighting with people, especially those she loved. She couldn't talk to Rick, to the point that he had moved out for about a week and stayed in Jack's place. She couldn't talk to Moira, to the point that she had not done almost any kind of work in shop since this had happened. It was a terrible place to be, mentally. And tomorrow she would have to go back to that courtroom and sit through the whole process all over again, except now David would be here too.

Somehow the idea of her brother being there for the trial was frightening. She didn't really want her family to know what had happened. It had been very convenient that her parents were away on an extended cruise of the Mediterranean for a couple of months and were difficult to reach. She didn't think she would have been able to stand seeing the hurt and anger in their eyes if they had known and she really didn't want to hear any "poor Jaye" from either of them. Her brother was just going to be an extension of that. It meant working to entertain him at night, putting up with conversations about the case, trying to find room for him in this tiny place where she and Rick already seemed to fill up every bit of extra space with their lack of real words and their tensions.

Jaye lost her appetite. She pulled out the plug and climbed out of the tub, grabbing a towel to dry off. She forced herself to look in the mirror and noticed how much thinner her face appeared to be. In the cupboard under the sink, there was a scale. The bathroom was so small there was no room for it to be on the floor all the time. She couldn't even remember the last time she had weighed herself at all.

Jaye put the scale on the floor and gingerly stepped on it, dropping the towel to the side.

She was five foot eight and the last time she checked, she had been about a hundred and thirty five pounds. Definitely not supermodel small, but she had an athletic body. She gasped out loud when the number popped up on the tiny digital screen.

"One twenty two, oh my god!" she whispered, her hand slightly covering her mouth. She didn't want Rick to hear her. It had to be wrong. She stepped off and waited for it to reset, then stepped on again. Still one twenty two. Good lord! Okay, so it shouldn't be such a shock, since the whole thing had happened, she hadn't been eating much since the incident, but thirteen pounds seemed a bit excessive. She hung her towel back up on the rack to dry, put the scale away and went into the bedroom to throw on her robe.

"Rick," she said, coming into the kitchen. "Have you noticed anything different about how I look lately?"

He looked up at her in surprise. "You mean besides your bruises and such healing and the fact that you're skinnier than ever? Why do you think I am so worried?"

"You never said anything about me getting skinnier until just now." Jaye reached into the box and grabbed some more pizza. Her appetite was still gone but she was going to make herself eat it.

"You've not exactly been the easiest person to talk to, you know. How would you have taken it if I just started telling you 'you're getting too skinny and you need to eat more'?"

"Probably not very well," she admitted.

"Damn right."

"Okay, I get it. Now who's bitchy?"

She smiled at him. It was so tiring to be angry all the time. Why couldn't they just be like this again?

Since David wasn't expected in until morning, they decided that Rick would drop her off and then come back to meet David and get his stuff into the apartment before heading back to court. It felt so good to chat and tidy up together. It was as if nothing had happened and they had just slipped with ease back into the way their lives used to be. After discussing the plans for David's arrival, they didn't talk about the case even once more that night. Instead, they curled up together on the sofa and watched a movie. Jaye concentrated on the feeling of Rick's fingers threading their way through her hair. It was the most relaxing sensation in the world. It almost made her want to purr. Finally, when she could barely keep her eyes open anymore, Rick helped her up and they went into the bedroom.

In about a month, they had not gone together at the same time until now. For the first little while, Jaye had been knocking herself out at night with medication, then, anger or disappointment had lived between them like a chaperone. It didn't make for good bedfellows. Unbelievably, she felt almost nervous to be getting undressed with him. Jaye slipped out of her robe and hung it on the hook on the back of the door. She crossed quickly and got into the bed, pulling the covers up tightly around her.

"I'm cold," she said.

"I'll warm you."

Rick got in beside her and snuggled over, putting his arm around her and pulling her into the crook of his arm. She rested her head on the natural hollow created by his body just under his shoulder and laid her hand on his chest.

"Are you comfortable? I mean this isn't too hard on your ribs, is it?" Rick spoke softly into her hair.

"I'm fine."

"Yes, yes you are."

Jaye felt him shift and she moved her head back onto her pillow. Rick had raised himself up on his elbow and was looking down at her.

Again, the nervousness rose up in her belly. The last time they had tried anything remotely intimate, it had backfired horribly.

"You're beautiful Jaye," Rick told her.

"No, I'm not. I'm too skinny and I still have bangs and bruises everywhere…"

"Shhh," he put his finger lightly on her lips. "To me, you're beautiful."

She bit her lip so as not to argue with him. Jaye closed her eyes as his lips came down to meet hers. Even after four years together, the feel of his lips still sent delicious chills up her spine. His mouth was soft, his tongue so gentle. She tried hard to relax into it, but it was difficult for her. In her mind, she kept picturing the last time they had been naked together, how aggressive she was, how angry Rick got. In her mind she kept hearing the words that were spoken in court. Touched with sexual intent...touched with sexual intent. Tomorrow would be the big day. Details were going to come out. Tomorrow she would find out just where she had been touched, and how, and by which one of those two grease ball boys.

Rick's hands were ever so slowly tracing the lines of her body. She knew this touch so well, had felt excited by it so many times. She could feel a war starting in the pit of her stomach. The desire to be with her man, the desire to run away as fast as she could, as far as she could.

His mouth was lower now, on her neck and the crest of her breasts. His hands encircled her, the tips of his fingers fluttering like butterfly wings on her back, her waist. She tried to kiss him back, but her lips felt wooden. He didn't seem to notice.

Rick had slid down on the bed now so that her upper torso was uncovered. He lightly kissed her breasts all over, letting his tongue flick and tease at her nipples, the way she used to love. Right now, she kept expecting him to get harsh and bite her. In her mind, she was sure it was just a matter of seconds before he hurt her. It made it impossible for her to relax fully into the motions.

Trying hard to at least pretend that she was into it, for Rick's sake, Jaye tried to banish the thoughts that were infiltrating her mind. It was going alright, until she felt his fingers slide in between her legs. Then it all felt horribly, horribly wrong.

"Stop," she said; her voice raspy.

"What?" Rick's head was buried in between her breasts. His voice sounded muffled. She reached down and grabbed his hand away.

I said stop!"

"What's wrong?"

Jaye sat up and pulled the covers back over her.

"I…I just can't. I'm sorry."

"I'm being careful."

"It's not that. I just…it feels wrong. I can't stop tensing up."

Rick muttered something under his breath, got up from the bed and headed for the bathroom.

"What did you say?"

"I said it was fine the other night when you practically jumped me…" he stopped short. "I didn't mean that."

"I know what you meant though. I told you, I don't know what got into me that night. And I don't know what's wrong with me now. I just, I can't do this."

Rick went into the bathroom and closed the door. She tried to think about what was making it so hard for her to relax with him, but her mind just kept on coming up blank. It was infuriating.

When Rick came back to bed, she turned so that she had her back to him.

"Hey Jaye?"

"Yeah?"

"When was the last time you saw Dr. Spiers?"

"I don't know, a little while ago, why?"

"You really should go talk to her again. You need help."

"That's what Moira said too."

"Maybe you should start to listen to one of us."

Jaye didn't answer him. As she started to drift to sleep, she couldn't help wishing that in the morning she would wake up and all this would be over.

Chapter Twenty Seven

Joshua Moody

That guy was right. Simms, our lawyer, showed up at the jail the day before we were set to start the trial. I knew something was up when I was showed into the interview room again and he was the only one there.

"Good Afternoon, Joshua," he said. He sounded slippery, like an eel. I didn't answer him.

"All set for tomorrow?"

Still, I didn't answer him. I guess he was used to me not talking by now. Whenever the three of us met, Frankie did all the talking. I usually just sit in my chair and listen. It's getting easier for me these days. I don't feel like I'm going to crawl out of my own skin anymore. I don't even mind being in here. The guys stay away from me, probably because of Frankie. But I hated hearing about that kid a little while back. And I hate that it always feels like everyone else in here gets how it works, and I don't. I'm not part of any groups, or any gangs. But I don't get into trouble with them either. I can feel them watching though. I can always feel them watching.

"I was hoping we'd get a chance to talk, you and I. How're you holding up in here?"

I kept my head down.

"Come on, Joshua, you gotta talk to me sometime. I'm your lawyer."

I still didn't answer. I really didn't want to be here with this guy. I knew that there was ways for the others to find out that we were even alone in the same room together. I didn't want Frankie to think that I was selling him out. I didn't want to sell him out. You don't rat on your only friend.

"Okay, kid. You don't want to talk, that's fine." He opened his briefcase and pulled out some papers. He slid a couple of them onto the table.

"All you gotta do is sign these."

I looked up at him.

"That's right. I'm going to do you the biggest favour of your life, kiddo."

What a joke. The biggest favour this guy could do for me would be to leave me alone. Just being in this room makes me nervous. I know they know I'm here.

"Look, I've read all the police reports, I've talked to Francis, I know you weren't the one who started the attack. You were just along for the ride, weren't you? So, it's his idea, he's the one who knocks her out and tries to rape her, for god's sakes, he should be the one doing the hard time."

He sits up, looking all pleased with himself, like he's just saved my life. But I know the truth. It's Frankie that saved my life. Saved it a million times. I owe him more than anything, even if it means longer in jail.

"I know, I know," he keeps going, as if I'm thinking this over. "You'll still have to do some time. You have those break-ins in Waterton and Cantabria and you stole a car...big deal. I'll plead you down to a year, three years probation and you're golden. We'll even make sure you stay in a minimum security place instead of getting transferred to the bigger prison. Believe me, kid, you don't want to go there." He holds out a pen to me.

I don't know what to do. If Frankie was here, he'd spit right in this guys' face. I pull the papers he laid out towards me and try and read them. That asshole actually sits back all happy-like, with his arms folded behind his head, like he's already won something.

I can't understand a damn thing on this paper. I barely went to school after I turned thirteen. I can get by with regular stuff if I have to, but this might as well be written in a different language. I don't understand any of it. The only words I recognize are my name. For all I know, I could be signing anything.

A sweat starts to break out on my top lip and under my arms. I don't trust Simms at all. He has told us right from the start that there's no way we're not going to do time for this. He is the one who told us to ask for trial with just the judge, no jury. Frankie didn't like that, but he said it was our best option for shorter sentence. A jury would take one look at us and one look at that lady and put us away for years. But that's what he says.

What do I know about how this all works? He could have been lying about that. He could be lying right now. And Frankie's not here to help me.

I push the papers back at him.

"No thanks." I say.

Simms stares at me for a few minutes. Then he puts the papers away and shakes his head.

"Shame," he says. "I thought you were the smart one."

He closes his briefcase and buzzes the guard to let him out and take me back to my cell.

I'm so glad this is over. I don't know how Frankie knew he was going to try this, but even without the warning, I wouldn't have signed that paper. It would be like signing a death sentence.

Back on the block it's quiet. Some of the guys are at their jobs, some out in the yard. The guard walking me down the hall slows down as we near my cell.

"You got tossed," he says. "better clean it up quick."

My cell is a wreck. There aren't even that many things in there to make a mess with, but it's a wreck all the same. First sight reminds me of the crappy place we were staying in just before we were arrested that night.

I get a small shove on the shoulder into the room and those bars slam home behind me. I still hate that sound. Inside I'm picking up my stuff. Blanket, pillow, even mattress. Some pictures I got from a magazine that used to hang on the wall are now in shreds on the floor. I look at my toothbrush. Wish to hell there was hot water in here cause I don't know what's been done to it since I left the room.

Trying to clean this up and thinking about who tossed the cell makes me nervous. I don't know if it was the guards or the other inmates or how much influence Frankie really has. Maybe somebody else in here is out to get me. Maybe it's all about this meeting, maybe it's all about nothing. Don't matter, I couldn't figure people out before and I can't now either. I don't even want to; I just wish I could talk to Frankie again. He always made things make sense for me.

I hate thinking this much about stuff. It makes my skin crawl again. It brings back that old feeling of needing something to take away all the pain and all the thoughts. I wish I had a bit of rock. Just a bit. I miss that brown and hazy feeling. I could just close my eyes and the world fizzed away on a cloud of nothing and I didn't have to think or worry or care. Just one little taste, is that so bad?

****

I didn't get to see anyone else until dinner. Again, there was no one at my table. The big guy who gave me the weed a while back is sitting with Frankie and his friends. I don't get it how he has so many friends in here. Outside, he hardly ever talked to anyone but me. I wish he would come sit and talk to me.

I hate this place. When I think about it, I've pretty much hated every place I've ever lived, if you can call this living.

Lying on my bed after dinner and trying to think of the last time I was happy. I don't have much memories. The ones I do have are strange. The only ones I like to think about are the ones where Frankie and me was in a house and warm and dry and pretending like we lived there. I want to go back to that. If I had a Big Bag I would burn it right up, let it ride my blood to my brain and fly away on it forever. It's a hard night. It's one of them nights when I just wanna check out. I look down at my feet. They don't give you shoelaces or nothing in here, probably so nobody will buy it before some judge can take away all their freedom first.

That's the one thing I hate more about this place than any other. They leave you alone in here with nothing but your thoughts and your memories and if you ain't got any good ones, and I don't know much people who is in jail who do, you're left with all your nightmares instead. I hate being left alone. That's why I stayed with Frankie so long.

The night gets deeper and longer and I can hear that most of the other guys are asleep. A lot of them snore. I still can't sleep. I keep thinking about things. I never thought this much before. I wonder if I will ever get to talk to Frankie again. I wonder if that lady is okay now, if she's still mad at us. She didn't look at our table in court at all. Frankie looked at her a lot. I still can't believe what he done to her. Right out in the middle of outside, with people around us and everything. I wonder if he's sitting in his cell right now thinking like I am or if he's asleep, not worried about nothin', cause he never did worry before.

I think about the girl whose car I stole. I wonder if she was okay. Funny that didn't seem to bother me then. It bothers me now. Now I feel like I'm no better than those scary guys with the nasty breath who used to come to me in the night. There were so many homes I had to stay in those years. There were many where I was beaten. There were two with demon 'fathers' who showed their true sides in the deep of night. I learned then to sleep with one eye open.

One thought keeps on coming back to me. The last house. It's where I met Frankie. I got sent there at fifteen after a summer spent in a work program. That's where they get boys like me and send us off somewhere for the summer to work and keep us away from all the normal people who want to take vacations with their real families and not deal with us left overs.

I got sent to the house where there were no kids at all but us foster kids. There were two girls and three boys in the house, including me. The girls were just little. They were sweet, but we hardly saw them. The 'mother' just kept dressing them up in little matching dresses and taking them out places. The boys were all older. Around my age. Only Frankie was older. I don't remember the other boys' name. He left soon after I got there.

It was Frankie who came to me after that first time. He kept me quiet, snuck me out to the garage. He showed me how to roll the weed and smoke it and he told me it would help.

He was right. It did help. It fogged the edges of my reality and soon I was smoking all the time.

It was clear that the 'parents' of this house were living two different lives. She lived for those girls, and he, he was a sonofabitch who lived for the night. We ran away once. He caught us and brought us back and Frankie took the beating so I could get some sleep. When I woke up in the morning, Frankie took me back to the garage.

We smoked and talked about getting out, really getting out. His eye was swollen and black and there was a trail of dried blood coming out of his ear. I didn't want to know what else he had on him, if this was what I could see. I didn't ask Frankie why he wasn't sitting on the step with me.

It took us another couple of months, but we finally left.

The rest is a blur of hard living and harder drugs. I have tried, since I got here and since I stopped using every day, to get back some more of the memories, but they just don't want to come. It's like there's a big black hole in my head where things should be, and I can't get in it. I don't really know if I want to get in it. What if I find a way and then I can't get out again? Can you get lost in the pit of your own head? I don't know if I want to find out.

I can't see the sun coming up, but I can feel it. It's nearly morning. You can feel things starting to change in the building every single day before they wake us up. You can hear the people coming and going, the old guys in their cells getting up and taking a piss against the steel toilets, the disgusting sucking sounds of the janitor's mop slopping up and down the halls. I wished I would have had some shoelaces. I wished I would have stayed under that bridge instead of going back to the pee smelling house. I wish I had a big pile of powder that I could bury my face in until the world was gone and everything burned and felt good at the same time. I can't stand feeling this much and thinking this much and I just want to check outta here.

But I'm not gonna check out, I'm gonna go to court. I'm gonna pray to fucking god that they don't leave me here for years with nothing but the dragons in my head to keep me alive.

I almost wish I had talked to that lawyer.

Chapter Twenty Eight

Jaye woke up shivering. Today was another day at the courthouse and she didn't want to be there. She couldn't stop the shaking in her body. Her brother was on his way and it just made things harder and harder. Rick probably meant well, but he was doing nothing to help her get through this ordeal and dragging her family into it just felt like a low blow. She looked to her side and noticed that Rick was not there. He had been spending a lot of time on the couch lately, that is, if he wasn't at Jack's apartment. After the thwarted attempt to make love last night, she doubted that he wanted to stay in the same bed as her.

A deep weariness came over her. Life just felt like it had taken a sharp turn from the path it had been on and landed down in the deepest and darkest of caves from which there was no clawing her way out. No matter what she tried to do or who she tried to talk to, she could not pull herself out of the deep residing anger that coated her brain with a voluminous roughness that made it difficult to keep focused and clear.

Hung up on the back of the door to the bathroom was her outfit for court today. It was a bland, nondescript kind of suit, the kind of thing her mother would wear and would have encouraged her to wear. In fact, this had been Rebecca's idea. It was important to dress appropriately for court, to reflect the seriousness of it and of course as the victim she should be soft and subdued. Loud colours or wild designs wouldn't do her any service here. Not that it mattered; Jaye hadn't felt like wearing any of her more outrageous clothes in weeks. She hadn't even bothered to re-do the pink streak in her hair, so that now it was looking washed out and sad. The bleached hair underneath the pink was showing through, making the whole effect like an old watercolour painting that had been found after years of attic storage. It was dull with no hint of its former vibrancy.

Jaye trudged into the bathroom. She studied her hair for a long time in the mirror. From this room she could hear Rick making movements through the kitchen. He was driving to meet her brother David at the airport this morning. They probably wouldn't even be back until nearly noon. The plan was to bring David straight to court and then the three of them would have dinner together later on that night. She didn't want any of it. She just wanted to climb back into her bed, pull the covers up over her face, stop shaking and stay there all day. She prayed hard for something to put a stop to this horrible roller coaster she found herself on.

Looking up once again at her hair, Jaye reached for the drawer to the left of the sink. There was a pair of scissors in there. She put picked them up and studied them for a second. The light glinted off the steel of the blades and it fascinated her. She reached up and grabbed a hold of the section of hair that had sported the once-proud pink. Just as she was raising her hand to hack off the piece, the door flew open and Rick poked his head in.

"Sorry, I just wanted to tell you…WHAT THE HELL ARE YOU DOING?" he bellowed.

"God, don't scare me when I'm holding sharp edges!" she bit back, dropping her arm to her side again. "I was just getting rid of split ends."

Rick shook his head. "Sure you were. Since when do they start at the scalp?"

Jaye watched him heave a sigh of irritation. She wished he would just quit ruining her mood with his high-pitched accusations.

"Whatever, Rick. Why don't you just go away?"

He reached out and took a hold of her arm, prying the scissors from her fingers with deliberation.

"I'm going. But I'm taking these with me. If you do this, you'll regret it right away. How exactly did you plan on covering up a bald spot right near your face?" He tucked the scissors into his pocket.

"Go away," she told him again.

"Do you want me to call Moira to come over and stay with you, drive you in?"

"GO away!"

"Fine. I'm outta here. Try not to cut anything."

"GO AWAY! GO AWAY GO AWAY GO AWAY GO AWAY!!" Jaye screamed. She started throwing things at him, but Rick had turned and left the room almost immediately. As soon as the door clicked shut Jaye sat on the floor, pulled her knees up to her chest and dropped her head down.

What am I doing? She wondered. This wasn't like her at all. She just couldn't seem to get a hold of her emotions. A thought entered her head and she sat up quickly, re-opening the drawer from which she had gotten the scissors and started fumbling through the jumble of items. Just before she had been released from the hospital, Dr. Spiers had written her a prescription for some anti-anxiety medication. Rick had filled it, as he did for every prescription that she herself inevitably would lose, and if he had, he would have put the pills in here.

A bottle of Ativan appeared to be stuffed into the back of the drawer. She grabbed it and fumbled with trying to get the childproof lid off. With the same frustration that she had been approaching everything else with, Jaye got mad and practically ripped the lid away from the bottle, causing the pills to go shooting all over the floor. She gathered them up and took a look at the little handful and for the briefest of seconds she contemplated swallowing them all. It would be so easy, she thought, just to put them all in her mouth and end the insanity of her swirling thoughts once and for all.

In the end though, she just dumped the entire contents into the toilet and flushed them away. It just wasn't worth it.

An hour later she sat in the back of the cab and stared out at the bleary sky once more. Heading back to the court seemed ever so slightly less difficult without Rick by her side, flashing worried thin-lipped smiles at her and trying unsuccessfully to be reassuring. She didn't deal well with that. It was bad enough knowing he would be back in court later on and staring at her from wherever he managed to get a seat.

The cab pulled up and Jaye noticed right off the bat that there were more cars there than last time. It was not a good sign. She really hated how many people knew about this. It was humiliating.

She hustled from the cab to the office as quickly as possible, nearly doing a double take when she noticed a man standing among the reporters who looked eerily familiar. His face rang such a bell, but she couldn't place it, nor was she in the mood to stick around and strike up a conversation. Trying to brush it from her immediate thoughts, Jaye ducked into Rebecca's office and shut the door behind her.

"Running from anyone in particular?" came the cheerful voice of Rebecca from somewhere behind her desk.

"Not really. There are just a lot of people here today."

"I know. Mr. Simms is going to speak a lot today; I guess people want to know what it is he's going to say about his illustrious clients."

Jaye looked uncertain.

"Don't worry, if it gets out of hand for so many people to be in there, or if it starts to really" she stood up straight and looked Jaye right in the eye, "and I mean really start to bug you, I can make a motion to have the courtroom cleared."

That was a load off. "Can we make that motion before we start?" Jaye asked her meekly.

Rebecca laughed. "I wish. Don't worry, today should be a little easier. I get to fire out a lot of objections- which I'm sure I will."

Jaye chewed her lip. If they could have a motion to clear, could that mean David wouldn't get to come in? Wouldn't that be heavenly?

Rebecca came up behind her and placed a hand on her shoulder. "You ready to go and do this?"

"As I'll ever be." Jaye answered, trying to smile.

"That's the spirit."

Finally getting together the last of her papers, Rebecca donned her black long robe, her white upside-down 'V' collar and motioned for Jaye to follow her out of the office and to their seats in the already full courtroom.

There were far more people here today than the previous days. Hardly a seat was available and Jaye noticed right off the bat that there were many more reporters here as well. She was just about to sink down into her seat when one face caught her eye above all the others. He was standing next to an older gentleman and seemed to be talking but Jaye could swear that she saw him studying her with a sidelong glance as she came in. He did not make direct eye contact, but there was something about him that struck her as familiar. Finally Jaye just sat down in her seat. Thoughts of the stranger in the back left her quickly as court got underway.

The defence lawyer was spinning a tale to catch the attention of every ear in the place. His performance was so emotional, despite the many objections from Rebecca to slow him down, that if Jaye didn't know any better, she would swear that had there been a jury present, several hearts may have actually warmed to the two boys facing judgment.

As Jaye listened to the lawyer spin the tale of abuse, orphans and sympathetic circumstances, Jaye found her gaze drawn not to the vultures of the back row but to the boys sitting at the table opposite hers. One of them appeared proud and cocky. As his lawyer spoke of him as merely a victim of the system, he kept his head and his gaze forward, locked on the judge in near defiance. The other one though, he never lifted his face. It was as if his greatest shame was being laid bare, and perhaps it was. To Jaye, he resembled a timid and broken bird she had once found in the back parking lot of her apartment building, stumbling to walk and sporting a severely broken wing. This boy, for he was not much more than a child, seemed to be much the same. If the story being told by his lawyer was true, then she was not the only one who had been violated against her will in this room. She was not the only one who had been damaged. What made it any less acceptable to be sitting in her chair? What was the big difference between the two of them?

As the lawyer finished up his speech, Jaye kept her eyes glued to the younger man. Then, just as his lawyer sat back down at the table, and only for a split second, Jaye saw him look up. His eyes were wide and black and she knew, just knew, that he had never meant to hurt her. That this one, this wild and wicked one was not the one who tried to break her. He was just the bird who had fallen from his nest and needed some help to get back on his feet. He just had a broken wing and no one had ever told him he could fly.

When Jaye left the building that day, she made sure to exit by the back of the building, the exact door where she had first laid eyes on the boys, when she had been so scared she had run away. There weren't many people about, as Rebecca had gone out the front to the main steps of the building to speak to the few reporters who had stuck around for the entire day and David had left with Rick to get the car.

Once again she watched as the boys were escorted to the police car that would take them back to jail for another night. Mr. Cocky Pants was practically strutting. Lord, didn't bad boys always think they were just too cool, even when in shackles. The other one was walking with a slow purpose behind him. This time Jaye did not want to run. She knew enough about this case and indeed both of these boys now that they no longer held that evil fascination for her. This time she watched them trudge slowly beneath the quickly blackening sky and neither of them noticed her at all.

Chapter Twenty Nine

That night a vicious storm hit Fayette, the likes of which had not been seen in years. Rebecca had phoned the apartment at six thirty in the morning to tell Rick that court had been postponed until the next day, as long as the snowploughs' were able to clear the roads in time. One of the hazards of living in a small town in the so-called snow belt was that when the rare snow storm hit, it usually rendered the town impotent for at least a day as everyone scrambled to deal with the influx of snow. By the time the phone was hung up, Rick could already hear the ploughs out on the roads doing their rounds. He glanced out the window in the bedroom and his eyes boggled at the sight of the thick blanket covering everything in sight.

Jaye was still lost in the deep undisturbed sleep of her medication. It made Rick furrow his brow. Sooner or later she would have to stop taking those pills or risk dependency. He reached over and turned off the alarm and got back into bed. No point in missing an opportunity to get some much needed rest.

*****

It was a quarter to ten when Jaye finally awoke. She first glanced over at Rick sleeping beside her. Well, at least he wasn't asleep on the couch. She had been missing the feeling of his warm body in the bed. When she saw the clock though, she bolted upright quickly.

"Rick! Holy shit! Did the power go out?"

She looked at the clock again. The power couldn't have gone out, the time seemed to be correct, it wasn't flashing or anything; Jaye quickly stepped out into the living room and looked at the time on the television. The time had to be right. So why hadn't the alarm woke her up?

"Rick!" she shouted, coming over to his side of the bed and shaking his shoulder.

"Mmmm? What's up?" he asked.

"Did you turn off the alarm? We're late for court. This is going to look so bad." Jaye fretted as she turned through the room searching for clothes. "GET UP!"

"Sweetie, settle down. It's fine," he started to say.

"It's not fine, we're so late, the judge is going to think I'm some kind of flake and he's going to wind up letting those assholes off the hook because I can't even be bothered to show up!"

She ran into the bathroom and turned on the water in the sink, as there was no time for a shower.

She began splashing under her arms and tried to wash her face with her right hand.

Rick came up behind her and put his hands on her arms, trying to settle her down.

"Stop...relax."

"Fuck you!"

"JAYE!"

"WHAT?"

"There is no court today. Rebecca called this morning, look out the window for Christ's sake."

Jaye stopped and walked towards the window in the bedroom. Everything outside was covered in more snow than she had seen in at least ten years. She slumped back down on the bed.

"Why didn't you tell me?"

Rick laughed bitterly. "Sure. You try telling you anything these days. I thought you might like to sleep in for a change."

He went back to the bathroom and closed the door behind him. Jaye stayed on the bed and stared at the bathroom door. She waited for David to say something from the living room, although knowing him, he was probably still fast asleep. Sometimes she really resented his ability to sleep through virtually anything and yet still manage to wake up with his cell phone as if that was the only sound that could permeate his sleep fogged brain. It was unfair.

She lay back down on the bed and pulled the covers over her head. The blankets were still warm. Jaye couldn't remember the last time she had stayed abed this late. Probably it was on a vacation or something, but then she hadn't taken one of those in a long time either.

She waited and tried desperately to fall back to sleep when the feeling of movement on Rick's side of the bed made her stick her head back out. It was her brother.

"Hey there sleepy," he said, tousling her hair.

"Hey," she muttered back.

"Did you get a load of outside?"

"Yeah."

"Okay then, breakfast. Gotta get you eating some more, you're skinnier now than you were when we were kids." He smiled at her good naturedly and gave her a small biff on the chin.

Jaye managed a thin smile back at him just as Rick came back out of the bathroom.

"Well," he mused, "at least you got her smiling again."

"That's because I said breakfast and she knows that means I'm going to make pancakes," David chuckled.

The guys left the room laughing and making jokes with one another. It was driving Jaye crazy already to see them like this. Sure, she appreciated that they weren't bringing up the very reason David had come down here in the first place, but acting like it was just any other old visit was making her equally nuts. She got up, closed the door over and put on some sweats and a big old t-shirt of Rick's. She wondered how long David was going to stay. Surely he couldn't have gotten away from his job for that long, could he have?

She was just about to join them in the other room when the phone rang. It was Moira. She was calling to tell her that she had decided to close the store down for the day, since nothing and no one was moving around the place and no creature in his right mind would get into a car until the streets were at least partially cleared.

She wanted to ask about dropping by for a visit with Jack that night.

She thought that supper together might be 'fun'.

Jaye thought hard. She had been pretty mean and rude to Moira the last couple times she had seen her. Maybe it wouldn't be such a bad thing to have her over and try to mend a few of those slightly battered fences. Plus, with David here, it would be good to have the extra people there as a buffer, and maybe then she wouldn't bite Rick's head off either.

It sure beat trying to do anything else in town; the storm had rendered it virtually a ghost town for a day. Of course now she would have to search her kitchen to see if she had anything that she could whip up on short notice.

"Jaye, you still there?" Moira's voice came over the line.

"Yeah, I'm here. It's fine, I mean, you can come over later."

"Good, make sure you don't make a heavy dinner, Jack and I are going to raid the store and bring a bunch of goodies." She could practically hear Moira smiling across the phone lines. Well, she'd have to start being around her friends again soon someday, might as well start now.

"I'll make something light for dinner. Come over for that around five, and bring whatever you like from the store, that sounds great," Jaye told her.

"Awesome, see you later!"

Jaye listened for the click on the phone that said Moira had hung up and then she put down the receiver. She didn't actually really want them to come over, but then again she didn't really want David there either.

Jaye pulled the covers back over her again and waited for her brother and Rick to beckon to her with the promise of pancakes.

The day was a fairly lazy one. At one point Rick and David disappeared to go for a walk in the snow and pick up a few items for dinner. Jaye spent almost the entire day in her bed curled up with a book. She didn't feel much like interacting with the boys and she was fretting over the evening's plans. She never really was one for the winter anyway. She really preferred the summer. Warm weather was so much easier to relax in. Cold just gave her a healthy dose of the shivers and a strong desire to stay in one place and not see anyone.

One year, early on in their relationship, Rick had taken her to Quebec on a skiing trip. Jaye had taken the obligatory lessons and had somewhat enjoyed them, but the blistering cold made her cranky. Rick had talked about working their way through the various runs until they were ready for the really big, steep ones. Jaye, in an effort to both show him up and a desire to get out of the cold, chose a black diamond run as her first hill after the lessons.

She shot down at a breakneck pace, nearly falling several times. About mid way down the hill, she started to get a feel for the rhythm and the slice of snow under her skis. Exhilarated, she straightened out her skis so that they were less of a hindrance to her speed. At the bottom, she lay back on the snow breathing heavily, a huge smile on her face.

When Rick joined her a few minutes later, she stared him down with the adrenaline still burning a fever in her eyes and they immediately left the slopes for the bedroom.

For the rest of that weekend, they would hit the hills in the morning, Jaye always taking off for the fastest, most dangerous runs on the mountain, skiing once and then waiting for Rick back in their room. She discovered a passion for cold champagne sipped in a hot tub and a mild tolerance for cold winter weather.

Mid afternoon, after the guys had gotten back from their walk, Jaye decided to run herself a hot bath. Again. David was evidently having a good time with Rick and she still didn't feel like talking to anyone. The only place these days where she stopped feeling so hostile was sitting immersed in the hot water of the tub.

It eased her physical aches and it almost seemed to wash away her need to lash out.

From the bathroom, Jaye could hear Rick and David bustling back and forth in the kitchen. They kept on bumping into each other. She distinctly heard David make a crack about needing more space and how impossible it must be to make any culinary masterpieces in a kitchen this small. No storage spaces, no real counter space.

Hmmmph, Jaye mused silently, my thoughts exactly.

She strained hard to hear Rick's response to this dilemma. How many times had she lamented loudly to him that she could not make him any proper dessert if she had to continually do battle with the terribly small workspace?

Rick was muttering something back to her brother, but unfortunately his voice was much quieter than David's. Jaye couldn't make out what he was saying at all. She heard David enthusiastically agree with something, and then he too became unnaturally quiet.

Probably trying to tell David that he's moving out soon. Maybe even already told him about the nights he was spending at Jack's house. And David thinks it's a good idea. Well, then at least I know where I stand.

Jaye pulled the plug and got out of the bath. She didn't much feel like sitting in it now anyway. Back in the bedroom she pulled on an old pair of sweat pants and a t-shirt. It was still quite chilly in the apartment so she threw an afghan over her shoulders like a sweater and finally ventured out into the main living area.

"Look who's finally left her cage," David teased as Jaye dragged herself over to the couch and slumped down on it in a heap.

"Hardy har har. You're such a comedian," Jaye told him.

"And you, dear sister, are such a grouch. Want to help us with the chicken?" David picked up a raw chicken leg and dangled it between his fingers at her. It looked ridiculous.

"No thanks. One more person in there is a fire hazard."

"Well, you're so skinny these days you probably don't count as a whole person. You're more like a toddler…a pouty one," David teased her.

"What is this? Pick on Jaye day?"

"Always," David chuckled and went back to dipping the chicken first in flour, then in an egg wash and then in a concoction of bread crumbs and herbs. His fingers were thick with the build-up of repeating this process. Every time he finished another one, he held it out to Rick, threatening to touch him with his messy hands, making Rick laugh. Rick, in turn was browning the chicken in a pan and then lining them up on the baking sheet for going in the oven.

"I got a question," David mused as he finished up the last leg. "If I'm the guest, how did I get stuck with the messiest job for dinner?"

"Luck. Plus, I can't do it nearly as well as you can," Rick told him playfully.

"Oh, so it was my amazing skills as a chef, huh?"

Jaye snorted. Her brother was no chef. Likely Rick didn't trust him not to burn the legs had he been given the browning chore.

"Ah, yeah. You got skills," She said, the sarcasm veritably dripping from her tongue.

"Hey! I resemble that remark!"

"Boy, do you ever," Rick muttered.

Even Jaye couldn't bite back the laughter. David flicked a fingerful of flour at Rick's back just as he bent down to put the sheet of chicken in the oven. It hit him in the neck. The splatter of white dust along Rick's shirt and dark hair was just too funny. Rick straightened up and tried to keep a serious face. He calmly reached behind him and grabbed his half full glass of water.

"You wouldn't dare throw that at me!" David squawked.

"Nope." Rick said, and slowly and calmly he raised it as if to take a drink, watched David's shoulders relax ever so slightly, and then poured the rest on his head.

Jaye tucked her feet up out of the way, laughing, as the boys tussled on the floor. She laughed when Rick banged his knee on the side of the couch and when David found himself pinned on the floor shouting 'uncle'.

"Uncle! Who's an Uncle?" Moira's voice entered the room before anyone of the three of them actually physically saw her. Jaye looked up in time to see her and Jack step in through the door and kick off their shoes. Jaye smiled back when Moira gave her a grin and a wink, but her best friends' eyes positively lit up when she noticed David.

"Oh my god!!!" she yelled. "You're here! Wait…does that mean…holy shit, Jaye are you pregnant?"

The whole room stopped and everyone stared at her.

"No, I am not pregnant. These two fools were just goofing off and David was pussying out as usual."

As the guys extricated themselves from the heap on the floor, introductions were made between Jack and David and food started to come out. Between the five of them, there was an easy lilt to the conversation and Jack talked extensively with David about his job in marketing. David ran his own business and it was fairly clear that the two would be setting up a meeting to talk professionally some time soon.

Jaye for the most part stayed quiet through the meal. She had a headache and was still dealing with that feeling of inexplicable rage burrowing its way behind her ears and threatening to jump out of her mouth at any moment. Far better for her to be quiet and seem maybe a little rude than to open her mouth and offend everyone yet again.

Dinner was delicious. The chicken was sumptuous and tender and David made frequent remarks as to his role in this. There were potatoes and a green salad, homemade rolls from the bakery. Moira had brought a sachertorte for dessert. While the guys cleaned up and cleared the food, Moira went picking her way through one of the shelves on Rick and Jaye's wall and came up with a Life board game.

"Omigod you guys, we have to play this! David, you remember."

David explained that when they were teenagers, the girls had once challenged him to the game when he had come home drunk from a night with his buddies. It was the only way they had agreed not to wake up the parents and rat on him. Of course, Jaye had won the whole thing.

Jaye eyed the game warily. She was already feeling like she would just love to get back into bed and stop this whole charade. She didn't want to play a board game. 'Life' was the worst; a perfect reminder of how things were supposed to go, and how nothing was going for her. Go to college/start a career at the beginning of the game was about the only path she had actually followed. She still didn't have a house or a husband or a family. She didn't want a game poking fun at that.

As the rest of the bunch hunkered down on the floor around the coffee table with their wine and good humour, Jaye lifted herself up quietly from the couch and went into her room. She closed the door behind her, climbed into bed and promptly bit back the salty tears that picked their way down her cheeks.

She heard the door open, but didn't look up to see who it was that had come in to check on her. Whoever it was had the good sense to back out and close the door again, leaving her alone. She squeezed her eyes tightly and willed herself to go to sleep, ignoring the sounds of laughter, of fun, of family coming from the other room and reminding herself that they were much better off without her.

Chapter Thirty

Rebecca answered her phone late. It was already after ten, but the call was from the judge letting her know that due to the weather, the trial would get back underway on Monday. She was grateful to have the time off. This case was a no brainer, it would eventually take care of itself, providing she kept her head on her shoulders and followed her notes. It wasn't the case that had her sitting up at her small desk this late; it was the fax that had come in on her personal line about two hours earlier.

It seemed that one of her ex-professors had taken a job consulting at a very large firm in Vancouver. The firm was headhunting some new blood and, thanks to his recommendation, they wanted her. She was floored. The offer was something the likes of which she probably would never see again. Rebecca had been staring at the fax for two hours, reading and re-reading the lines. In it, she was told to expect a follow-up email with more details, and she was practically chewing her nails to the bone waiting for it to come in.

The phone call had practically made her jump through the roof. She managed to keep herself calm and professional and then called over to Jaye's home and spoke to Rick, letting him know that they had a bit of a break coming to them. As she hung up, she mused that snow putting a halt to civilised life was something she probably would never have to put up with again if she took this job.

If…what if? Rebecca hated it here in sleepy little Fayette. The only reason she had taken this job to begin with was to find a shortcut to getting ahead in her career faster than she would have starting out in a big firm, in a big city. Now she had some real clout and real court experience. Now she was a real asset. Here was the opportunity she had always wanted, a way out of town, upward and onward in her career being handed to her on a silver platter. It was glorious.

She scanned her eyes over the fax one more time, and from the corner of her eye noticed a change on her computer screen. The email had finally come through.

It was idyllic. The position was junior partner, where she would be mentored by a senior partner and would be working on actual cases. Corporate law. Something she had always wanted to focus on, indeed the exact course where she had excelled and whose professor was the one offering the chance in the first place. The money made her drool. The benefits made her swoon. She couldn't have come up with a better offer if she had handwritten it herself.

And then, she saw the flaw; the one flaw in the otherwise perfect job offer. They wanted her there in a week to begin meeting all the members, associates and partners and to get acclimatized with the office and the firm in general. One week.

This wouldn't have mattered to Rebecca if she wasn't involved in the case. She had no family to speak of, no husband, no children and an open lease on her duplex. There was nothing tying her to town at all except for the case. Possibly, it could be finished in a week, just possibly. Maybe even days if the storm didn't come back and dump more snow on them. But there was still sentencing and closing up the files and at least two and a half to three more weeks of work to do. To leave now would jeopardize the entire thing. At worst, it would cause a mistrial; at best Jaye would lose what little grip on her sanity she still had left. Either way it was a no go.

Her cell phone buzzed beside her but she ignored it. Her eyes were busy still racing through the information on the screen and her brain was working overtime. They were offering a generous bonus in exchange for the hasty move. Rebecca made decent money, she could afford to hire help to pack up and ship the contents of her place. She could stroll into the airport right now if she wanted and book a first class flight to Vancouver. If it wasn't for that lousy timing.

Again her cell phone buzzed. She had left it on vibrate. She glanced quickly at the screen to see who it was.

Daryn.

He was texting her, something he had been doing for days now, ever since he had come into her office that day. She cursed herself for letting things get to that place again when she had finally begun to separate herself from him. Now it seemed like he assumed things were back to the way they were, booty calls and all. Well, she wasn't his booty call anymore. He was toxic for her. A man who took as much as he could get and never gave anything in return and dammit, she was better than that.

At the bottom of the email was a contact number. She glanced at her clock again. Ten thirty. That was only about seven thirty on the coast. She picked up her cell and dialled.

It was strange to talk to Professor Clarke and call him Brian. But he had insisted. He explained that the firm was newly merged; two private practices that had teamed up to form a firm together and already had some impressive clients. He explained also the urgency in getting her up there. Rebecca had excelled in corporate law and they were sitting on a pretty major case. She also had a small amount of court experience and she was a woman, something that they felt would, in this particular instance, be a great asset.

As they spoke, Rebecca became more and more intrigued and excited by the prospects. She explained the case she was in the middle of in town and asked for some leeway in timing.

Her phone kept on making those little split second sounds, and she knew that Daryn was still messaging her, but she forced her mind to stay focused.

Brian said that he understood, and, as she was their first choice, he would speak to the partners and see if they would settle for having her in three weeks instead of one. As they wrapped up the conversation, Rebecca prayed that they would agree to this. The opportunity was simply too good to pass up. Brian ended the call by offering to be the first to take her out for dinner when she got there. He told her to get online and start looking up places to live. She smiled as she hung up the phone.

Fancy him inviting her to dinner. Well, he was only fifteen or so years older than her, and she had always had a hunch that he was sweet on her back in school. Maybe there was an opportunity there.

She frowned at her phone. Five more messages. Good Lord. Dinner with Brian sounded increasingly appealing, the chance to interact with a grownup, instead of this little boy who kept on pestering her. She decided to have a hot shower and then crawl into some comfy pj's while making notes on what she would need to facilitate moving quickly.

It took the water forever to get hot in this place, so Rebecca went into her bathroom, got naked and turned on the shower. She wrapped a towel around herself and then went into her office and grabbed her laptop. Carrying it downstairs, and leaving her cell phone upstairs, she plodded down to the kitchen for a drink.

The water would be at least ten more minutes to get hot enough to wash, so she pulled up a real estate website and started checking out apartments and condos. Who knew, maybe now would be the right time to think about buying. She had plenty of savings. She always knew she would never own a property here in Fayette. Which reminded her, she needed to make a note to write a letter to her landlady with her official notice. God, it was so exhilarating to be planning a big change in her life. It was time to move on.

Rebecca put the laptop down on the sofa beside her and ran back up to check the water. Still lukewarm. She thought she heard some banging coming from downstairs. Probably her crazy neighbours again. Either that or the old pipes were worn out trying to come up with a way to heat her water and were finally going into revolt. She bounded back down and headed for her kitchen again. She felt like celebrating. Since she never had champagne in the house, the only option left was some chocolate ice cream in her freezer. She reached in and grabbed it, giggling, and scooped some straight from the carton with a spoon.

Again she heard a banging, but this time it was evident that it was coming from her door, not the neighbours or the pipes.

She went over to it, wondering who on earth could be here at this time of night, in the aftermath of a vicious snowstorm. Holding her ice cream carton in one hand, spoon in mouth, she opened the door.

"Thank god, I thought something had happened to you," Daryn blurted out as he pushed straight past her and into the house.

"Daryn, what the hell are you doing here?" she demanded, now fully aware that she was standing there in nothing more than a rectangle of terry cloth.

"I need to talk to you; didn't you get my texts, or my messages? And why aren't you answering your phone?"

Rebecca sighed and shut the door. "Daryn, I'm busy. You should go home." She moved to open the door again for him but he grabbed her wrist.

"No, I need to talk to you first."

"What about and why can't this wait until tomorrow?" she asked him.

He stopped and turned his head for a minute, listening. "Do you have water running?"

"Oh shit. Yeah, I was going to have a shower."

He seemed to notice her for the first time. The wicked gleam she knew so well crept into his eyes. "Seems a shame to waste that hot water, I remember how hard it is to come by here," He mused. "Can I join you?"

"Absolutely not. I'll go turn it off."

She started to head back up to the bathroom, but Daryn's voice cut her off. "Don't bother; you might as well take your shower first. If you turn it off now, you'll never get any hot water back until tomorrow."

Damn, he was right too.

"Fine, I'll be a few minutes. Don't touch anything."

"I can wait."

She ran the rest of the way to the bathroom and shut the door behind her. This was going to be the fastest shower in history. She didn't want Daryn pulling anything on her like suddenly appearing naked in the shower with her, his body making it so hard for her to tell him that it just wasn't on.

Five minutes, and she even managed to wash her hair. It must have been a new record. Rebecca dashed into her bedroom and put on the most unattractive things she could find. Old sweat pants and a t shirt with tweety bird on the front. She wrapped her wet hair up in a towel and threw on some old sweat socks to boot. She didn't want him to see anything that might suggest sex.

When she came back down, Daryn was standing in front of her computer with a scowl.

"Why do you have real estate in Vancouver on here? You checking something out for a client?"

"Nope. I'm checking it out for me. Now what do you want?"

"Wait, hold on a sec, what do you mean you're checking it out for you?" He reached for her hand but she kept them folded under her chest. "Becks, are you moving?"

She sat down and took a deep breath. "Yes, I am probably moving. And don't call me 'Becks, you know I hate that."

She watched in disbelief as he reached out and took her hand. "I'm sorry. Look, I didn't want to come here and piss you off."

"I'll bet. You probably came here to try and get laid."

"Well, I certainly wouldn't say no to that, but that's not why I came over either."

"Then what's going on? You want to tell me about whatever it was that happened between you and my client?"

She relished watching his face react to that one. Ha ha! Didn't think she knew about it, by the looks of it.

"Well…I… um…okay, I can explain that. She came on to me, I didn't start anything."

"Don't worry, I'm sure you didn't rush to stop it either. But it's okay."

"It is?"

"Yeah. I don't own you. I don't even care. Who you choose to fool around with is your business, not mine."

Daryn reached for her hand again but Rebecca shifted and tucked them out of his way. She was going to make sure she wasn't sending him any mixed signals this time. She would not let herself get suckered into sex with him again. Or anything else for that matter. She was simply too good for him and she was finally ready to admit that to herself.

"Babe, listen to me, this is important for Christ's sakes." Daryn grabbed her hand again but this time he got a hold of it before Rebecca was able to snatch it away.

"Stop it," She said, trying to twist her wrist to make him let go. He only held on tighter, squeezing her a little too sharply. "You're hurting me," She told him.

"Sorry," He muttered. His grip relaxed but only a little. He was still staring her down. Rebecca didn't like this, it was just a little out of her comfort zone.

"See, the thing is, I think, I mean I know, I want to be with you again. That thing in your office the other day, that was so damn hot. We're so perfect together, babe. Come on, don't you know that?" He leaned towards her and half pulled her in by the wrist he was still gripping.

Rebecca watched in horror as Daryn tried to come in for a kiss. Good lord. As hot and attractive as he was to her, yes, even just days before in her very own office, she had finally turned some kind of corner and wanted nothing to do with him. Only a sleaze ball would let a client make out with him. Under any circumstances. Plus she liked Jaye and didn't want to see her get mixed up with Daryn.

"I'm sorry," she told him, pushing him back and pulling hard to free her hand. "I'm not interested. Come on, Daryn, we went over this ages ago. We're not right for each other, we want different things. You know it as well as I do." She stood up and walked over to her door.

Daryn jumped up off the couch and ran up on her so fast she didn't have time to react. He pinned her arms over her head and pressed himself in close to her. She could already feel the heat rising from him, but surprisingly didn't feel her body responding, as it always had.

She tried to turn her face to the side as he once again came in for the kiss. He must have interpreted it differently though, for as soon as she moved her head, he began to kiss her neck. Too hard. Rebecca struggled to get free, but he was holding her too tightly. The position of being pushed with her back into the wall made it so difficult to get in any way wrenched to the side or in a position to get out from under him.

Keeping her head turned firmly to the side, she tried to shimmy out to the side.

"Oh yeah," Daryn murmured into her hair. "That's the way, baby."

Shit. He probably thought she was trying to grind on him. As Rebecca searched her brains to find a way out of this predicament, Daryn moved his hands so that one was now holding her two wrists together and the other one started working on her breasts.

"Stop it," She said. She was getting pissed. He pressed his now hard erection into her pelvis, jabbing her with it and hurting her.

"I said stop!"

He ignored her still, his hands now reaching lower on her body.

Suddenly, Rebecca remembered what part of her was not fettered. She raised her knee up swiftly and connected it with the most persuasive part of Daryn's anatomy. He immediately fell back on the floor, cupping himself and moaning.

Rebecca looked down on him with disgust. "Aren't you police officers the very ones who teach women that no means no? I said stop. Twice. What the fuck has gotten into you?"

"You bitch! You don't know how good you had it. I was willing to take you back," he spluttered from the floor.

"What happened, Daryn? Strippers stop sleeping with you or something?"

She bit back the smile as he turned beet red. "It's that cow client of yours. She went and made friends with a bunch of them and now they hardly talk to me."

Go Jaye! She thought to herself.

"And you thought that was reason enough to come over here and try and 'take me back', huh? I'm not a pity case, Daryn. I'm not someone you can just 'decide' to be with because your other options failed." She watched him struggle up onto his knees and then to his feet. "You need to go home."

She reached over and opened the door for him. The second he was clear, she slammed the door shut and locked it.

"You're nothing but a cold frigid bitch, Rebecca. You're getting past it and you're never gonna find a man like me. Forget about me taking you back, bitch, now or ever!"

Daryn's screams faded as he walked down the driveway away from her house. She listened until she heard the sound of a car door slam, an engine turn over and the squeal of tires as they pealed away in shame.

Poor Daryn. At this rate he would never be truly happy with anyone but his own self. Rebecca giggled. She sure hoped he was into self-lovin. By the sounds of it that was all he was going to be getting for quite some time.

She went back into her kitchen and reached out for that ice cream again. Mmmm she thought as she spooned a generous portion onto her tongue. Deliciously sinful. Then she sank back down in front of her laptop and began scrolling through the properties to rent.

Leaving Fayette would be the easiest thing she'd ever done in her life. She wasn't going to miss one thing.

Thirty One

After Jaye went to bed for the night, Rick decided to talk frankly with Moira, Jack and David.

He was getting so frustrated with how to deal with Jaye; he just didn't know what else to do.

Trying to keep his voice low, Rick decided to first bring up the other subject that had been plaguing him a little in recent days.

"So Moira, I uh, met someone I think you know the other day. Or knew, anyway."

"Oh yeah?" she asked, trying to figure out which path in the board game would garner her more money. "Who's that?"

"Some guy named Colin? Reporter. He was at court the other day."

Instantly, Rick was sorry he mentioned the guy at all. It seemed that the blood had drained from Moira's face in an instant.

"You okay?" David asked her.

"Yeah...I'm fine. So, what did Colin want?" she nodded weakly towards Rick.

"I don't know. Not much. He said he had just come back to the area recently and was a reporter. He's covering the trial, though I don't know which paper he's working for. He mentioned that he knew you, or at least knew of you. I didn't talk to him for long."

Rick felt bad; if he had known that this was going to be a sore spot, he never would have brought it up in the first place.

"New topic. Who wants to talk about this anyway?" The jovial mood of the evening had been tarnished. Rick got up and grabbed and opened a new bottle of wine from the kitchen. He began topping up the glasses.

"So, who's turn was it?" he asked, false cheerfulness forcing itself from his throat.

"Jaye was right, this game is stupid. It just perpetuates stereotypes." Moira stood up from her spot on the floor and moved to the chair in the corner. She inclined her head towards the bedroom door. "She asleep?"

"I'll check," David volunteered. He peeked in the bedroom door and came back out a minute later with a sad kind of smile on his face. "Yeah, she's done."

"So, what are we going to do about her, then?" Moira wondered.

"Why? What's going on?"

The question came from David. Rick looked at him and sighed heavily.

"You know how I told you on the phone she was having trouble coping?"

"Yeah, but who wouldn't? She's been through an ordeal and a half. Anyone would have trouble with that. It hasn't even been more than a few weeks, give her time."

"We're trying, but she's been doing some really out of character stuff lately," Rick explained.

"I think now is the perfect time to explain to me what you mean by that," David said. "Should I call our parents?"

"No, no, no. I think this is something we can handle."

Rick looked at Jack, then Moira. They nodded at him.

"Okay, here goes. She's been hanging out at a strip club," he began.

"What??"

"Not...not all the time, but a few times. She gets plastered drunk and I don't know whether or not she's mixing her pills with the alcohol." Rick had a large lump in his throat that didn't want to go down. It was hard to talk about Jaye like this with her not even there to defend herself.

"That's not all, she's been avoiding work…I mean, which I understand, at first she couldn't even pick up a bowl without dropping it, because of her wrist," Moira put in. "But when she does show up, she's mean and harsh and usually leaves in an absolute huff."

"That doesn't sound like Jaye," David said.

"I know. One day she left and she went and got a tattoo, right out of nowhere."

"Really?"

"And she's taken off once or twice as well. Panic running around town in the dead of winter without a coat or anything." Moira's voice was so worried. Rick wanted to squeeze her hand. She had known Jaye so much longer than he had, it was probably really hard for her to see her like this.

"I don't like the sounds of this. Rick, is she talking to you at all?" David inquired.

"Not really. Sometimes she talks, but mostly she just winds up getting mad or yelling at me. I can't tell you how many times she's told me to fuck off in the last month." He sniffled and excused himself to go to the bathroom. Passing through the bedroom, he noticed that Jaye was lightly snoring. There was no way she would be aware of the conversation going on in the other room.

She looked so damn lovely sleeping, it was almost painful to stare too long. The fights and the frustrations were getting so out of hand, so hard to predict and to deal with that he just didn't know what was going to become of them. That thought in itself was one of the scariest feelings he had ever known.

Coming back into the room, Rick smiled at his friends.

"Look, Jack was just saying that the counsellor he saw after his father's death was really great with him. What if we gave you his contact information?" Moira asked.

"No good, she already has a doctor that she sees...or at least that she is supposed to be seeing. It was a hard enough battle to get that going, I doubt she is going to want to go to your doctor, Jack. Besides, wasn't it a man?"

"Well, yeah, but he specializes in grief, and I really think that Jaye is grieving for whatever part of herself she feels she lost that night," Jack put in.

"You're probably right on some level, but getting her to talk to a woman doctor is hard enough. I can't see that she is going to be trusting a man right now, a man she doesn't know at all. No offense."

"None taken."

"Hey Rick, you said you guys were having some kind of argument when...well, on the night in question. Do you mind if I ask what that was about?" David tipped his head to the side.

"I bet I can guess." Moira's voice was quiet. "It was about the house thing again, right?"

"How did you know?"

"She talked with me about it a bit, you know...before," she tried to smile as Jack put his hand on her knee.

"Yes, it started because of the house. It went on the market that day."

"What house?" David and Jack spoke in unison, prompting Rick to crack a wry smile.

"There's a house near where Moira's mother lives. Jaye loves this house. She talks about it, she probably even dreams about it." Rick got up again and started to pace. "I mean, look around here, guys. Would you want to live here for four years?"

They didn't answer him. Of course they didn't need to. The apartment was grievously small, anyone could see that.

"Hey Moira, how did you know? Besides the fact that she's talked about it before?"

"I was at my mom's that morning. My nana hasn't been well this winter, so I sometimes go there in the morning to check up. I saw them put the sign up on my way home."

"Yeah, well I saw it up on my way to work," he dropped his head. "and here's the worst part. I was being mean about that house on purpose. I wanted to piss her off so," he sniffled loudly again. "so it would be a surprise."

Almost as one, the three friends turned to him in unison with a look of curiosity and perhaps even a little anger. Rick knew they must be thinking that he was nuts. Why on earth would he want to make Jaye mad on purpose?

He took a long swallow of his wine and a deep breath. "I called the agent that morning as soon as I got into the office. I found out the asking price and was just arranging things with the bank so that I could make an offer. He was going to hold any other inquiries on the house for me for one week so that I could get things figured out and surprise Jaye."

It was hard to come clean with this. It had been weighing on him and eating him up for weeks now.

"Gosh," Moira said. "That's one hell of a surprise, Rick"

"I know. The owners moved out of the country. That house is vacant. We could have moved right in."

"So, what are you waiting for? Why don't you call him back and make an offer?" David wanted to know. "Don't you think that's exactly the kind of thing that might help snap her out of this....funk she's in?"

"I can't."

"Why not?"

"Because he said he'd hold it for a week. That was three and a half weeks ago."

"That doesn't mean anything."

"Yeah, but the sold sign does," Moira put in.

"Oh, shit," Was all David could say.

"I know. I guess it just wasn't meant to be."

They were quiet for a bit, each of them chewing over the information in their own way. Rick felt like such an asshole.

"Rick?" Jack asked.

"Yeah?"

"This might be a kind of personal question, but were you really in a position to buy a house like that? I mean, you said you were talking to your bank, right? I assume you'd be applying for the mortgage alone," Jack spoke tentatively.

"You're right Jack, it's none of your business." Moira shot him a look. "Sorry Rick, ever since the inheritance, Jack has been taking an overt interest in the financial goings on of people he knows."

"It's just a question, he doesn't have to answer," Jack said.

"Actually, I'm curious too," David piped.

"I'm comfortable. You guys know what I do for a living. Plus, we don't have any kids or any dependents. We don't really spend a lot. I save a lot of my money. Have been ever since I started working. I'm in a good place."

"Wow," Moira mused. "Maybe I should marry you."

Rick chuckled against his inclination. Then everyone started to laugh.

"Thank god, this party was becoming too serious," Moira laughed. "There still is one more thing I would like to discuss though, since we're all here."

"What's that?"

"I still think we should do that intervention. She needs help. She's not taking it from any of us and she's digging herself into a private little hole. I don't want to see Jaye, the real Jaye, get lost in this."

"I think you're right. And I think we should do it soon."

"You'll have to count me out then," David told them. "I have to get back to work. But I'll be here for the sentencing. You can count on that."

Rick reached out and patted David on the knee. "Thanks, brother. That means a lot. It will mean a lot to Jaye as well, even though she may not be the one to tell you that."

They smiled at one another.

As they tidied up, plans were made to confront Jaye about some of her more reckless behaviours and soon. If they could do it before the case was finished, so much the better. Rick and David bade Jack and Moira a good night and then they too settled in for some much needed sleep.

"Hey Rick," David said as he exited the bathroom from brushing his teeth.

"Yeah?"

"I hope you will someday, you know," he grinned. "Be my brother."

"I know. Me too."

Rick watched David walk slowly back out to his bed on the couch and then finally climbed in beside his sleeping beauty.

It was a terrible thing, to watch someone you loved deconstruct. He only hoped that between them, their little family of friends could make her finally see how loved she was and just how much they missed her.

Thirty Two

Jaye woke on Saturday morning with a bit of a start. Yet more snow had fallen in the wee hours of the night and there was a delicate web-work of frost clutching the bedroom window. She sat up in the bed and tried a simple stretch. Her ribs were still quite achy, and this cold weather was doing nothing to help that. Although her wrist was healing, it was still sore and tender, especially first thing in the morning. Probably in her sleep she was still lying on it at some point of the night. A reflex, one that she wished she had not ever picked up on, or at least that she could train her body out of doing while it finished getting better.

Today she had a meeting with Dr. Spiers, and not one she was looking forward to. Since the trial had begun, it seemed that the good doctor just assumed that Jaye would be needing her more than ever, when in fact it was just the opposite. The longer it went on, the less she wanted to talk to people about it, especially people she hardly knew, professional or not.

She tiptoed into the living room, not that she needed bother being quiet with David there. He could sleep through a parade in the living room.

Pouring herself a glass of juice, Jaye noticed that they had cleaned up last night. A welcome surprise.

She went back to her room with her glass and into the bathroom. The scars were still there on her head. Probably always would be. She traced the line with her finger, pressing down into the groove of the stitches which had begun to dissolve. It was so ugly.

This morning's appointment to meet with Dr. Spiers was at her office, which, thankfully, was very close to her house. After grabbing a few bites to eat, Jaye dressed quickly in some warm clothes, located some clean and dry gloves and wound a scarf around her neck. Then, without checking to see whether the boys were up or not yet, she quietly let herself out of the door and quickly began to walk down the street.

Fayette looked like a ghost town. Gone was the usual bustle of people generally to be found on any given morning, including in the winter, off to their various places of call for the day. The few cars that were parked along the sides of the street were now buried behind walls of snow created by the plough's first run through after the first drop of the white stuff the day before. It seemed that not even the birds were out and about this morning. Shivering, Jaye could understand why. It was bitingly cold out; the kind of cold where you prayed for there to be no wind, lest your very bones rattle inside your body. It was the kind of cold where a person's nose went cherry red within minutes and you could feel the whites of your eyes get even whiter.

Jaye hated winter. But for some reason she was not bothered by this particular day. Even with the frosty temperatures and the lack of people, something about the barrenness of it all appealed to her.

She checked her phone again for the address that Dr. Spiers had sent to her in an email. It indicated a building about four blocks from Jaye's apartment, suite number 301. As Jaye neared it, she thought that she must be mistaken. This place didn't look like a place of business at all. It looked more like a residence.

She walked up to the main doors, let herself in the first set of doors and looked at the list of occupants.

This building was in fact some kind of residence. It had to be, for there was no indication on Dr. Spiers listing that she was anything other than just a tenant. Along with the seven other names, it simply read: K. Spiers. Jaye pressed down on the buzzer anyway and waited for the response.

"Yes?"

"Um, hi.   It's Jaye.   I'm here for my appointment."

"Come on up." And the door buzzer sounded.

Jaye grabbed the door and pulled carefully. It opened and she quickly let herself in and immediately went up the stairs.

The second thing she noticed about this place was that there were only two apartments per floor. If it was residential, then Jaye was about to walk into one of the largest apartments in the entire town.

She knocked on door 301 and barely had time to put her hand back down when Dr. Spiers herself answered the door wearing comfortable sweats and a towel wrapped around her head.

"Come on in!   You're exactly on time." She said, holding the door further open and gesturing to the inside with a sweeping motion of her hand. Jaye stepped in past her and shrugged out of her winter gear.

"So, um…this is your office?"   Jaye asked as she bent down to undo her boots.

"Sort of. It's my apartment, but I use the living room for certain clients when the need arises or when I'm just getting sick of my office at the hospital.

Sometimes it's easier to relax in a less formal setting, don't you think?"

"I guess."

"So, sit down, I'll get this thing off my head and grab us something to drink. You a coffee or tea girl?"

"Tea would be nice, thanks."

Jaye watched her leave the room and immediately began taking stock of her surroundings. There were pictures and books everywhere. Medical books took up most of the large bookshelf that was against one of the walls, but she also noticed that there were paperbacks tucked in and around them and a few of them on various other surfaces of the room. So, the doc liked to read, huh? Jaye bent down to pick up one that was sitting just under the coffee table when Dr. Spiers walked back into the room, this time with her damp hair hanging down and a bright smile on her face.

"Aha, I see you found my weakness," she said. "I just love those Harlequin romances."

She ducked out of the room again and Jaye could hear running water.

"You ever read any of those?" she asked from what must have been the kitchen.

"Nope, can't say that I have. I don't usually have time for reading, but when I do it's hardly ever romance," Jaye told her.

"You don't know what you're missing," The doctor said, coming back in once again with a tray, which she laid down on the table in front of Jaye. "That one is particularly good," She added with a wink. "There are pirates in it."

Against her better judgement, Jaye laughed out loud. The sound surprised her.

"I want you to call me Kate today. I know, I've asked you before, but we're here in this nice cosy place and there's no need for formalities. Okay?"

"I guess."

"How do you like your tea?"

"One sugar, no milk," Jaye said, and helped herself to one of the small scones that were on a plate on the tray. It was the grocery store kind. She stifled a small inward groan.

"So, tell me how the case is going? You getting through it okay?" Kate wanted to know.

"I guess so. A lot of it feels like it's over my head so I try to just sit there and think about other things."

"What kinds of things?"

"I don't know. Whatever."

Kate took a sip of her tea and waited. Jaye sighed. "Things have been kind of weird with me and Rick lately," She finally said.

"How so?"

"I don't know; we fight a lot. I get mad at him a lot. Plus, I think he's talking about me behind my back."

"With whom?"

"Moira, Sloane, Jack, my brother David. I just get the feeling that they're always having some conversation about me that I don't get to be a part of. I don't like feeling like they're…you know, sneaking on me, living around me but not with me."

"That's pretty astute. Sounds like you're holding onto some pain."

Jaye reached up and traced her scar again absently. "I guess you could say that."

"This has not been easy for you, I know. Have you tried asked Rick or your friends about their conversations?"

"No, not really."

"Why not?"

"It's hard. Whenever we talk, we always wind up getting in a fight."

"Who does, you and Rick or you and your friends?"

"These days, me and anyone I talk to."

"Well, we're not fighting right now, and we're having a pretty decent conversation," Kate pointed out.

"Yeah, but you get paid to listen to me and not to pick fights."

"Good point." Kate smiled at her.

"Let's go back to Rick. Tell me what kinds of things trigger fights with him."

"Well, I get mad or I need to get out and he freaks out on me. He practically had a meltdown when I went to the club."

"Which club?"

Jaye blushed and dropped her head a little. "'The Club'. The one out by the highway. You know…"

Kate was still looking at her with a questioning face.

"Oh for crying out loud, the strip club, okay. I went to the strip club."

"Hmm. Interesting choice for a single woman out on the town. Why did you pick there?"

"So I could have a few drinks where no one knows me. I don't know anyone who goes there. I could sit by myself and no one would pick on me or baby me or ask if I was okay."

"And the women are in total control of who they talk to, who they sit with and who can touch them. Sounds like a logical choice to me."

"Yeah, well, nobody else seemed to see it that way," Jaye muttered.

"Have you tried to explain it to them?"

Jaye avoided her question by taking another sip of tea. She didn't really like where this line of conversation was going.

As if reading her thoughts, Kate changed up the questions again. "Are you still taking medication to sleep?"

"Sometimes," Jaye admitted.

"What about pain meds? Still taking any of those?"

"If I need them."

"Is the pain really still that bad?"

Jaye stood up and started to pace the room a little. "I don't know, sometimes, okay! Sometimes I just feel like…I just get so…." She bit her lip. Freaking out in front of her shrink was probably the last thing she should do. What would happen if her notes were subpoenaed?

"It's okay; say what you need to say," Kate said.

"I get mad, right? And I feel like, I don't know, hitting someone," Jaye started. It felt kind of good to get this out. "My skin feels like it's crawling and whoever I'm talking to, I...I just can't stand the sound of their voice. Rick is making me crazy with always asking me how I'm doing and trying to do stuff for me and babying me and Moira...she's trying to be all...mother-y. Then I want to take off and run away from them so that I won't have to deal with how they keep on treating me like glass when I'm fucking fine!!"

She swallowed hard against the lump in the back of her throat. Kate was still sitting on her couch sipping her tea. She hadn't written a note and she hadn't spoken a word yet. It was remarkably relaxing. Jaye went on,

"I mean, what does it matter if I want to take off sometimes and be on my own? Rick should get that, he left the apartment and left me for about a week. Did I tell you that? That he wants to leave me now? He's just waiting for this stupid trial to be over, I know it. And Moira doesn't want me in the shop anymore, she has her mother and sister and even Jack in there helping her out. Jack can't cook his way out of a soup can and she's letting him in our kitchen! Don't even get me started on that cop either. What a sonofabitch he turned into. Do you know I practically threw myself at him and he did NOTHING!? Well, almost nothing, I mean he did kiss me back and stuff, but whatever. I don't need that guy, he's such an asshole! And to top it all off I don't know when it's going to stop feeling like this and JUST GO BACK TO BEING ME!"

Jaye stopped and realized that she had been pacing the room and twisting something in her hands. It was the romance novel that she had picked up earlier. The cover was now a wrinkled disaster and several of the pages were bent and twisted from their original bindings.

"Sorry," she said.

"It's absolutely not a problem. I've read that one at least twenty times already anyway." Kate said. "You want to come back and sit down?"

"Sure." She stepped back over to the couch and sank down in it.

"Sorry," she muttered again.

Kate sat up straight and poured her some more tea. "Don't be. That was probably some of the best work you've done since we started seeing each other." She winked at her and slid the newly filled cup back to her. "Told you this place was more comfortable and freeing."

"No shit," Jaye retorted. "You call that rant 'good work'?"

"Yes! It's the most you've ever said to me, it was real, it was honest and it's a real step forward. Look, you're supposed to be feeling all these things right now. You should be angry and be pissed off. But you need healthy ways to express it. Not running off to get drunk at a strip club or kissing people who aren't your significant other. That kind of behaviour is not going to help you heal and is just going to push away the people you love."

"Thanks a lot," Jaye said with heavy sarcasm. "What the hell do you suggest then? Let them make me feel like a fifth wheel all the time? Let them talk down to me like a two year old and then go punch a few pillows when I get mad at it?"

"No, you'll find something that works for you. It just may take a bit of time."

"That's kind of a bullshit answer, Kate," Jaye told her.

"I've never claimed to have the answers, just trying to help you find some."

Jaye bit her lip. The session felt like it was turning into 'let's all fix Jaye' time again and she just felt like she had to get out of there.

"I'm going to go," she said, standing up and heading for the door.

"Okay, that's fine. Listen, you really did do good work today. I can see that you're getting upset again, and that's okay too. I just want you to know that this was a positive meeting, and I hope we'll have many more of them."

Kate smiled at her as she finished putting on her outerwear. Jaye just shrugged at her and left.

Positive meeting, huh? Well, if that's what she wanted to say. Actually, she did notice her anger seemed to leave her almost as quickly as it had come on. That had to be a step in the right direction....didn't it?

As she walked back through the snow-laden town, Jaye fervently hoped so.

Thirty Three

Some of the businesses were beginning to open back up now that the bulk of the snow was getting cleared and no new snow was falling. Jaye made a point of stopping in at The Ink Spot to say hello to Levi and to show him her recently healed tattoo. He gathered her in another of his monstrous hugs and sent her back on her way, with a promise that he would absolutely call in the store for a cake sooner than later. Jaye didn't have the heart to tell him that she was barely, if ever, there anymore. It was just one of those things she didn't feel like addressing yet. Maybe when the trial was over, perhaps.

The Bean Post was open, and Jaye decided to nip in for a coffee. One thing about this weather, it made you crave hot drinks like an addict. She could think of nothing better at the moment then delaying her return to the apartment with a hot and frothy cappuccino. She rounded the corner and went in through the front door.

Instantly, the aroma of hot fresh coffee made her mouth water. Jaye went straight up to the counter and ordered a large cappuccino with foam from the girl working behind it. She was just starting to dig for change to pay for it when a large arm reached from behind her and slapped a five down on the counter.

"It's on me," said a deep voice.

Jaye turned around slowly. She found herself staring into a face she had not seen in a very long time.

"No thanks," she said, and finally located and then dropped several coins on the counter. "I got it."

"Still stubborn, huh?"

"As ever. What are you even doing here?"

He motioned for her to join him at his table, and, with a little reluctance, Jaye did, although she found herself staring quickly at all the other customers in succession first to make sure there was no one else she knew in there that could possibly report back that she was fraternizing with the enemy. She sank down in the seat and took a good look at Colin.

"So?" she asked him.

"So what?"

"What are you doing back here? I thought you were never going to come back to Fayette."

Jaye took a sip of her coffee, but her mind was whirring. Colin; one of Moira's first boyfriends, and absolutely her first in a series of bad experiences with men. She wondered if Moira even knew he was in town. It wouldn't be pretty if the two ran into one another.

"I moved back. Just about a month and a half ago. I was finished with Calgary anyway and my mother isn't doing very well. I agreed to come and take care of her for a year."

"That's nice of you." Jaye didn't even try to hide the sarcasm in her voice. She remembered this guy all too well from high school. He was a smooth talker, far too good looking for his own good and far too aware of it for the good of any woman. In some ways, he reminded her of Officer Daryn, but without the sharp edges to his features. How was it that men like that learned that their looks seemed to give them some sort of pass to treat women like shit? Jaye would love to have the secret to that. Actually, what she'd rather is that guys like that just got a dose of their own medicine. Preferably by some very beautiful woman who would just walk all over them and then leave him in the dust.

"How are you doing?" Jaye was shaken from her thoughts by the question.

"Well, let's see. How am I doing? I imagine you know all about the court case, being back in town just before it happened."

"I know some stuff. I work for the paper now, so I'm actually covering it."

Jaye stiffened. She wanted to leave right now. "I hope you don't think you're going to get an exclusive or anything from me?" she said icily.

"No, no. I already know you're not giving interviews."

"How would you know that? This is the first time you've talked to me."

"I talked to your boyfriend at court one day."

This was news to Jaye. Rick had not mentioned talking to any reporters, let alone to one with whom she had a past connection. It was infuriating.

"Ah, I see he didn't mention it." Colin looked smug. It made Jaye want to hit him.

"Maybe he did, maybe he didn't. Look, I should go. I have things to do you know."

She got up from the table and started putting her arms back into her coat and slipping her hands back into her gloves.

Colin stood up and touched her arm. "Hey, I didn't mean to piss you off. I was just wondering though, do you know if Sloane is still living at home?"

Well, if any question could have stopped Jaye in her tracks, that was the one.

"Why?" her word was as biting as she could make it.

"Just wondering. I thought it might be nice to look her up." He tried smiling one of his billion watt smiles at her but Jaye knew better.

"She's married," She told him flatly. "Why don't you go find some other sucker...I mean girl, to hit on?"

"Now Jaye, that really wasn't necessary. I thought we were old friends."

"I hate to tell you this, Colin, but we were never friends. You dated my best friend, and then her sister. You were never a friend of mine."

"Ouch, harsh. Look, I'm sure I'll find a way to bump into her sometime and say hello. It was nice to see you again, despite you biting my head off," He chuckled. "Take care of yourself, Jaye."

"Hey, just because you may know me a little from years and years ago, that doesn't give you license to print a bunch of shit about me in the paper. Stick to the facts of the trial."

"You know, I can promise you that, and I will, but you should know I'm not the only reporter there. I can't do anything about what they write....or where they get their sources."

"That sounded like a threat."

"Nope, just some friendly advice."

Jaye left, not wanting to waste another breath on him. This was just great. If she were to be in debate about it, she could probably trace Colin back to the first guy that messed Moira around so badly that she stopped trusting guys altogether. Having him back in town was bad news.

She looked back in time to see Colin leaving as well. Just as he was raising his hand to wave, and she was raising her finger, her cell phone went off. She couldn't help notice that Colin's did as well.

"Hello?" she said, fumbling slightly to keep the phone under her ear, with the gloves making her fingers thick and clumsy.

"Jaye? It's Rebecca. I just wanted to let you know, court will be back in session first thing Monday. We should be getting ready to wrap it up soon. Okay?"

Jaye mumbled an okay and a goodbye. Her eyes were still fixed on the sight of Colin talking on his phone too. He hung up and called out to her.

"I guess I'll see you tomorrow then, huh?" and with a wink, he took off in the opposite direction and Jaye turned and headed for home as fast as her feet would carry her.

Thirty Four

As pleased as Rick was that Jaye had gone out to see her psychiatrist, he sure didn't like the mood it had put her in when she came home. He spent most of the rest of the day trying to avoid her. When they did bump into one another, she either didn't speak to him at all or bit his head off. Rick wasn't sure if she was nervous about going back to court, or angry with him or about something that had come up in her session, but he didn't want to ask. Far better to stay out of her way when she got like that. It made him sad though, he hated seeing her suffer and not come to him to work things out. They had always talked through their issues together, whatever they may be. Finally Rick just grabbed a notepad and sat down to write out his victim impact statement, something he had promised Jaye's lawyer he would do.

It was hard work, trying to find the words that would let the court know what had become of Jaye since this attack on her so many weeks ago. Rebecca had insisted that this would lend huge credence to the sentencing, especially since Jaye herself would not talk; they needed to hear first-hand from someone who loved her what this terrible thing had reduced her to.

It took him hours, but Rick finally finished what he thought was a pretty decent account of Jaye, then and now. He was just finishing when Jaye came out of the bedroom and sat down on the arm of the chair where he was working.

He was aware that she was looking over his shoulder, scanning the page, but figured it was probably far better for her to see it now then to hear it for the first time in court the next day.

"What's that?" she asked him.

"It's, um, a victims impact statement," he answered.

"Oh, and what are you a victim of?" She squinted a little. "That's my name on there."

"Well, yeah. It's for your case," he told her.

"Who said you were going to speak about it?"

"Rebecca asked me to do it. She thinks it will help…"

"Nice." Jaye bit out, "just fucking nice." She made a grab for the page.

"What are you doing?" Rick demanded.

"I'm going to tear that up," she said, calmly.

"Like hell you are! This took me almost two frickin' hours!" Rick jumped up and hugged the notepad to his chest.

Jaye looked like she was going to lunge for it again but instead she just sank down in a chair and started to cry.

"Will you at least listen to it before you decide that it needs to be destroyed?" he asked her gently.

Jaye waved her hand towards him, which he took to mean yes. Well, at least that was a start.

Rick took a seat again and cleared his throat.

"Okay, here goes. Your Honor, my name is Richard Abbott and I am the common-law spouse of Jaye Spencer. I would like to speak to the court today on the impact this terrible crime has had on my partner.

"Jaye has always been a free spirit. She lived life to the fullest and she put her entire self into her work. For years, Jaye has been a pastry chef and a baker and for the last few years she has been in a business partnership with the local bakery known as The Cakery. She runs this business side by side with her best friend and she gives all of her ability to her work, and all her passion, every day."

"Just over a month ago, on our way home from dinner, these two men, Francis Archer and Joshua Moody, robbed, beat and broke this woman. She suffered multiple injuries and wounds. She was unable to work and required rehabilitation."

"Worse than the physical injuries have been the changes in Jaye herself. For someone who had loved life with such zest and verve, for the last weeks, it's been like living with a total stranger."

Rick stole a glance upwards at Jaye, who was not even looking at him. Her head was buried in her hands and her shoulders still shook with silent tears.

"Jaye has become withdrawn, angry, irrational and sometimes hostile. She hasn't worked for more than two hours in over a month. She has taken off without telling her family or myself where she is. As a matter of fact, she hasn't volunteered any information on the incident to her family at all. Currently, her parents are still unaware that anything out of the ordinary has transpired. She has engaged in behaviour that is not only out of character for her, but also sometimes dangerous. In short, she is not the Jaye that I know, not the one I fell in love with…not herself at all.

"I truly believe that had this incident never occurred, these changes would not have come to pass. Jaye was content with the life she had. She was happy, she was a hard worker and she loved her friends and family fiercely. Now she is withdrawn, she does not work except at pushing us away."

"I would like to request, on behalf of Jaye and myself, for the sake of her healing process, that the two assailants receive the maximum penalty available." He took a deep a deep yet shaky breath. "Thank you for your consideration."

There was a stony silence. Rick was almost afraid to look up at her.

"Well…?" he finally asked.

"Well what?" Jaye was still speaking from behind her hands.

"What did you think? You think this will help get a huge sentence?"

"I don't fucking care."

Rick sighed. He still wasn't getting through to her at all. It looked like it might be time to put Moira's suggestion into action.

"I'll tell you what," he said, trying to change the subject and sound a bit more cheerful. He jumped up and looked out the window. "Looks like most of the roads are clear now. Let me take you out to dinner tonight."

"What for? I'm just a hostile person who pushes you away."

"Well, hostile person, do you feel like cooking tonight? Cause I don't," he smiled at her.

"Don't try and butter me up. That 'statement' is way too personal. I don't like it."

"It's supposed to be personal. It's supposed to shock the court into knowing how bad this whole thing has been for you."

She stood up. "Well, I don't want the reporters to hear it."

Rick nodded. So, she had finally noticed that there were reporters in the court room. "I'll ask Rebecca to make a motion to have them taken out of the room for this, but it might be hard to get the judge to agree to one this late in the proceedings."

"Can we do that?"

"We can do whatever we want," he said, coming over beside her and putting his arms around her. She pushed him off.

"Where do you want to go to eat?" she asked.

"I have an idea," he said.

One hour later Rick was pulling the car into the little spot next to the alley, exactly where they had parked that fateful night. He tried to ignore how white Jaye's knuckles were on the arm rests.

"What are we doing here?" she asked through gritted teeth.

"Replacing a bad memory with a better one," he said. He had already texted Moira earlier. They would be waiting for them by the time the meal was done.

"I don't want to go in," Jaye said.

"Come on. I called ahead, we have a reservation."

"Rick, I don't want to."

This was going to be harder than he originally anticipated. Rick turned to face her in the car.

"Look, I get why you don't want to do this, but I don't want you to get upset every time we go by this place for the rest of our lives. Come with me, I'll hold your hand and make sure nothing happens."

"I don't need you to hold my hand," she barked at him.

"Good, then let's go."

They exited the car and walked side by side into the restaurant. Rick went to give his name to the hostess and was surprised when the manager, or owner, he wasn't sure which, came up to him and pulled him aside.

"Good evening. I just wanted to let you know, on behalf of myself and the staff, that we are deeply sorry for what transpired the last time you were our guests. I am honoured to have you and your lovely companion back, and please allow us to serve you dinner on the house."

Rick was stunned. He nodded and said his thanks but decided not to get Jaye involved in the conversation. He wasn't sure how her ego might hold up to something that she would most likely view as charity.

They were seated and went through the motions of ordering. Rick winced when Jaye asked for a double martini, but he was picking his battles tonight. He didn't want to do anything that might set her off. It was crucial to keep her there so that they could all talk to her later, show her how loved she was and hopefully start to bring back the old Jaye.

It had been so hard to try and get her to talk. Rick had found that as angry as she had made him feel lately, more often than not, he was just holding back the tears to keep from crying. It wasn't fair. He should have been the one that came out of the restaurant first. He would have been able to handle it much better than Jaye. He probably would have at least heard the guys coming and could have stopped anything from happening. It was maddening to him that she had to be the one to deal with it, suffer through it, and relive it in the court room. He hated that she had to know where that fucking junkie had put his hands on her, where he had touched her, how and what he probably would have done had Rick been just thirty seconds slower.

As he watched her sit in silence with her meal, Rick only picked at his own. He wasn't really hungry. His mind was churning with thoughts of how Jaye would handle this little group meeting later. He just hoped that she would understand why they were doing it.

The owner himself tended their table later, and brought them the take-home containers for food that might have been the greatest food in the world, but for the mood of the night might as well have been sawdust.

Rick thanked him, shook his hand and promised to return before too long.

Now, it was time to do some quick talking.

"Let's go get dessert," he said, as he and Jaye walked back to the car.

"Really? I didn't even want to really eat my meal."

"I know, but I think we deserve something sweet before tomorrow. Come on, we'll go to the shop."

"I don't know, Rick. Moira might not like me going in there after hours without her."

"I bet she won't mind at all. Besides, it's partly your shop too. When was the last time you were in there?"

"Fine," she said, sitting in her seat and buckling her seatbelt. "We'll go. You can pick out a cookie. Then I just want to go home and take a bath."

"It's a deal," he told her. Rick, he told himself, I hope to hell you know what you're doing.

Thirty Five

They entered the door and immediately Jaye was faced with the presence of her friends.

She stood and faced down her friends, perched on various seats of the empty store.

"What's going on?" she asked suspiciously.

Rick approached her first and put his hand on her shoulder. "I'm sorry babe. I just didn't know what else to do," he said to her. He turned to Moira. "Maybe this wasn't the best idea."

Jaye's face was burning hot. She could feel the last lingering stitch in her ribs from where they had broken pinching her as she took deep breaths to try and calm herself down. She could feel the swirling sensation in her head taking over. Just like when she was a girl caught in the tow of the waves.

Wildly she looked around the room. All of these people looking at her as if she was someone to be pitied. Someone to be taken care of and feted. Well, she was having none of it, thank you very much. She crossed her arms over her chest, as well as she could, and fixed her glare on Moira. Of all people, she would have expected Moira to understand, to let her heal in her own time and her own way. How disappointing to see her looking as though this was all her idea. As if she was the one with all the wounds needing mending.

"So, this is what? An intervention? Do you all work for A&E now?" Jaye continued to stare down her friends. So-called friends.

"I'm not on drugs and I don't see any cameras, so what the fuck is this all about?" She shrugged Rick's hand from her shoulder. He didn't make an attempt to put it back, but instead took a few steps back and collapsed into one of the chairs in the café side of the room.

"We're worried about you, Jaye," Moira told her. "You're not yourself anymore."

"Oh yeah, well who am I then?" she countered with spirit.

"Jaye, did you talk to anyone? That counselor that I recommended to you?" Jack asked her gently. "I know it seems like a lot of bullshit, but honestly if you give it a chance, counseling can be really helpful." Moira squeezed Jack's hand. The intimate gesture made Jaye wince. She hadn't let Rick touch her like that in a while.

"I don't need a counselor. I'm dealing with this in my own way," she told them.

"Yeah, by not dealing..." Sloane said under her breath.

"What? Got something to say, Sloane?"

Sloane stroked her small belly bump. "Yeah, I do. I think you're being a selfish bitch."

Moira, Jack and Rick cast each other looks. Rick opened his mouth as if to reply to the remark, but Jaye beat him to it.

"Oh really?"

"Yeah. You're dumping on Moira and me all the time, you don't show up for work. You keep taking off on these ridiculous little 'adventures' which, I'm sorry, are nothing more than you trying to get yourself killed and worry all the people who care about you. Selfish bitch."

Jaye's face twisted into what might have been called a smile, but was much too bitter.

"Isn't that a bit of the pot calling the kettle black, Sloane?" she spat at her.

"Be fair Jaye. Sloane's changed a lot. You were the first one to say it," Moira said softly.

"Stay out of this Moira," Jaye barked.

"NO!"

"What?" Jaye took a step towards her dearest and oldest friend with nothing but bitterness in her eyes and bile in her mouth.

"I said no. This is not about you and Sloane getting into it with one another. This is not about Jack or Rick or I ganging up on you. This is about you. You're not dealing with the fallout of this terrible thing that's been done to you. You're being self-destructive and you're pushing us all away. We're not here because we're mad; we're here because we love you."

Rick approached her again and tried to put his hand back on her shoulder, but Jaye swatted him away.

"You all feel like this?" she gritted out through clenched teeth. "You all think I'm not 'dealing' with this? Well screw you! I am dealing. This is how I deal. While you're all moping around trying to think of how to put kid gloves on around me, I'm out there, living my life again. Living it better and facing my fears. I'm probably the only one who's dealing with it. The rest of you are just stewing."

Jaye was shaking with anger. How dare they? How dare they all accuse her like this? Jeez! She would get enough of this if she decided to read an impact statement at the trial. She didn't need it from her so called friends.

"This is a fucking joke. You all forgot what's it's like to live life. You're all safe in your little worlds with your marriage and your business and your work." She indicated Sloane, Moira and Rick each with nods of her head and a finger pointed at each in turn. "I'm the only one who's getting out there and seeing what's going on in the world."

"Oh yeah," Rick spoke up quietly. "What about your business Jaye? This is part yours too and you don't care about it anymore. And what about your relationship? You've been leaving me in your dust for weeks now. You're not you anymore."

"At least I'm finding this out now. Don't hold back, Rick. Tell them what you really feel."

"I am, I'm telling you. You're not Jaye anymore. You're this angry person who keeps trying to find new ways to either hurt yourself or hurt the rest of us," Rick blurted.

"So, I'm not good enough for you anymore, is that what you're saying?"

Rick studied his hands for a moment. "I just want you back to the way you were."

Jack shuffled his feet. "Look Jaye, I think Rick is just trying to find a way to say what we're all feeling. You haven't been yourself for weeks now. We all just want to see you get better."

Jaye heart was beating so hard it felt like it was going to burst out of her chest.

"How dare you!" she shouted. "You barely know me! You have no right to speak for Rick or for Moira for that matter."

She stared them down again, her hands clenching and balling into fists at her side. Rick wouldn't catch her eye, Sloane was standing with her arms crossed in front of her and Moira was staring at her with tears in her eyes.

"What?" she demanded. "You want to say something now?"

"I don't want you to come in like this anymore. You're angry; you hide in the kitchen and barely do anything but bite my head off. I want you to take some proper time off and get better," she whispered.

"Fine. FINE! You're all going to get what you want then. You don't want me around, Rick? You got it. I'll move out tonight." She turned towards the door and then whipped back around to face them again. "You think I'm fucking up the store? Buy me out. I don't need any of this shit from any of you anymore!" she screamed.

Jaye had her hand on the door before any of them could catch up to her and try and stop her. She tore out onto the sidewalk where the night was settling on the town with a intensity that was blinding.

She didn't know what to do with herself. Tears were burning hotly behind her eyes but she blinked them back and tore off towards the bridge once again. She could hear the voices of Moira, Jack, Rick and

Sloane behind her, chasing her down, calling her back. No way was she going to let them try and tell her that she was wrong or broken.

Her wrist was aching. Clenching and unclenching it had put strain on the injury that was still healing and her chest throbbed with the effort of breathing hard under the still healing ribs. She broke into a run and headed further away from the pain of the words that had been thrown at her.

It was so unfair. Here she was trying so hard to be tough, to get past the pain of recovering from her attack. Trying to find a way to prove that she was still alive, still fighting. All effort she had put into proving her spirit to herself, to her friends, all of it had been taken the wrong way. None of them understood. Jaye could feel the thoughts swirling around her head in a dervish of pain. Her head hurt and her heart was broken. There was no way she would go running back now, showing weakness and falling into Rick's arms like a helpless little baby. She would leave. Leave Fayette and start over somewhere completely new. She'd find people who wouldn't care that she was tough. She'd show them all.

The sound of her feet pounding on the snow packed sidewalk was soothing in a strange sort of way. She could still hear the sounds of at least one or two of them following her but she didn't care. Jaye ran and ran, letting the burn of her muscles drive her farther away from the hurt of the confrontation in the store. She heard Rick from somewhere behind her, crying out her name.

For a brief moment, she considered turning back to him. Something in his voice was tugging on the deepest part of her heart. The part she buried when she found out what those two vagrants had done to her. She dug her fist into her eye, rubbing the hurt away, trying to shut out the desperation in his voice.

"Jaye….come back. I love you!" he hollered from somewhere behind the fog of her thoughts.

Jaye shook her head hard to try and block him out. She stopped running and collapsed in exhaustion on the side of the road.

Rick ran up and dropped down beside her. He was crying. She had never seen him cry this hard before. Not even when she was in the hospital, broken and bruised. He began to draw her in for an embrace.

"I need you, don't go and don't run," he tried to choke out.

"No…NO…NO!" she screamed. "You don't want me; you said you didn't want me like this." She pushed herself up from the curb and ran out into the road.

The car that slammed into her wasn't going very fast, but it knocked her sideways with a sickening crack, and Jaye swam back into the hateful blackness of unconsciousness once again.

Thirty Six

Jaye lay crumpled on the road with her body curled in and her leg at a strange angle. She wondered if she were dead. She couldn't feel anything, couldn't hear anything and didn't seem to be able to open her eyes. She squeezed her eyes tightly in an effort to try and do something, anything to assure herself that she was still here.

A loud roar sounded in her ears. She struggled to place it. It sounded like the crash of waves, but that couldn't be so. Then she began to hear the voices. They seemed to be coming at her from all directions, over her, around her, behind her, everywhere. She didn't like it. It felt like she was drowning in a sea of sounds, none of which were comforting or appealing. Someone was yelling. She tried to lift her hand to shush them, but it wouldn't budge.

There was a hand on her face, and then one on her arm. It was squeezing her wrist. Why? Oh, her brain clicked into gear, probably checking for my pulse. Am I that bad? The voices started to slide into place as the roaring in her ears subsided. She could make out Rick's voice, Moira's and a few others from whom she had run just seconds ago. Or was it seconds? Maybe it was hours, she couldn't tell. There was another voice, a sobbing one. Someone kept insisting that it wasn't his fault. She didn't understand.

Jaye made up her mind that she was not dead, but that she had to make herself open her eyes and see what was happening. Lying here in this limbo wasn't going to help her at all. With massive effort, she wrenched open one eye, and then the other. Immediately she regretted it. It was far too bright. All she could see were sun spots bouncing around in front of her. Finally, her vision slid back into place and she looked directly into Rick's face, which was right beside hers.

"Thank god!" he breathed. "Don't move the ambulance is on the way," he told her.

Ambulance? And then she remembered. The fight in the shop, the horrible things she said to Rick, Sloane, Moira and Jack. Her family. She had run away and run into the road. The voice she heard was probably the driver of the car that she ran into. Tired of facing a reality in which she was the bad guy of her own nightmares over and over again, Jaye faded back out into the black.

When Jaye awoke in the hospital this time, there were no police waiting to interview her. There was no nurse cheerily bustling around the room and no doctor waiting there with news to put her life on tilt. There was only Rick, sitting at the side of her bed, one hand resting on the bindings on her leg.

She watched him for a few minutes before he noticed that she was awake. When he looked up to her, they locked eyes and she saw how red and puffy his were.

"It's broken," he said, indicating her leg. "You're lucky that car was in mid-turn. If it was going full speed, it might have killed you."

She opened her mouth to answer him, but he held up his hand. "I don't want you to talk yet. You'll just say something that you'll wind up regretting." He took a breath and stood up. "I've always loved you. Loved your strength and your spirit. But this is not the Jaye I know. The Jaye I know wouldn't run in front of a car after running away from the people who mean the most to her."

"You have a strong heart, Jaye. It's fierce and loyal and it's one of the things that makes my heart sing when I look at you. You keep thinking that you have to be this strong fighter; that you have to prove something. I don't know who you're trying to prove it to. I don't know why you keep pushing me, all of us, away." He looked down at his hands. "I always thought they'd be strong enough to hold you when things got hard. I thought they'd be strong enough to fight off those bastards who attacked you. I thought they'd be strong enough to hold you up while you healed." He clenched them, and shook his head. "I wanted to be your strength when you were broken, but you just kept pushing me away."

Jaye kept her silence as Rick poured out his heart. She was so tired. She just wanted to curl up into his arms, but she couldn't make herself reach out for him.

"See, what you don't know is that you have a grace and elegance as well. You never want anyone to see that part of you. It's a shame too, because it's the most breathtaking thing I've ever seen. But you want to bury it with all your pain and it's clear now that nothing I can do will bring that back to you. I can't watch you get hurt anymore. I can't watch you ruin yourself and expect me to just stand by, not help you or hold you. So I'm going to do the hardest thing I've ever done."

Jaye watched Rick reach down to the floor and pick up a bouquet of flowers. Jasmine, her favourite. He untied the florist's twine from them and laid them down on the table by her bed.

"You told me we were going nowhere, remember? Well, you're finally right. You don't have to move out, Jaye. I'll be gone by the time you're released."

He turned towards the door, leaving Jaye on the bed with tears falling freely down her face.

"I'd like to be your strength for a change, Jaye. I'd like to be the one you lean on. But I won't chase you for it anymore and I won't watch you kill yourself this way. This time it's up to you."

He crossed the threshold of the room but turned for one last second to face her.

"If you really wanted to prove how tough you are, you'd learn when to ask for help. I'll be there when you're ready."

He left and Jaye sat in a stupor, tracing the top edge of the cast that was holding her leg together. The sun had long since sunk down behind the trees and the sky was inky black. From her room, Jaye couldn't even tell if there were stars shining above her. She reached for the flowers, splayed out along the top of the rolling table at her side. She pulled a handful of them onto the bed with her and drank in their scent and simplicity.

A card dropped out onto her lap and she picked it up.

Jasmine,

A flower of grace and elegance

That which you do not realize you embody

Wholly, completely

I love you Jaye

She wanted so very badly to get up and bring him back to the room. But there was no way she would be able to get out of the bed. Perhaps too late, she realized that she might have driven away the greatest man she had ever known.

Not even a second later, Rick dipped his head back in, catching his eye on the chair in the corner of the room. "I forgot my jacket," he mumbled, crossing quickly to retrieve it.

It was now or never, she realized. Time to stop being so pushy to him, time to swallow her pride and grab a hold of him before he was gone forever.

"Rick," she said quietly.

"Yeah?" he turned towards her.

"I don't want you to go." Her voice sounded almost alien to herself. It was too quiet, too timid sounding. But maybe some humility was finally called for.

Rick came over to the bed and stood over her. "You'll have to speak up, Jaye. I can barely hear you."

"Don't go!" she choked. "I don't want you to go. Don't leave me, don't move out and don't go," she cried.

It felt like the weight of a thousand years of bondage was falling from her with every word she uttered. She kept on babbling at him.

"I love you, I need you, I'm sorry. You're the only man I've ever loved my whole life and I don't want to lose you."

Rick sank down onto her bed and buried his face in her neck. He held her while she sobbed and murmured the same words over and over again into his hair. It felt so good to touch him again, to hold him and smell him. She wanted to breathe him in forever. She wanted to drown in him.

"I lost you," he said when he finally sat up again, his hands holding her face, running through her hair.

"I'm here. I'm so sorry," she whispered, drawing his face down for a kiss.

It was the gentlest, most tender kiss she could remember them sharing in a long, long time. Rick brushed her lips with his own so tenderly, so carefully. She pressed her own against his a little more firmly. With near shyness, she carefully opened her mouth and ran her tongue around the outside of her mouth, of his. A sob escaped from her throat, but she stayed with him, letting their mouths and their tongues say the words that had been so difficult for so many weeks now.

They broke apart and Rick gently lay down beside her on the bed, careful not to disturb the casing of her leg or make her uncomfortable. He tucked one of his arms underneath her and pulled her in so that she was nestled into the crook of his arm, her head resting in the hollow of his chest. It was her safe spot. The one place she could be calm and restful and wash away all her cares.

"You can't leave me," she whispered to him. "Because if you're gone, all the meaning to my life will have gone too."

She felt him pull her in just a little bit closer and closed her eyes. It was time to start to heal.

Chapter Thirty Seven

Jaye was told by Dr. Mayer that she had to remain in hospital again for five days. The bone that had broken in her leg had been set with two pins and they needed to make sure that she was going to be following through on the aftercare that was prescribed. She had a special cast on at the moment that Rick had fashioned for her himself. It held her leg together, allowed for the pins to stick out without catching on the bindings and gave enough support that she would be able to get around on it on her own, eventually anyway. For now, she was under strict instructions to use the wheelchair for anything farther away than the bathroom in her room.

During the day, Jaye finally met with Dr. Spiers, who kept insisting that she call her Kate, and started to talk about the events over the last month. Jaye had a hard time believing when she looked back on it, that it had only been one month. It felt more like an eternity. She was relieved about so many things. That both men had been caught and put into jail was probably the biggest load off her mind. Rebecca had called her in the hospital that morning and told her the outcome. Sentencing, she said, would come in about a week. In the meantime, though she didn't say as much to anyone else, Jaye fully planned on going to the jail at some point and talking to the quieter of the two boys who had so changed her life. Something about seeing his face that day in the courthouse had made her think of those frightened animals you see in rescue commercials for the humane society. His eyes haunted her. She was sure that the defence had been honest in its portrayal of him, and she wanted the chance to talk to him herself. She planned to talk to Kate about it after the fact.

*****

Rick spent those five days running around planning the greatest surprise he had ever planned in his life. He rallied together Moira, Jack, Sloane, Moira's mother and grandmother and a whole host of other people. He even called Jaye's lawyer, although the skeeving little creep Daryn was auspiciously absent from the list of people he pulled together. He still couldn't stand that guy.

The nice thing about Jaye finally taking the time to meet with her psychologist was that there were large portions of the day that he was expected to be away from her. He had also arranged for Rebecca to go in and spend a few hours with her doing 'wrap up' from the case. It meant that Jaye was not suspicious of him being gone for hours at a time. Of course, she knew him so well that she had no doubt figured out that he was planning something, but he was willing to be that she would never be able to come up with this...nor would she be expecting it. It was part of what made it so special.

With all the attention that the incident on that fateful night had gotten and the intrigues still happening over the most high-profile court case the town had seen in years, Rick found that he could pull together in just five short days what people spent months, hell, even years trying to do. By the time Jaye was ready for release, he was ready too, and it was all he could do to keep from giggling or blurting out the whole secret. Or for that matter, from yelling from the car as he drove through the town, just how much he loved this woman.

Rick arrived at exactly three pm sharp on Friday afternoon to pick her up. As he sauntered down the hallways of the hospital, it was hard to keep the bounce out of his step. Rick stepped into the elevator humming to himself. There was an elderly couple in there already looking gloomy. Rick flashed them a smile but they did not return it.

"Great day isn't it?" he asked them.

The older man nodded at him, but the woman just continued to stare straight ahead. They exited the elevator on the third floor. Oncology. Well, that would explain the sour looks. Rick forced himself to remember that there were still hard things going on in the world around him, but that there was always a reason to feel okay with it. So, one of those two people was dealing with cancer. Or else they knew someone who was. But they still had each other. If nothing else, Rick had clung to the knowledge that despite what he and Jaye might go through together in the years to come, they would have each other, and that was in itself, the greatest reason to be happy and to believe that life was worth it. She might have worked really hard to push him away, but in the end, it was exactly the tonic he needed to finally understand how much she meant to him.

Rick got off on the fourth floor and headed straight to Jaye's room. He could hear her from the hallway, talking to Moira and, yes, she was even laughing. It sounded like music.

*****

"Honestly it's ridiculous, Moira. I would never wear something like this." Jaye was looking at the selection of clothes her best friend had brought for her to wear home.

"It's my grandmother's. Don't insult her by dismissing it; she wanted you to leave this hospital in style. Like one of those old movie stars from the forties. Besides, I think it actually suits you," Moira teased her with a grin.

Moira had brought in a beautiful satin dress in the most stunning shade of pink and a white fur cape. The dress, she had explained, was so that Jaye would feel glamourous even with the large and cumbersome cast on her leg. The fur was to keep her warm. It was February after all.

"Besides, I couldn't bring you in any of your clothes, almost everything you have is jeans and cargo pants and to get them on, I'd have had to cut up the legs. I didn't think you'd want me to do that," She winked at her friend.

Jaye looked mutinous for a second, and then laughed. "I guess you're right. I don't want you cutting up my clothes. But you could have just grabbed me some sweat pants and cut them up, honestly, I wouldn't have minded. I feel so...conspicuous in this."

Jaye looked down at herself. Even though she was putting up the token argument, she couldn't deny that the dress looked and felt beautiful. The material was so soft and luxurious. It felt like clouds whispering against her skin.

"I still don't know about the fur though, isn't that kind of, I don't know, tacky?" she wondered.

Moira shrugged. "Does it matter? I think it's kind of perfect and dramatic. Besides, you can't wear just any old coat over a dress like this. I'll take it back to her after we get you home. One twenty minute trip is hardly going to make a difference, is it?"

Jaye studied her friend's face. She was up to something, but it was hard to tell what.

"Okay, you win. I'll wear the darn thing."

Jaye swung the heavy fur over her shoulders just as Rick walked into the room. She smiled at him. It was a miracle that he was still here for her after she had tried so hard to push him out of her life. She was grateful.

"You look like a painting," he told her, coming over to kiss her. "Shall I lead you to your chariot?" he asked, indicating the wheelchair in the corner of the room.

"Lord, I can't wait to get going with my physio. I hate using this thing." Rick helped ease her into it.

"Got everything?" he asked.

"I have most of it," Moira piped up, holding up the bag she held with Jaye's clothes from the night she was brought in, her paperwork and her toiletries that had been brought in. "Just don't forget those." She pointed at the bouquet of jasmine that Rick had brought to Jaye just a few days ago. "Here, Jaye. You take these. My hands are full."

Moira placed the flowers in her friends' hands and then started to walk out of the room. Rick followed her, pushing Jaye in the wheelchair.

They exited the hospital and Rick helped to settle Jaye into his car out front. Moira had already gotten into her car and taken off without as much as another word. Jaye figured that she was probably hurrying back to the store. Probably didn't want to leave Sloane in charge for too long. Not that Jaye blamed her; Sloane was good for them, but not ready to run the place solo for any length of time yet.

The air was almost humming, Jaye felt. Perhaps it was just because she was so happy to be on her way home, or perhaps it was because she was finally starting to feel like her old self for the first time in a month. Rick was fussing over making sure she was tucked in properly and then he too got into the car and turned the ignition.

"Ready to go home?" he asked her.

"Yes."

He winked at her and she grinned back. Now she was sure that he was planning something, though nothing in the world could have prepared her for what happened next.

Rick didn't follow the roads that led to their apartment. Instead, she found herself watching the scenery of Moira's mother's street fly by the window. She assumed that there was some kind of welcome home party planned for her there and began to relax. Trust Rick and Moira to rope Angela into planning and hosting some kind of shindig for her at that beautiful house of theirs. Jaye sat up a little higher in her seat. It would certainly explain the fancy dress anyway. And the way Rick looked like the cat that swallowed the canary. She hadn't seen him look this pleased with himself since they had signed the lease on their apartment four years ago.

But the car went right past the Ryan house and kept on going down the street.

"Rick, where are we going?" she asked.

"You'll see," he said.

She was going to get nothing out of him. Rick loved a good surprise. Jaye started to wrack her brain for what or who was down this area of town. Some place that they could have a great ol' party. She wasn't coming up with any answers and was about to ask Rick again what was going on when she saw it...the house. The one that she loved. The one that had gone up for sale and had started the big fight they had had on the night when everything went wrong. There was a sold sign on it. There were cars all around. And their car had slowed right down.

"Rick...what's going on? What are we doing here?" She swallowed hard. There was a large lump in her throat.

Rick turned off the car in the driveway and got out without saying a word. He came around and helped Jaye out. The air was so crisp that Jaye's breath was billowing from her mouth with the effort of getting to her feet. Rick reached into the back of the car and pulled out a sturdy looking silver cane, which he handed to her.

Jaye watched with wide eyes as Rick next grabbed the bouquet of flowers and used the wide white ribbon on them to tie them to her cane. Together they walked slowly towards the front door. It started to snow.

Jaye opened and closed her mouth a few times, trying to come up with the right question to ask. She had never seen Rick look so happy. When they reached the door, Jaye instinctively reached out to the doorknob to turn it, but Rick stayed her hand.

"Let me," he said, gently. He reached up and knocked three times. For a moment, Jaye experienced a stab of pain. For the briefest of moments, she had allowed herself to fantasize that the house was theirs.

That Rick had pulled the most elaborate and amazing surprise on her of all and bought the house for them, but he wouldn't knock on the door of their own house, would he?

She was stunned when the door opened and a minister stepped out.

"What?" she started.

From around the side of the house, friends and family appeared and began to gather behind them.

Rick dropped down on his knee in the snow.

"Jaye. My amazing, strong, beautiful Jaye. You are the love of my life. In one month, I've nearly lost you twice, and it seems like the only reason I came so close to losing you was because I was afraid. Afraid to really and truly have you. I don't want to lose you." He reached down into the pocket of his coat and pulled out a small box. "I'm not afraid anymore and I don't want to lose you ever again, and I don't want to take you across the threshold of our home until I can carry you over it, as my wife. Will you marry me?"

Jaye watched with astonishment as Rick opened the box and held up a ring. She could hardly believe what was happening. She looked around her at the crowd that had gathered. Moira and Jack, Sloane and Martin, Angela, Siobhan and Rebecca. Her doctors, her friends, even customers from the store and a couple of nurses from the hospital. Standing in the back of the crowd looking so proud was her brother David. She could hardly believe it was real.

Rick sniffed, and she snapped her head back to him.

"I would love nothing more than to marry you," she said.

Rick stood up. His knees were soggy from the snow but he looked so happy that Jaye laughed out loud through the few tears that had slipped from her eyes as he slid the ring on her finger.

She took his hand in hers and they turned to face the minister in the doorway. Moira and Jack stepped forward from the group and took up their places beside them. Jaye gave her friend a hug and whispered a thank you into her hair.

Epilogue

The winter I was twenty seven years old, I nearly died. Twice. I was attacked by two drug addicts who just wanted money for a fix and then I was attacked by my own bad choices. I've done a lot of things in my life that I'm not proud of, but that month, I nearly lost everyone I've ever loved due to my own need to be strong.

As I sat in my new house on the night of my wedding and watched the people I love eat the beautiful wedding cake my own best friend had made, I thought back to the summer that I was a little girl and my own daring had nearly destroyed me in the ocean. I've always been one to live according to my own rules, and I've always thought that it was something to be proud of. But I'm proud of different things now.

This house looks almost barren of things. We hardly fill up the main floor with our small furniture from the apartment. But this house is full of something far more important. It's full of possibilities. I am watching Rick now, my husband, talking to my brother. He spoke to me of being afraid, but I was the one who was afraid. He is the oak in whose branches I will play. It's not the hard road of mending my wounds that I see ahead of me now. It's the memories we will build together. He looks at me and for a moment I can see that he feels the same. Changing is not hard. Changes happen all around us every day. True strength is learning to ride the waves instead of crashing with them on the shore. There are oceans of possibilities out there waiting for us...oceans. And I am going to dance on them, together, with my love.

The End

Winter Jasmine